Napoleon's
Vampire Hunters

BY THE SAME AUTHOR

The Quest of Frankenstein
The Triumph of Frankenstein

Napoleon's
Vampire Hunters

by
Frank Schildiner

A Black Coat Press Book

Acknowledgements: Paul Féval and Brian Stableford.

Copyright © 2017 by Frank Schildiner.
Cover illustration Copyright © 2017 Mariusz Gandzel.

Visit our website at www.blackcoatpress.com

Introduction

The chief protagonist of *Napoleon's Vampire Hunters*, the steadfast Jean-Pierre Séverin, is the creation of French writer Paul Féval (1816-1887) and was introduced in his novel *La Vampire*, translated by Brian Stableford under the title *The Vampire Countess.*[1] *The Vampire Countess* was first published in a volume called *Les Drames de la Mort* (*The Dramas of Death*) in 1856. It was later reprinted in 1865 with some slight amendments to the original text.

Paul Féval trained for the legal profession, qualifying in 1836 while not yet 20 years-old, but two year later, he abandoned his budding legal career to become one of the leading popular authors of his times. Many of his early stories were fantasies, often based in the folklore of his native Brittany, but it was in the production of popular fiction for serialization in newspapers that he truly shone, alongside his peers Alexandre Dumas and Eugène Sue. His best-known series began when the editor of *L'Époque* commissioned him to write an imitation of Sue's *Mysteries of Paris* entitled *Les Mystères de Londres* (*The Mysteries of London*) (1843-44). That novel set a pattern which was to dominate Féval's contributions to the *roman feuilleton* in building its plot on the foundation of a conspiracy which is part-criminal and part-political. He mined this vein with *Les*

---

[1] Available from Black Coat Press (ISBN 978-0-9740711-5-2).

Compagnons du Silence (1857; *The Companions of Silence*) and *Jean Diable* (1860; *John Devil*; book 1863)[2], which formed a prelude to a series of seven melodramatic novels collectively known by the title of *Les Habits Noirs* (1863-75; *The Black Coats*).[3] This series tells the long and convoluted story of a vast conspiracy run by the prototype of all criminal masterminds, the seemingly immortal Colonel Bozzo-Corona.

Although popular fiction did not carry quite the same stigma in Paris as the "penny-dreadful" in London, it was regarded with considerable disdain in literary circles, and the sheer pace of Féval's production won him a reputation as a hack. With the aid of hindsight, though, we can now recognize that he was an enterprising, ingenious and historically significant pioneer of several modern popular genres—as significant in that respect in France as Edgar Allan Poe was in America—but nobody knew that at the time, and conventional academic disdain for popular fiction has ensured that he has never received the credit he deserves, even in his native land.

The Vampire Countess was not reckoned among Féval's most successful endeavors in his own day. Like the contemporary critics, Féval was not in a position to guess the likely import of his own innovations, and he may have underestimated the importance of some of the

---

[2] Available from Black Coat Press (ISBN 978-1-932983-15-9). *The Companions of Silence* will be available in 2018.
[3] The entire series, comprised of 1. *'Salem Street;* 2. *The Invisible Weapon;* 3. *The Parisian Jungle;* 4. *The Companions of the Treasure;* 5. *Heart of Steel;* 6. *The Cadet Gang;* and 7. *The Sword-Swallower,* is available in translation from Black Coat Press.

things he attempted to do in that novel. After all, forty years were still to pass before Bram Stoker's *Dracula* was to usher in the new era in vampire fiction that extends to the present day.

Féval was almost certainly commissioned to write *The Vampire Countess* because of the recent success of a play by Alexandre Dumas called *Le Vampire*, penned to cash in on the success achieved by John Polidori's *The Vampyre* (then widely misattributed to Lord Byron).[4]

Féval must have been aware that Dumas had failed to find a way of making the supernatural acceptable to the audience for serial fiction. On the one hand, he must have been tempted to place the entire melodramatic emphasis of his plot on criminal conspiracy and sadism (as he usually did); on the other, he must have been tempted to see if he could succeed where Dumas had failed. The end result is that *The Vampire Countess* is in effect, a crime story with an ambiguous supernatural component grafted on to a domestic tragedy in order to serve as a protective vehicle for some mildly contentious political commentary.

The Vampire Countess is important as an early crime novel, with several interesting and innovative features—including its hero's capacity to move from Clark Kent mode to Superman mode merely by holding a section of broken fishing-rod as if it were a sword. Even if all the scenes featuring its antagonist at work are delusory, it is also important as a novel of the supernatural, because the scenes in which the vampire is active set several significant precedents as well as conjuring up a magnificently feverish quality. It is important, too, as a

---

[4] Dumas's play is available from Black Coat Press under the title *The Return of Lord Ruthwen* (ISBN 978-1-932983-11-1).

precursor of soap opera, not merely by virtue of its genre-compounding but by virtue of some of its set pieces—most importantly the sequence of written messages impotently hurled at a closed window by its hapless heroine.

From a post-Stokerian perspective, *The Vampire Countess'* status as an important item of vampire fiction is compromised by the fact that the eponymous vampire is not a drinker of blood—but the novel's relationship with other vampire stories published in the same era is both obvious and interesting. The vampire's manner of predation is unique, but other aspects of her alleged nature are much more closely related to certain prior works of vampire fiction, yet Féval's novel set at least two crucial precedents for vampire fiction to come.

With vampires so much in vogue, it would not have been surprising if Féval had come up with the idea to write a vampire novel himself, but the hesitancy of *The Vampire Countess* gives the impression that he was in two minds about the propriety of the exercise throughout the time he was writing it, so it seems more likely that he was specifically asked to write a vampire story set in Paris. Having been commissioned to do that, however, he must have made up his mind that he would produce something distinctly different from the English school of vampire fiction, whose focus was on *male vampires*.

It was during that time that Féval happened upon the idea of a series telling the stories of individuals and groups featured in the expositions of the Paris Morgue. Although mortuaries in general answered a legally-enshrined precautionary requirement to let corpses lie for a while before they were interred (the fear of premature burial, widespread in the 18th and 19th centuries, reflected the difficulty of finding reliable criteria of death), the principal function of the Paris Morgue was to display unidentified corpses so that they could be inspected by the relatives of missing persons. The practical difficulties of this process—which became obvious soon after its founding in 1722—necessitated the Morgue becoming a pioneer of refrigeration; by the beginning of the 19th century, when a thousand corpses a year had to be put on display, the temperature of the corpses was carefully controlled: after initial cooling to -15 degrees Centigrade they were stored at -2 degrees.

The necessity of opening the expositions to all-comers also demonstrated the macabre pulling-power of such displays; the Morgue became a place of popular entertainment, capable of drawing big crowds when an unusual number of corpses were delivered at the same time by some kind of catastrophe. The fact that some members of the crowd would indeed be relatives of the deceased, whose terror would give way abruptly to horror and grief when they found their loved ones, added considerably to the entertainment value of the spectacle for those crowd members who were there purely for recreational purposes.

The idea of linking a series of stories by means of a Morgue-keeper who also happened to be an expert swordsman must have seemed entirely natural, and the notion of setting one such story at the moment when the original Morgue, near the Châtelet, was being replaced by a new establishment on the Marché-Neuf must have seemed inviting.

The Vampire Countess is set in 1804, in the days immediately before Napoleon Bonaparte—who had led the Consulate since the 18 Brumaire coup of 1799—declared himself Emperor. This was material that required careful handling as the novel was published soon after Napoleon III had proclaimed himself Emperor in November 1852. One of the consequences of this event was a period of unusually rigid censorship, so Féval's readers would have been acutely sensitive to the double implication of any comments offered by the book as to the legitimacy or otherwise of the first Napoleon's institution as Emperor.

Also, in 1802, Napoleon had abolished the Ministry of Police, forcing the notorious Joseph Fouché into "retirement," although he continued to command the loyalty of many of his former colleagues and spies. This, too, was a significant element of *The Vampire Countess'* background, which made much of the assertion that the various factions of the police were so busy watching and plotting against one another that, by 1804, they were incapable of efficient action against crimes and conspiracies committed under their very noses!

Jean-Marc Lofficier & Brian Stableford

Prologue

"No, please!" '

The young street tough's wail was the whimpering of a beaten child. His name was Gabin Dury and he was dying. A member of the King of Beggars' new Court of Miracles, he made a living as a housebreaker and occasional leg-breaker. But his favorite sideline was far more sinister. Using the sewers and back alleys of the city, he was a predator. His prey was the young, the innocent and the weak. It didn't matter whether they were boys or girls. It was the power he felt when he grabbed one, beat them a little and sodomized them for an hour or more. Then he'd dump them, content in the knowledge that they'd keep their mouth shut. Nobody wanted to admit they'd been used that way.

"Yes, I think so."

The voice speaking was cultured and soft. "You are perfect. Bathed in blood and corruption. A fitting meal before visiting mass death upon the mewling masses of nugatory peons. But in the end, the proper order shall return to this world. Be content, you are a meal that will herald a golden age."

"He smells like food."

A rasp of talons across stone drifted to Gabin's ears, causing him to shiver. But a hand of iron held him in place, preventing any chance of fleeing.

"Soon, my pet. Very soon. First, I take what I need. Then you shall feed."

11

There was a slight loosening on Gabin's arms as he was slowly turned to a deeper, darker part of the back alley.

"I have money! You can have it all! I can get more, give you anything you want!"

Gabin tried to reach for secret pocket in his belt. But the grip on his shoulders tightened and he gasped in pain.

"Money? Is that all you rustics think of? No thoughts of duty? Service to your betters? Just filthy coins! And a desire to use them to rise above your proper station! This is why a Corsican *parvenu* is about to place himself as a ruler. No! It shall not be allowed! Not ever!"

A pair of hands clamped down on Gabin's head. Their grip was pure agony, lancets of pain shooting through his skull like icy knives. He opened his mouth to gasp, when a wide maw clamped down and drowned out the sound. Rows of sharp teeth tore through his lips, filling his mouth with blood. He tried to shriek in pain, but the jaws fastened down over him seemed to suck the air from his lungs.

But the suction within Gabin's chest didn't abate. In fact, if anything, it seemed to increase. The young rapist struggled in vain as he felt the small bits of air, which he was trying desperately to pull in through his nose, being stolen and consumed by the other. Blackness entered his vision as the mouth continued to prevent him from breathing. There was a sensation that more was being taken, like his very soul was being ripped from his body.

A moment later, Gabin Dury slumped and was dropped to the ground. His face was a torn and tattered ruin, a mask of shredded and split flesh. The Parisian rapist was barely alive and sinking fast. He had mere seconds left to live.

"Feed, little one. Feed to your heart's content. Then dump his body into the Seine. We have so much to do. We have a coronation to prevent. Soon you'll be dining on the flesh of the First Consul, little one. Flesh not good enough to be a king, but it will serve as an adequate meal, despite the nouveau riche flavor."

The sounds of teeth and talons tearing and chewing drifted through the alley. The horrific dissonance continued for quite some time into the night.

CHAPTER I

Paris, November 1804

The Paris Morgue was a new facility. Clean, built along scientific lines, it was another example of the modern world as interpreted by the leadership of the French Empire. The Citizen employees operated under a rigid standard, rules that cost them many employees at first. The old habits of pocketing valuables were strictly prohibited. All items, even tattered clothing, were duly recorded in the huge ledgers provided by the new director. A system was now in place, efficient and precisely what the Revolution had promised back in 1792.

At precisely 8 a.m., said director walked into the mortuary. He was a tall man with light colored hair and pale eyes. His clothes were always freshly laundered, but looked well-worn. He was an older man, in his middle forties at least, with a scarred, lined face that caused even the most belligerent citizen to pause. His name was Jean-Pierre Séverin and it was said he was friends with First Consul Bonaparte.

As was his habit, Séverin greeted the staff as he headed for his office. There was a calm to him that translated to the Morgue employees, all of whom worked with impressive efficiency. The nightly log was brought before him by Blaise Leroy, the long-established deputy medical examiner for the city of Paris. Leroy was a tall man with rounded shoulders and wispy white hair. He'd been a medical examiner since long before the Revolution, surviving because of a complete lack of political sense. His work upon the dead was correct and exact, if completely uninspired. His only vice was said to be a love for street theater, puppet shows, mimes and performers.

"A fine lovely morning, Citizen Director," Leroy said, placing the night log before Séverin with a slight flourish.

He remarked upon the weather in this manner every day. It didn't matter if the weather agreed with his morning sentiment. To Blaise Leroy, it was always a fine day, whether the environment agreed with his statement or not.

"A bit cold, but I like such weather," Séverin replied, always attempting to hold to the facts in their morning conversations. It was his habit, precision.

"Only two corpses brought in last night, Citizen. The first was a poor, elderly seamstress, Madame Masson. Her son reported that she had refused to quit working, despite several fainting spells lately. I examined her myself. No signs of flux or any ailments. Symptoms of a weak heart. The second was somewhat odder. A young drowning victim. The fish and other river creatures feasted well upon his corpse."

Leroy almost sounded delighted as he spoke of the grim happenings of the night. This was often off-putting to many, but not to Séverin. He knew and understood that this was an armor that his subordinate had built around himself after a lifetime of being surrounded by death in its myriad forms. By presenting a happy and friendly outward appearance, Leroy was untouched by the daily dark events of the Paris Morgue.

"How is a drowning victim odd?" Séverin leaned back in his wooden chair and studied the man. Most believed Leroy to be a fool, but Séverin prized the man's perspicacity.

Leroy smiled with open delight. He liked nothing better than these morning exchanges with Jean-Pierre Séverin. Often the coroner of Paris was a position for a civil servant. Most of those appointed were there as either a step to a higher position, or as a last job before moving to the country to grow roses or some other nonsense. But Séverin was different. He behaved as if he was in this job because it was an essential facet of life. No death was considered unimportant. The man was willing to examine the corpses of frozen beggars if he doubted their method of passing. A good man. And a very intelligent one.

"A drowning victim presents certain simple signs. Pulled from the Seine or one of its many banks. Bloated body from the immersion. Water in the lungs and a body consumed by various marine life. Or, if found outside of the river, by rats, kitties or doggies. When any of these elements are missing, I mark the discovery as odd," Leroy explained with the calm of a schoolmaster explaining a particularly difficult lesson to a favored pupil. But there was no condescension in his tone.

"And what is missing from this unknown victim?"

Séverin watched Leroy closely, absorbing the lesson. Leroy possessed an astonishing range of knowledge and one profited intellectually when he explained the details of his profession.

"Several. The corpse was not bloated from the water. Odd, but the man may have been in the water only for a brief time. The stench of the river was upon him, but weaker than I would have expected. And the corpse was in terrible condition. He was quite literally torn apart."

Leroy ticked fingers off his hands as he discussed the ghastly minutia of the previous evening.

"And the lungs?"

Séverin sensed he was meant to ask this question. And he complied, allowing the older man his moment of triumph.

Leroy raised a finger, pointing to the ceiling. The pose was theatrical; the mummer's version of a leader making a point that will save or condemn the life of another. A universal gesture, but one rarely used in the real world.

"Therein lies the true oddity, Monsieur! The lungs—they are gone!"

Leroy's smile widened and he seemed to glow as looked down upon his supervisor.

"Gone?" Séverin repeated, knowing this would lead to the full tale.

Leroy wished to present the details in a method worthy of an opera. There was little reason to deny the elderly man his moment.

Leroy nodded, his head bobbing rapidly. He resembled one of the puppets he loved so well as his nearly bald pate waggled. Comical, but his words were not:

"The lungs, liver, kidney and heart were gone. Torn away. I presume a particularly nasty pack of wild dogs are loose in some part of the city. The damage was quite significant."

Séverin rose, a fluid gesture of liquid grace the belied his age,

"Please show me this oddity, Citizen Leroy. I'm quite intrigued by your account. Lead the way!"

Leroy gave another sketch of a bow. He scooped up the ledger and led Séverin through the corridors towards the main chamber. But suddenly he shifted away, turning to an older portion of the building before opening an anteroom door.

"I surmised you might wish to examine the poor gentleman yourself. Therefore, I placed him in this chamber. The light is far better than the holding area and the stench is less formidable. Additionally, I placed several lamps within—if you need further illumination for your examination."

"Well considered."

Séverin gave Leroy a nod and stepped within. The stench struck him immediately, an invisible force that almost staggered him from his feet. The scent was that of blood and meat, the smell of a butcher's shop, but there was also an underlying scent, a corrupt rot underlining the redolence of flesh and death. A horrible aroma, one all too familiar to those who worked at the Paris Morgue.

With a flourish worthy of a street theater actor, Leroy pulled the long sheet from the corpse.

"As you can see, the poor man is in a most terrible condition."

And he was at that. If anything, Leroy had been kind regarding the condition of the body. The form on the table was that of a man, thought that was difficult to determine at first glance. The face was a torn and tattered ruin, with most of the lips and nose missing. The missing flesh caused the teeth to be fully visible. This gave the dead man a rictus grin, an abhorrent smirk from beyond the grave.

But it was the body that held Jean-Pierre Séverin's full attention. The chest and torso were a ripped ruin, a shredded mass of shattered bones and mangled meat. The skin had been cleaved apart, revealing an anatomy with many missing organs. Whole sections of the frame were simply empty, as if internal parts of the body had been wrenched out by mighty talons. The sight was nightmarish, gruesome and grisly.

Yet, Séverin appeared unmoved. Pulling a tiny brass magnifying glass from his jacket, he examined the visible wounds with silent care. He moved slowly about the corpse, starting at the facial disfigurement and finishing below the sternum. Finally, he straightened up, his normally placid visage replaced a somber expression.

"Why is there oil upon the forehead of the corpse?" he asked, pointing to the dead man's skull.

Leroy's eyes widened in surprise. The oil was quite dried up by now, but Séverin had detected it regardless.

"My apologies, Citizen Director. I forgot to mention it. The representatives of the Papal States are in town. They are making arrangements for the forthcoming coronation of our First Consul. Well, to make a long story short, one the delegation requested to perform the last rites on all those who passed away while they were in town. Not an unusual request when the Papal Representatives visit our city. It was approved, of course."

"Of course."

Séverin's response was distant and he appeared to be concentrating elsewhere.

"Monsieur Leroy," he said, "please check your records and see if any other odd bodies occurred prior to this one. And if any others appear, please contact me immediately. Day or night."

Leroy appeared surprised for a moment, but then merely shrugged and gave his half-bow again.

"If that is your wish, Citizen Director. What shall we do with this poor man?"

"Send him to the charnel house and have the remains buried. Not merely sent to the pauper's burial, if you please."

Séverin stared at Leroy as he gave his orders, his pale eyes boring into the older man's watery brown orbs.

"As you wish," replied Leroy. "That is slightly unusual, usually reserved for bodies well past the stages where eventual burial is possible."

Leroy opened the ledger and wrote down his superior's orders in flowing script.

"This time, it is necessary as well," said Séverin. "I will explain all in the distant future. I must go for now."

Séverin stepped towards the door, but then looked over his shoulder at his colleague.

"One further detail: the priest? Was he a tall young man with green eyes and red hair?"

Leroy shook his head: "Neither the priest nor his assistant could be described in such a manner. The holy man was close to my age. Quite round and jolly. Execrable accent! I believe he was a Roman, or some such. Still, was quite gentlemanly in a Roman way. His companion was younger, not more than twenty or so, taller, quite handsome."

"A Roman as well?" asked Séverin who wanted as much clarification as he could receive. Every detail might be critical in the near future.

Leroy shook his head.

"No, not at all. He spoke little, but judging from his accent, I would say he was Swiss, or some kind of German. He had a harsh way of emphasizing his vowels. Is it important?"

"Not at all. I'm merely curious. You miss little, Monsieur Leroy. At what time did these holy men arrive at our little establishment?"

Leroy pulled out an old and somewhat battered repeater watch and replied:

"At precisely six forty-five a.m. They were never late by more than a moment or so. And never earlier either."

"Just after Matins.[5] That makes some degree of sense. I shall return then and meet these men personally. Remember what I requested. Send word of any similar corpses either prior to this date or from this day on. You may leave word at my house."

Séverin headed for the door. He would be back in his home within the hour and would pen a quick note. It was rare he requested the attention of the First Consul, but so far, Napoleon had never rejected one of his pleas.

"And he will provide me with anything I require. For, if I am correct, the nightmare of nine years ago is returning to both of our lives. Not to mention every living soul in all of France."

On that terrible though, Jean-Pierre Séverin increased his pace. Few things in this world frightened him, but the corpse in the Morgue heralded a terror that still caused him to quake with fear when alone in the dark. Some horrors seemed impossible to put to rest.

---

[5] Matins is the monastic nighttime liturgy, ending at dawn, of the canonical hours. In the Roman Catholic pre-Vatican-II breviary, it is divided into three nocturns. The name "matins" originally referred to the morning office also known as lauds. When the nocturnal monastic services called vigils or nocturns were joined with lauds, the name of matins was applied at first to the concluding morning service and later still to the entire series of vigils.

CHAPTER II

Paris, September 1795

The air was unseasonably brisk as Napoleon Bonaparte wound his way through the morning streets of Paris. For the fifth time he read the words. His publisher was delighted by his novel *Clisson et Eugénie.* His tale, a tragic romance of a military officer and his wife, was barely a work of fiction. His beloved fiancée, the lovely Désirée Clary, possessed many of the characteristics of the tragic Eugénie of his novel. But unlike Clisson, Napoleon would not meekly go to his death with a broken heart. That was the way of the tragic hero, not a true military man.

But it was the next letter that caused him to frown and sigh with annoyance. His request for a transfer to Constantinople had been rejected and he was officially removed from the active list. A blow to his future, certainly, but one he had anticipated. Someone within the new Directorate wished to destroy his career, prevent his rise.

First had been an offer of a post in the Army of the West. Did they really believe he would meekly accept a demotion to a mere infantry command? A plea of ill-health dealt with that quite effectively. But then, they had blocked his only path back to true command, back to proving that, despite his being only 26, he was one of the premiere military leaders of this new age.

This thought did not come from mere conceit, this much Napoleon knew in his heart of heart. His skill in battle had been proven time and time again. The proper use of artillery was one of the essential points. Many viewed the lovely field pieces as items to merely be pointed in a direction and blaze away. But a precise use of the guns transformed them from loud occasional menaces to infantry into weapons capable of decimating the enemy as a body. This, combined with his knowledge and belief in his own fortune, had led him to a simple conclusion: to effect true change, he needed to command. First the military, then the country. For who was more worthy?

But once again, he was being hampered by the worst adversary of all, secret enemies. Politicians with no more comprehension of battle than the high officials in the Church. Somehow, Napoleon knew there were individuals who wished to re-establish some version of the old order of life. The Directorate, like the Committee for Public Safety, were just men seeking to make themselves the new kings, princes, dukes and counts. That would not do.

When the glorious Revolution had come to his adopted homeland, Napoleon Bonaparte had embraced it happily. Not because he believed in the absolute equality of mankind. That, in and of itself, was a mere tale spun by the lesser to pull down the greater. There were always superior men in the world. These were the true leaders, the geniuses, who directed those not born so gifted. But this did not come from blood, or breeding. Greatness was a birthright, one of the few received from nature. Napoleon was one of those men.

Therefore, the Revolution was the best means to rise, to use his talent to become his country's leader. Traditions of nobility and ancient history had been, prior to the transformation of the social order, a barrier for him to achieve his justified prominence. By throwing down the ancient ways, France became a land in which he could flourish. His military genius, as well as his knowledge of better methods of dealing with politics, would make France, and eventually the rest of the world, a true paradise. But only if he could prove his worth.

He wasn't fool enough to believe the true path was through the previous leadership either. The so-called Committee for Public Safety was little more than a tool of terror, a weapon for the crazed to attack the formerly great. Some of the Jacobin ideals were wise and correct. Universal male suffrage, abolition of slavery, and a fair legal system. These were laudable aims. But they had been forgotten when Robespierre, Saint-Just, and their writer compatriot Marat had lost sight of the truth. They had the chance to make a world in which excellence could rise above the common rabble. Instead, they had chosen to become little more the street thugs, bully-boys drunk on blood from their slaughters. Rather than trans-forming France into a utopia, the country had become a charnel house. One where crazed peasants had rampaged through the streets, denouncing any who crossed their path. Napoleon still remembered a harridan at one of the many executions being held on the Place de Grève. She was knitting as she watched the killings of the innocent with cold satisfaction as housemaids and seamstresses were guillotined for no reason other than her inner rage. This was the legacy of the Committee, rabble rule, mob justice, and a fountain of blood stolen from the lives of the innocent.

The difficulty was that the new regime, the Directo-ry, had come with a new set of complications. They were inefficient. Barras and his body of men were a well-meaning pack, rejecting the excesses of the previous regime. They had established a better system of justice and restored the currency to a worthy level. But the Directory was still a body of men, each possessing their own ideals, their own desires. And these desires were often in conflict with others' from the ruling party. Take Carnot, a man of brilliance and skill, a mathematician and organizer par excellence. Instead of using his talents and skills to improve France, he was forced to spend his time in futile battles with Barras. And intrigue was to Carnot as land-walking was to whales. A waste of time, and improper. That was merely one example of what needed to be corrected. Barras alone could fill volumes of treatises on incorrect behavior of government officials.

These problems appeared out of Napoleon's reach. At least, for now. But something had to change; something would have to occur soon. He knew, in his secret heart, that his dreams of power were no mere fantasies. They were a reality; a future he would seek to achieve with the same military genius that he had used to rise to the rank of general by a mere 24 years of age.

His thoughts were interrupted by a shout from below, on the bank of the river. A pair of men, a boy and a gray-haired man, were leaning over the fallen figure of a body. Their slight frames shielded the corpse from view, but they appeared both surprised and revolted by the sight. In need of a diversion, Napoleon walked down a flight of stone steps and was soon at their side.

"Is there a problem, citizens?" he inquired.

The stench coming from the two men was terrible. A noxious combination of river pollution and the harsh odor of the sewers. Napoleon was grateful for his artillery training. His time with the great guns had taught him to ignore all foul smells and analyze them for danger signs. This pair reeked, but they were harmless—

unless they touched your coat. Then one would have a difficult time removing the scent that exuded from their very being.

The older man pulled off his woolen cap and elbowed the boy to do the same.

"Sorry to disturb you, Monsieur le General," He said. "My grandson and I found this poor soul after we finished our rounds. We check the sewers and make sure there's nothing plugging the openings."

Despite himself, Napoleon was surprised by the man's reaction. He was dressed in civilian clothing, a well-tailored blue suit and white shirt. The only symbol of his possible connection to the military was a pair of soft, well-made Hessian boots he received as a gift from his brother, Joseph.

"You know me, Monsieur?" he inquired.

The older man bobbed his head and gave a sketch of a salute.

"I was a sailor in Toulon, General. I saw you on the fort with the cannons. You saved our lives from the English and made them run away like rats. We cheered you good that day."

Napoleon smiled, remembered the glory of that day. Lifting the siege of Toulon had been the first step in his path to glory. A good day.

"Thank you for your kindness," he replied. "What is your name, Monsieur? And what have you discovered?"

The man touched his forelock again.

"My name is Paul Bernard, General. This is my grandson, Hugo. And we found a body, torn up something awful. Move aside, lad. Let the man see."

Hugo, a thin, dull-eyed lad not yet in his teens, shuffled aside. He possessed a muddy brown hair and a spindly frame. Napoleon, as was his habit, assessed the lad and knew he was probably best used where he was at this time. Too small to be a soldier and too slow-witted to learn the skills of a sailor. As a sewer worker, he would be efficient and unimaginative, if odiferous.

The corpse was that of a man, soaked and smelling of the river. His face and torso were in ruins, shredded and barely recognizable as human. This was a state Napoleon knew all too well. A man dies and the animals, clever-eyed beasts which lurk in the shadows, begin to consume the remains. Horrible, but a sight well-known to any warrior who had served in a battle.

"Sad," Napoleon pronounced with a shrug. "He probably fell in some time back and the rats fed on his innards. Call the watch and they'll send him for burial."

Paul Bernard shook his head and sighed.

"Sorry to be rude, but the General doesn't know much about bodies in the water. This man didn't drown. He hasn't been in the water more than a day or two."

"Explain," said Napoleon who had a sudden inkling that Paul Bernard possessed layers unseen beneath the grime of his current profession.

Though he had no interest in matters naval, Napoleon knew some details of the skills required. To survive as a sailor, and no mere rope-puller, a man became a craftsman of impressive skill. To denigrate them because they were lower rank was against his nature. One could learn much from those who did not hold the rank of officer.

Paul Bernard pointed a horning and slightly twisted finger towards the face of the corpse.

"Look at his face, General. Not all bloated. If he'd drowned and got eaten this much, he'd be all puffy. And his skin was firm and not all rotten and mushy. If he'd been in long enough to have this much chewing on him, he'd be falling off the bone. And all this chewing? I've seen men chewed on by sharks that didn't look this bitten. I think he, like that man last week, was chewed and then dropped in the water. Maybe a pack of big rats or wild dogs? No bears or wolves around Paris. But my brother's wife's brother said he saw a pair of white wolves just outside Nice..."

Napoleon squatted down beside the body and examined the extent of the damage. The buzzing sound that was the sewer keeper was like that of an insect to his ears. Napoleon possessed the ability to focus on a subject to a degree unheard of by most. Combined with his fast-moving mind, he could analyze a situation at an uncanny rate. This had led him to become a successful artillery general, as well as allowing him to see all facets of a battle. This was another reason he needed to rise beyond the common herd.

When applied to any situation, Napoleon was often able to determine details and discover a method of proceeding at an impressive rate. Which was why he stared at the many wounds all over this dead man. There was something odd there, and he knew that a careful examination would yield the answers to the disquiet he was suddenly feeling.

The trauma upon the corpse was extensive, but no more than one might see on a battlefield. The facial area was ruptured around the mouth and nose—a series of fissures reminiscent of metal fragmentation. The body was equally ripped, with large internal sections seemingly scooped out. Napoleon had viewed similar images in Italy. Modern weapons were not for the faint of heart. A true soldier learned to accept the results of their use, the horrific destruction of his fellow man.

But this was not the feature that caused his disquiet. Staring for a full moment, the details in question formed in his mind. It was the clothing the dead man was wearing. While damaged by the water, the shoes on the man's feet were well-made, expensive leather, from a cobbler of impressive skill. The stockings were torn, but quite obviously made of silk, and the jacket was well-used, but had once been expensive. This was no mere tramp, murdered and tossed into the river to be forgotten. This was an individual of some worth, at least at one time. The atrocities perpetrated by Robespierre and his compatriots had caused many of the nobles to flee France. But with their fall, some were apparently returning; Napoleon believed this man may have been one of those *émigrés*. This made his death all the more puzzling.

Straightening up, Napoleon cut off Paul Bernard with a quick look.

"Send your grandson to find the gendarmes for this district," he ordered. "I will wait with you to ensure the remains are properly dealt with and sent to the Morgue."

A short time later, two gendarmes appeared, a mean-eyed man named Sicre and a younger recruit whom he didn't know. Napoleon knew their type all too well from the army. Time-wasters, more interested in getting an easy pay and taking advantage of underlings than actually performing their duties. But in the face of command, and possible danger to their position, they became subservient and compliant.

"I am General Napoleon Bonaparte. You will have this body taken to the Morgue. There are areas of concern that must be addressed."

Napoleon used his best officer's tone in addressing the gendarme. His voice was calm, but clearly brooking no argument or further discussion.

Sicre appeared inclined to debate, but caught the steely look in Napoleon's eyes. Though a tall, powerful, if somewhat corpulent man, the gendarme was no fool. He was a bully, a blackmailing wastrel more interested in accepting free drinks and feminine charms than performing his duties. But he also knew there were some men never to be crossed. This round-faced general with the harsh accent was such a one.

"Of course, Citizen General," Sicre said.

He spat out some orders to bring a fallen door as a replacement stretcher to his junior partner, them inquired:

"Shall I shall tell the Morgue attendants you plan on calling?"

Napoleon nodded and gave the man a slight smile:

"Yes, do that. I shall mention your hard and quite excellent work."

Sicre found himself saluting Napoleon, a fact he would discuss in the years to come. As an elderly man in the distant future, he would tell over and over of the day he had met the great Napoleon Bonaparte and was entrusted with very important duties by the future Emperor. For his part, Napoleon soon forgot the fat, fool, but he remembered the gendarmes' willingness to obey his orders, which was one reason why their duties and numbers in the days of his rule flourished.

Heading deeper into the city, Napoleon felt his sense of disquiet spreading within his mind. It was not the death of a man, in and of itself. No, that he could confront with ease. A part of him, the hidden portion of his mind which helped him in the face of danger, was invoked. Something was wrong here, and he did not know what it could be.

Then, a face from the past intervened, a familiar individual of whom Napoleon thought during periods of confusion. A calm, controlled man who had once predicted that he, a young army officer, would rise to unimaginable heights of power.

A man who had seemingly appeared out of nowhere and now stood before him.

"Maestro Séverin," said Napoleon, surprised.

Then he smiled and extended his hand to the taller man.

"You are looking well."

"Am I? How surprising!"

Séverin's words were said in a light tone of voice, but beneath the humor was a degree of melancholy that Napoleon sensed instantly.

He normally would have wished the man a pleasant day and move along, but Séverin was a swordmaster and a deep thinker. And he, too, appeared lost in dark emotions. The solution was, in the mind of a military man like Napoleon, to present Séverin with a task. Nothing better to fight back the darkness of the soul than the work of the mind and body.

"I had considered presenting myself to your academy," said Napoleon. "A terrible incident has me disturbed, which is surprising since violent death is my profession..."

"Shall we walk? You intrigue me, Sire. Excuse me, General."

Séverin waved in the direction Napoleon was strolling and stepped besides the shorter man.

Napoleon related the events of the dead body in short unequivocal sentences. He may have been preparing a report of the results of a battle for a general like Lazare Hoche. Hoche was one of the few men Napoleon admired and respected. And in his opinion, Séverin possessed a mind even greater than that military genius.

"An interesting puzzle," Séverin said, finally. "A well-dressed man is cleaved by persons or creatures unknown. And none of the important people of Paris appear to be seeking a missing family member. I believe we must examine this body for additional information."

Séverin changed directions, leading Napoleon towards the Morgue.

"What of your academy, Monsieur Séverin? Are you not required to be there for your students?"

The first meeting between Napoleon Bonaparte and Jean-Pierre Séverin had occurred at the latter's fencing academy—a small but impressive facility. Maestro Séverin was a true expert with the blade, demonstrating skills in both the formal styles and the street brawling systems generally not taught in fencing schools.

"My assistant will attend any students showing up today. I told him I may be away for the day. My restless demeanor is somewhat strong these days. Additionally, certain details of your description of the wounds have me concerned. But, if the Lord is kind, my theory will be incorrect. Sadly, the creator is not often so obliging."

Séverin shortened his long stride and they marched at a quick pace through Paris.

Napoleon glanced at the taller man:

"You have heard of such happenings before?" he asked.

Séverin raised an open palm in response.

"I traveled a great deal in my youth. One of my swordmasters, a former imperial officer named Kronos, taught me much about the unusual. He, his close friend, who was a scholar of some renown named Grost, and Kronos's daughter, fought a terrible evil in the Zdanice

Forest. Though our time in Muskovy was even more terrible. That is a tale I will never tell another. Since that time, I keep my eyes open to the unusual."

"I had no idea you were so well-traveled. Or a student of the darker aspects of the world. I have little time for such things. My world is the here and now, and I will carve my way to my goals. No mumbling mystic or walking corpse will hinder or assist my progress. Still, I imagine this is an area others may find important."

Napoleon's dismissal of matters such as this was unsurprising. He was a realist, despite his belief that luck often was the difference between success and loss.

"It would take far too long to explain the unique path I undertook in life. One day, perhaps, I shall do so, but for now, I ask that you take my word with some faith. Or lacking faith, trust. If I am correct, the lives of every soul in Paris are in danger. As well as France herself."

Séverin was very emphatic as he explained his position. But secretly, he said a prayer, hoping he was wrong, though in his heart of hearts, he knew he was not. And that meant a future of blood, death and horror.

CHAPTER III

Paris, November 1804

Claude Donat was a man with a mission, a holy crusade. His work was in God's name and his toil was all that stood between the holiness and the return of the archfiend whose name must never be spoken. Unless he served with unswerving faith, disaster could befall all life.

Wringing the cloth in his leather bucket, Donat began scrubbing the scuff marks on the marble tiles leading to the sacristy. Such desecration of the holy was unimaginable, a true insult to the dignity of the Lord. Notre-Dame was, in Donat's mind, God's station on Earth. This was the new holy land, the lands formerly of that name long since lost to evil unbelievers. This much was confirmed as His Holiness himself was here in Paris to crown the First Consul as Emperor.

Above him, the four hundred children that made up the choir sang with a beauty that almost made Donat weep. But he forced back his tears, knowing they might stain the holy ground which he was cleansing. All tears must be saved for later, when he would be away from this, the Lord's home upon the Earth.

At the other end of the cathedral, Donat spied two men. They were exalted personages, beings who existed at the feet of God's chosen. And they were so vastly different in appearance and behavior. Perhaps this was the Lord's method of distinguishing the great, making them vastly different and unique looking. Perhaps not. But they were important men and were no doubt speaking of major events that would affect the coronation of the Emperor.

The first man was tall, lean as a blade, and possessed dark, curling ringlets of hair which framed his face and neck. He was dressed in the white uniform of a Marshal of the French Army. The garment was covered in masses of gold piping, medals and lace. Even his sword was gold and covered in complex designs and traceries. He was Joachim Murat, Marshal of France, known as the "First Horseman of Europe." He was Napoleon Bonaparte's brother-in-law, closest advisor, and one of the most important men in the Empire.

The second man was a contrast in every way. Older, graying, squat built and broad-shouldered. There was a dangerous air about him, an animalistic predatory danger in his gaze and his sinewy movements. He was dressed in a plain gray tunic and matching pants. His sword was well-worn and clearly a weapon used in battle. This was Major Jost Alois Pfyffer von Altishofen, second in command of the Pontifical Swiss Guard. He was a professional soldier, a warrior raised in battle and surrounded by death for most of his forty-five years. The life of a protector of the head of the Church was positively refreshing compared to fighting as a mercenary for the English, French, Prussians, Russians and Austrians.

"I will send you a bottle tonight. You'll find no wine equal to that of the Bordeaux region. Absolute ambrosia," Murat said.

He scanned the cathedral, missing few details of the ancient building, the holiest location in the whole of the Empire.

"My thanks," replied von Altishofen. "I will send you a Venetian vintage from a Cardinal whose family once sat in the seat of St. Peter. The Commandant is particularly fond of that wine. He will bring several cases when His Holiness arrives next week."

He spoke French with a marked Germanic accent, but his voice was smooth, almost melodic in quality. This was quite at odds with his scarred face and panther-like motions.

"That will be enjoyable to sample," said the Marshal. "My wife, the Emperor's dear sister, will be holding a ball next week in honor of the coronation. I will see you receive an invitation."

Murat found an easy comradery with this man. He knew the Major was one of the most important men in the Papal States, possessing the power of a deputy governor and a military position that made him one of His Holiness's inner circle.

Major von Altishofen gave a little bow as both thanks and a salute.

"There will be a small troop the Pontifical Swiss Guard in the Cathedral. The Noble Guard, the Papal States' cavalry, will merely escort the Pontiff here. I believe you plan on surrounding the Emperor-to-be with your men?"

Murat ignored the slight jibe, a reminder that Napoleon was still First Consul until the coronation. The Papal States forces were small and elite, but they held a slightly inflated sense of their place in the overall power of Europe. Important, but hardly a force the French army needed concern itself with should they fall into contention. But this was not the time or place to remind the Swiss Guard of such critical details.

Instead, Murat shrugged in a very Gallic fashion.

"His Imperial Highness will be guarded by the heavy cavalry. They are known throughout Europe as the

Grenadiers à Cheval de la Garde Impériale. Security will be provided by the elite consular guard. They are called the Gendarmes d'élite de la Garde Impériale. The Emperor will be well-protected."

Major von Altishofen merely nodded in response. He found the new powerful men of France to be almost as worrisome as the previous madmen that had executed their poor king. The new blood of this country was not the fat, complacent nobles he had known from his years in battle throughout the world. They were lean, hungry men, with eyes like wolves and the desire to emulate the great families of history.

"Oh," added Murat, pulling a slip of paper from his tunic, "One of the agents of the Prefecture passed along an odd bit of information. Why is there an Austrian among your troop? You do know that we are at war with his country, no?"

Major von Altishofen chuckled and shook his head.

"He is not my man. I requested he be left behind in the Vatican, but Pope Pius VII disregarded my request."

Murat replaced the note in his tunic and straightened his cuffs.

"None-the-less, his presence concerns us. Please tell me why His Holiness required the presence of an Austrian. Was it to insult the Emperor?"

Major von Altishofen shook his head, though more emphatically now.

"Not at all. That man possesses no interest in the politics of the Papal States, let alone Europe. His name is Baron von Karnstein and he is from Styria. The Pope made him a member of the lesser order of Exorcists. He investigates unholy happenings in the name of the Church. You need not worry about him sending any information to his fellow Austrians."

"How so?"

Despite himself, Murat was interested in the answer.

"Because he views the Hapsburgs as latter-day pretenders. According to my information, his family predates the Holy Roman Emperor, Charles the Great. No, that one only seeks witches, warlocks and monsters. He matters not at all," concluded von Altishofen, waving a hand, indicating the lack of importance of the Austrian exorcist.

Murat frowned, finding the answer to be slightly odd. But one didn't discount the terrible, dark areas of the world. Even though he was a man as firmly rooted in the principles of the modern world, Murat knew there were aspects of the world that were ancient and terrible. He had seen as much on 13 Vendémiaire, a secret he and the Emperor had agreed he should take to his grave.

"So be it," he pronounced

He took the Swiss Guard deputy commander out of Notre-Dame. The joyous voices of the choir were an omen. The coronation would proceed perfectly.

CHAPTER IV

Paris, September 1795

The guard outside the Morgue was going to be difficult. He was fat, unshaven, sweaty, stank of cheap wine and foul tobacco. He stared at both men through the bloodshot eyes of one suffering from a life of constant indulgence. His face then broke into the sneering smile of a bully. This was not a brawler or killer. This was a man who sought out the weak and only attacked from a position of strength. He would bash a man over the head with a chair the minute his back was turned. Or trip a child into a puddle of mud, and roar with laughter as the youngster wept. A hyena in human form.

And that made him everything Napoleon Bonaparte despised. He'd seen such men in the army. Usually they were non-commissioned officers, but he'd encounter a few in the officer ranks as well. He broke them, all of them, as he rose through the ranks. Such men were secretly cowards and no benefit in battle.

"Good evening, citizens. The Morgue is closed. And even if we were not, we do not allow visitors," said the guard.

He looked at both men and took in their clothing. Séverin's outfit was utilitarian, making him resemble a minor clerk or a functionary. Napoleon wore civilian togs, mud-spattered and somewhat threadbare. Neither looked particularly prosperous. The guard sniffed and lifted his nails, contemplating something only he could view.

Séverin gave a small bow.

"The Morgue is a public building, open to all citizens, I believe."

"Not at this hour, except those who've been summonsed. Please find your way out. Unless you hand me twenty francs. Each. I know what you wish to do to the corpses. Just clean up after you are done."

The guard belched and pulled out a clay cup. He poured a small measure of wine from a brown bottle and drank it up in one gurgling gulp.

Napoleon stared at the man for a heartbeat. His arm then cocked back and he backhanded the cup out of his hand. The clay shattered as it struck the brick wall, the wine dregs running slowly towards the stained floor. Before the guard could react, the General scooped up the wine bottle and dashed it to the ground. The shards exploded across the room, echoing through the empty halls.

"What are you doing? I'll kill you! I'll summons the gendarmes!" the guard spluttered.

"Yes, do that," Napoleon said, calmly.

Here was the controlled tactician who had led armies so successfully in his short years.

"Then you can explain to them why you demanded a bribe from General Napoleon Bonaparte and Sword Maestro Jean-Pierre Séverin," he added.

The guard rose up, his face transformed from anger, to fear, to canny assessment in seconds.

"I… ah... citizens, I think…" he muttered, trying to straighten up, but at a loss as to how to react.

"Citizens? You dare to call us that when you are as bad as the autocratic monsters we defeated in our grand Revolution?" said Napoleon. "You dare to abuse your authority, granted to you by the people? You worm! You contemptible cur! Find a broom and clean up this mess and hope I do not tell your superiors of your dereliction of duty."

Napoleon watched as the guard withered before his eyes. Like all bullies, he was easily defeated by a strong, intelligent response.

The General and Séverin strode past the guard, who was even now running for a closet and pulling out a broom.

After a short walk down a hallway, they spotted a man seated at a desk. He was a fleshy man, but tiny in size. Shaped like a ball, with tufts of wiry hair along his head and face, he was peering at a small pile of papers through large, thick spectacles. Looking up, his watery brown eyes looked enormous, but he smiled and showed them large yellow teeth that were very even and straight.

"Hello, citizens! How may I help you?"

He placed the papers down on the table and stood up. A head shorter than Napoleon, he was almost dwarfish and elderly, but radiated a youthful energy.

"A body was brought in today. Very damaged. Pulled from the Seine. If it is not too much trouble, we would wish to examine it," said Séverin, giving the older man a sketch of a smile. "Might I ask who I am addressing?"

"My name is Leo Perrin," the man replied. "I'm the one of the Assistant Medical Examiners. Today's dead body? Yes, that one is still with us. The other four were claimed or sent for common burial. Please follow me."

"The other four?" Séverin didn't bother to hide his concern as he followed Perrin down a flight of stairs.

"Oh yes, my friends. Five poor people. Terribly mangled in the last three days. Quite horrible. All pulled from the river and sent here. I remarked it was rather queer, but Doctor Roche, the Chief Medical Examiner, declared there to be nothing strange about each case. As a humble servant of the Republic, I had no choice but to agree. Still, in all my years working at the Morgue, I have only seen such dreadful damage on four occasions. Quite awful."

Perrin fished out a ring of keys and opened a door, leading them inside. He turned up the light. A body was on a stone table, covered in a blood-stained sheet.

"If I may?" Séverin looked to a Perrin, who nodded.

The sword master pulled away the sheet. The scent of decay suddenly flooded the room along with alcohol and several other unidentified odors.

"That is the man" said Napoleon. "His shoes were expensive and well-made. I found that odd. One does not expect the wealthy to be pulled from the river. Unless they choose death as a romantic gesture," he mused, remembering the tales of young lovers who chose to drown rather than face life without the one they loved.

He found such notions cowardly and foolish. Love, while important and wonderful, could be found again if one looked hard enough. But if not, death in battle was the courageous means of seeking an end.

Séverin examined the trauma to the body for several moments without comment. He retrieved a small looking-glass from an interior pocket and leaned closer, taking a closer look at the edges of the wounds. After a time, he frowned and studied the face before exhaling and nodding once.

"You have an excellent eye for details, General," he said, replacing the looking-glass in his pocket. "That man is, or rather was, a nobleman, more specifically the dispossessed heir of the Vicomte de Meilcour. He fled during the Terror. He was a libertine but a competent swordsman. I believe he hoped to bring back the Bourbons."

"A Royalist? Are they still not considered outlaws?" said Perrin, wringing his hands and looking distressed.

He quickly covered the body again with the sheet and shook his head over and over.

"I should think so" replied Napoleon, frowning. "This de Meilcour is known to me. He fled when General Hoche defeated the Royalists. I remember his name. Reports held he was one of the worst and cruelest among that pack of fiends."

Séverin rounded on Perrin.

"The other bodies. You stated they were claimed or taken away. Was there anything remarkable besides the damage to the corpses?"

Perrin frowned and then shook his head.

"They were vastly different, the poor souls. One was a young girl. Another, a beggar. A third was unknown, but he too did possess expensive foot wear. Which might be what you meant, is that not so, citizen?"

"It is," Séverin frowned. "Possibly two former noble, and each murdered by remarkable means."

Perrin, still wringing his hands, hunched his shoulders slightly.

"I was unable to determine the means of death. Doctor Roche declared they were consumed by the river's bottom dwellers, but I am unsure. And must now ask that you leave."

Napoleon was about to object, but Séverin intervened.

"Yes, I think that is a reasonable request. I thank you for your kind assistance, Citizen Perrin."

Moments later they were back in the open air, heading away at a rapid pace. Finally, Napoleon asked Séverin:

"You discovered something."

The swordmaster looked off in the distance for a full minute. Finally, he focused back on the Corsican General.

"I have a nickname."

From any other man, Napoleon Bonaparte might have demanded clarification. But Papa Séverin was no common citizen. There was power within this man. And a clear-sighted vision that was rare among all men. Their training sessions had been a transformative moment. For Napoleon, that is. For Jean-Pierre Séverin, that was merely another day in an impressive and very colorful life.

"You have a nickname?" Napoleon cocked a head and waited.

Séverin nodded once.

"*Gâteloup*. That was what I was called in the past."

"Spoiler of wolves? You hunted the beasts? Where?" said Napoleon, intrigued despite himself.

"Several places. In the Gévaudan and the Black Forest, to name but two. But the beasts in questions were not the poor animals which are rarely seen anymore in our modern world. No, these were once humans. They lost their souls to darkness..."

Séverin studied Napoleon's face.

"You are saying you hunted...?"

Napoleon could not manage to say the word. He was a man of his time, rejecting the superstitions and tales of the ancient past. But part of him believed there was some truth to the legends and lore of evil in the world.

"*Loup-garous*," Séverin confirmed. "Among other monsters, as I indicated earlier today. The body you discovered bears the mark of one of the worst of that breed of foul creature."

"Werewolves," said Napoleon, having difficulty believing he was saying the word out loud. "We are about to undertake a hunt against a creature created by Lucifer himself?"

"If only it were that simple," Séverin replied, taking Napoleon's arm and leading him away. "I fear evil is about to attempt to rear its head in a terrible way. Dark days are ahead for Paris, if not the world..."

CHAPTER V

Paris, November 1804

Jean-Pierre Séverin waited. He knew the priest and his black-clad follower would appear sooner or later to the Morgue. The building was as silent as the proverbial tomb, with only the scratching of Leroy's pen audible. Many would find the hush in the presence of the dead quite disturbing, but not Séverin. To him, the quiet was restful. The dead were rarely a difficulty; they were merely shells of once vital beings. Only a bare few were a danger.

Checking the battered silver time piece he always kept tucked in his vest, Séverin smiled as a pair of feet sounded down the hallway. Exactly 6:45 a.m. Just as Leroy had indicated. Tucking away the watch, the tall swordmaster clasped his hands behind his back and waited. The sounds of speaking voices floated his direction, words spoken in rapid Italian.

Two men stepped into view and stopped upon noticing Séverin's presence. They were a picture of contrasts, opposites in so many ways, resembling characters in a mummer's play, the opposite men who conduct an amusing conversation to lighten the forthcoming tragedy. Despite himself, Séverin smiled.

The man in the lead was short and barrel-chested. A vast round paunch extended in front of him, causing him to resemble a serpent after swallowing an enormous animal. His hair was short, closely cut and iron-gray in color. His clothing was black and red and quite sumptuous and well-tailored. A gold crucifix dangled from his wide neck, jangling as he moved. He glanced up and smiled, his brown teeth and dark eyes flashing and giving him a beatific appearance.

The second was taller, younger, and astonishingly handsome. Equal in height to Séverin, he was rapier-thin and moved with a slow, lugubrious style that suggested cat-like reflexes. His hair was a curtain of darkness, the darkest Séverin had ever viewed outside of visitors from the Far East. His eyes were light blue and large and his skin was very pale. There was a scar across the right cheek, a slash that Séverin knew came from no blade. He was dressed in black, with only a sweat-stained white shirt providing a dash of color.

"Good morning, my friend!" said the priest in French with a thick, though educated and smooth, Roman accent. "Would I be correct in presuming you are the head of this establishment? The one called Jean-Pierre Séverin?"

Séverin bowed.

"I am he. Whom do I have the pleasure to meet? I quite approve of your kind actions on behalf of the deceased of our fair city."

The priest chuckled and waved a hand to indicate a dismissal of such gratitude.

"I am Monsignor Lorenzo Pisani. His Holiness, the blessed Pope Pius, wished to lend my small services to your wonderful city on this joyous event. Our Lord believed that blessed are the downtrodden. A prayer for the dying or deceased is the least the Holy See can do this day."

Séverin bowed again. He could tell the priest was entirely sincere in his beliefs. There were truly holy men and women in this world, individuals who tried to live

47

by the tenets of their faith. To find one attached to a major religious figure, such as the Pope, was a surprise. Usually, only the politicians of the church rose to such spots. To discover an actual man of God in such a place did give one a trace of hope for the future.

"This silent gargoyle at my elbow is Franz von Karnstein," the priest continued. "He's an Austrian, but we try not to hold that against him. He is a member of the lesser Order of Exorcists. The Swiss Guard insisted he accompany me for protection. I find such a request quite amusing and indulge our Swiss friends and their funny notions of danger."

Father Pisani chuckled again, gesticulating in wide, broad motions as he explained the situation.

Franz von Karnstein nodded and clicked his heels in salute. He was holding a small leather bag, a battered, elderly item that appeared to be a soldier's bullet container. Father Pisani reached in and pulled out his surplice, which he prayed over, kissed and lay around his neck. He reached back in and removed a small stone bottle with a cross etched across the flat sides.

"There are two in need of your services, Father," said Séverin waving towards the hallway at his rear. "An elderly man and a woman. They died in a small fire in their home. The smoke caused them to expire as the flames were extinguished."

The priest nodded gravely and headed past the taller Séverin. He pulled the sheets, exposing the faces and chests. Crossing himself, he knelt and began to pray, the soft words of Latin filling the air. Séverin, recognizing the prayer for the souls of the dead, stopped listening. Instead, he turned his focus upon Franz von Karnstein.

"Forgive me, Monsieur, but—if I may?—what is the Order of Exorcists? I know of the holy rite against evil, but I did not know there were men who devoted their lives to such a pursuit."

Séverin knew full well the details of the minor Order of the Roman Catholic Church, but this seemed to be a good method of engaging this man. He sensed there was a story to be learned.

"We are an order beneath the priests, deacons and others of the priesthood. We prepare infants for baptism. Very rarely we perform an exorcism."

Karnstein spoke French with an Austrian accent. His tones and method of speaking were very precise and educated.

"You seek to become a priest?" Séverin cocked his head, studying the man closer.

The scar on his face was not new. And he spotted the trace of another at the edge of Karnstein's collar.

"Perhaps."

Karnstein wasn't meeting Séverin's eyes. Instead, he appeared to be scrutinizing the older man's hands.

Séverin realized that it was time to surprise him. He knew the name Karnstein well, having learned about their long and frightening history from his old teacher. They were an ancient clan, one with a history that terrified all those who knew of the dark paths of the world. Jean-Pierre Séverin was one of them.

"Karnstein. Might you be a relative of Countess Mircalla of Styria?" said Séverin smiling.

Karnstein stared at him for a moment and looked both angry and afraid at the same time.

"A distant ancestor" he replied. "She died centuries ago."

"Did she?" said Séverin. "I heard otherwise. Does that make you the titular Count?"

Séverin was impressed by the younger man's self-control. Most men his age would be reaching for their weapon, looking for a duel. By bringing up his infamous ancestor, Séverin was in truth challenging the honor and family of Franz von Karnstein.

The younger man seemed to be wrestling with answering or not. His handsome face remained impassive, but there was a storm within his pale eyes. And the tension rose across his shoulders and arms. But finally, he appeared to relax slightly and answer.

"No. I am Baron Karnstein and Baron Vordenburg. I am heir to the title of Count. Why do you ask?"

Karnstein's voice held none of the tension still visible in his eyes and body.

"Mere interest," shrugged Séverin. "When I studied several esoteric subjects, your family name was mentioned at length. I assume that is the reason why you serve the Church. But please, forgive me; I did not wish to intrude upon your privacy."

Séverin stepped back, having heard Father Pisani complete his prayers and move to the corpses. He would be finished soon enough. Also, Séverin believed the discussion with the young nobleman required greater privacy.

"On behalf of His Holiness, I thank you." Father Pisani grinned.

They both knew Pope Pius would neither learn, nor care, about the Monsignor's charitable actions. But the pomposity of the statement was required, at least for politeness's sake.

"On behalf of the First Consul and Emperor-to-be of the French people, I thank you for your kindness. I hope to see you both again."

Séverin bowed to both men and was unsurprised to see that Karnstein was studying him with angry eyes.

Watching them leave, Séverin left the Morgue and returned home.

The name Vordenburg was in his mind. Pulling several books from his library, he was struck by the musk of the leather-bound volumes. This tome was Grost's masterwork about vampires, one of the few complete copies of the late professor's life's work. The subject was surprisingly wide and the depth of his teacher's knowledge still managed to astonish Séverin years later.

The chapters on the Karnstein family weren't difficult to find. Neither were their connection to the Scholomance and the Deep School, and the rumors of vampirism. According to Grost's research, Mircalla Karnstein was executed by her lover, a vampire hunter named Baron Vordenburg. This was interesting. Franz von Karnstein was an example of dualities in one man. Young and handsome, but dour. Dangerous, if the visible scars were anything to judge by, yet serving a spiritual power. And possessing the name of a family devoted to darkness, yet also holding the title of a warrior against monsters. Odd, but interesting.

I think I need to speak to the young Baron soon, thought Séverin. *I believe we have a great deal to discuss.*

Séverin pulled a small sword and a saber from the rack near the books and left his home. First, he would speak to Napoleon. Then, to the young Baron Karnstein.

CHAPTER VI

Paris, September 1795

Leaving Napoleon to seek out his contacts in the army, Séverin strolled the streets. He sought a specific target, an easy proposition theoretically. But, as in all things, when one searched for something, it was often hardest to find. Therefore, he allowed himself to simply walk the more crowded avenues. His eyes roamed the many people, tradesmen, soldiers, common people, which he encountered.

And then he sighted his prey, so to speak. A man, his face swathed in bandages, his left leg a small stump. He held a battered, tarnished tin cup in a woolen gloved hand, rattling the few coins before the passerby. He called out to the people in a harsh croaking voice, his barely visible eyes roaming the crowds.

Séverin sensed the hunger within the man, the lust for the goods carried by the people. The life of a beggar was a harsh one. They were the ignored refuse of society. People spat upon them, viewed them as monstrous and mad, but often they were merely victims of birth or circumstances. Séverin, as a good Republican, tried to assist them whenever he could, but he knew this was a Sisyphean struggle, a battle against mankind's behavior. A tragedy, one with little chance of a remedy until men transformed their soul to reach a higher degree of enlightenment.

Stepping before the beggar, Séverin held up three new and shiny coins. Dropping one in the tin cup, he rolled two more across his knuckles. The action of a street performer, a conjuring trick Séverin had picked up from a dagger fighting expert he had trained under in Naples.

"Two questions. A coin for each answer. And ten more if your information proves correct. Nothing dangerous, mind you, but important."

Séverin watched the man's eyes, seeing the intelligence within the nearly hidden orbs. Some beggars were simple beings, lost within their minds because of illness, disaster, or birth. This one possessed the light of intellect, a keen mind despite his ruined body.

"I don't know you."

The response was spoken in the same harsh tone. A grating sound that assaulted the ears.

"My name is Jean-Pierre Séverin. You may ask your people about my reputation. I am no informer or gossip. The information I seek is one that will benefit all involved."

Séverin straightened his back and took on a casual pose. The beggar stared for a moment at the taller man, his keen eyes assessing him.

Soon, he waved over a small boy and whispered something in the child's ear. The waif ran off, vanishing into the crowd. A full hour passed, the beggar continued to plead for remuneration. Séverin stood nearby, watching the current of men and women as their numbers slowly dwindled as evening approached.

The child appeared from the throng, the tiny being's dull eyes were unfocused and blank. Looking into this poor being's orbs was like gazing into a muddy puddle, a thin pool with no true depth. This was one of the lost, forgotten by society and abandoned. The beggars raised and fed such sad creatures, among the few willing to accept the forgotten children of unknown parents.

"Jonas say you can trust him. He say that one not bad."

The child's voice was as flat as his eyes. A being alive, yet not truly living.

The beggar handed the child a small coin, patted the youngster's filthy head and waited until the child vanished from sight. He rounded on Séverin and shrugged dramatically:

"Ask your questions."

Séverin dropped the first coin into the cup.

"Where is the Court of Miracles these days? And yes, I know it may have another name since the original is long destroyed. But you understand the question's meaning, I believe."

The beggar smiled, revealing a set of broken brown stumps where teeth should exist.

"I do, Citizen. Had you not phrased it in that way, I might have sent you to the site of the old Court, but you are a wise man and I shall not mislead. The Court of Miracles, for that still is our name, is in Les Halles, off the Rue Morgue. You will find it easily enough, I believe."

Séverin dropped the second coin in the cup.

"Who is the King of Beggars these days? I knew the one who called himself Cardinal Salmon. He died two years ago."

The beggar sighed and shook his head.

"Ah, Salmon! Such a kind man. Died a good death, in bed with a fifteen-year-old whore. I miss him. He took me in after I lost my leg. Run over by a cart."

Séverin raised an eyebrow, surprised by the demonstration of honesty on the latter's part. Most beggars wove tales of battles and heroism. Their lost limbs became symbols of formerly great times, a sentimental assault upon the masses. The beggar caught his surprise and guffawed:

"No reason to try and trick you, Citizen. You'll pay me just the same. Jonas, the head of this district, doesn't vouch for just anyone."

"I'm grateful to him for his kindness."

Séverin didn't know who this Jonas was, but that was no surprise. The beggars often hid behind pseudonyms, usually the names of saints or biblical figures. Perhaps Jonas was a former friend or contact of his.

The beggar guffawed yet again, a donkey's bray more than an expression of amusement.

"Don't be grateful. Jonas, despite his name, is not saint. He's a good protector of the guild. Salmon took him in. Made him one of us before he got his head chopped off for head-bashing. The one you're looking for is known as the Antipope. That's the king. Salmon made that one his second-in-command some years back. He's good, almost as good as Salmon."

Séverin added another coin in the cup.

"After I'm done, I will give you ten more. Can I find you here each day?"

The beggar nodded.

"Day and night, all seasons. I'm called Silas. Silas One-Peg."

Séverin gave the man a slight bow.

"You know my name already. I may consult with you again in the future."

Silas shrugged again.

"As long as you pay, Citizen. You seem a good sort, but money first."

"Agreed and understood," Séverin replied, giving Silas One Peg a wave.

Next stop was the infamous Court of Miracles. Possibly the most dangerous place in Paris that didn't involve politicians.

CHAPTER VII

Paris, November 1804

Séverin checked the forms a third time. He bowed at the First Consul's second secretary and left. The soon-to-be-Emperor was still one of the most efficient men in the world.

They met in his office and, after listening to Séverin's thoughts, Napoleon issued a quick series of orders. There was a military precision about his actions, no wasted seconds.

Seconds later, the swordmaster was propelled from the office and watched as one of the important under-lings of France's leader wrote out the directives. The new seal of Napoleon Bonaparte was affixed to the bottom and the results were presented to Séverin.

Napoleon's orders were a temporary commission in the army. This was a roving inspector's post that would allow Séverin to call upon the resources of any and all bodies of the Government in the event of an emergency. Very effective, very Napoleonic in style. There was no listed reason for such an extraordinary post. None save the two of them needed to know the true reason.

Returning to his former fencing school, Séverin changed into the light, slightly threadbare tunic he used for training. He knew he wouldn't have long to wait. Some factors were inevitable. In this case, the results were as predictable as the seasons.

The knock of the door was insistent, but not pos-sessing the force of anger he'd expected. Good. He'd hoped for better with this one. Perhaps this would not end up in another disappointment.

Opening the door, he smiled and waved his visitor inside. The latter bowed and walked in, taking off his cloak and following Séverin into the training hall.

"You expected me?"

Baron Karnstein didn't sound surprised. He stopped and examined a long rack of unusual weapons, obtained from various places abroad.

"I did," replied Séverin. "My only concern was that you might wish to challenge me to a duel. I did bring up your less than savory family history."

Séverin waited for the young nobleman, then led him deeper within the room. The training hall was an octangle chamber with clean white walls and flat, wooden floors. This was his personal training apartment, one which he had rarely allowed students to enter in the past. Though a Republican through and through, Séverin was also a maestro. As such, one needed an area for self-practice and reflection.

Baron Karnstein rounded on Séverin, but he was suppressing laughter.

"I may be young, Master Séverin, but I am no fool."

"Please explain," said Séverin, cocking his head.

Karnstein nodded and looked at the other man's hands.

"Your hands. I've seen such calluses thrice before. All three were swordmasters. They also possessed your calm and self-possession. Challenging them, or yourself, would be a poor idea."

"You're an observant young man," replies Séverin, with a bow. "Allow me to offer you a similar observation. That scar upon your face? That was not caused by any blade, but by a claw. Or should I say, a talon?"

"Talon is accurate," said Karnstein, meeting Séverin's eyes. "You know what killed those people."

"I do; do you?" said Séverin, raising one pale eyebrow.

"A werewolf. A member of the species called *loups- garous*. Violent and very dangerous. They feed on the innards of people—and their brains."

"Correct. Did you learn this from your training as an Exorcist?"

Séverin stepped deeper into the training room, his back to the young Austrian nobleman.

"No," Karnstein replied, following him into the room, but stopping a short distance away. "You have fought such monsters in the past?"

"I have," answered Séverin.

His back was turned to the other. He pulled a saber from the rack and tossed it to Karnstein, who caught it. Séverin then pulled a matching one and saluted.

"Let us exercise as we speak."

Karnstein saluted and assumed a fighting pose. They engaged in several passes before he spoke again:

"There is only one in Paris now. *Loup-garou*, that is."

Séverin disarmed Karnstein with a flick of his wrist and handed the young man his sword again.

"Correct. Otherwise there would be many more corpses. But the werewolf is of lesser importance. We must seek its master."

Karnstein swung wildly and was knocked to his back by Séverin. He rose, bowed, and assumed another fighting stance.

"How do you know he has a master?"

Séverin blocked the flurry of attacks from Karnstein. His blade barely moving as he parried each slice.

"A *loup-garou* possesses very little self-control. The Seine would be choked with bodies if he didn't. The creature would feed day and night. Their appetite is bottomless. But these werewolves, when controlled, will feast sparingly. However, very few beings possess the power necessary to control a rampaging beast like a *loup-garou*."

Karnstein stepped back, his face and body covered in sweat. He bowed deeply to Séverin.

"My thanks for the lesson. Both with the blade and the dark realms of the Earth."

Séverin returned the bow and placed the swords back on the rack.

"You seem to have had little training with the blade, Citizen Baron. How did you manage to survive against monsters without that essential skill?"

"I've had other training. May I ask why are you so ready to trust me? You do know the history of the Karnsteins. Still, I'm sure there are many secrets of which you are unaware."

Karnstein accepted a towel and mopped his face and chest. Séverin spotted a second scar on the young man's neck. The harsh gray crease stopped just above his heart. The swordmaster chuckled and shook his head.

"You forget, young man, that I have confronted the darkness for far longer than you've been alive. My information on the subject is deep. And I researched your other title. As I remembered, Baron Vordenburg was the man who executed the Vampire Countess Mircalla Karnstein over one hundred years ago."

"My parents were descendants of both," nodded the young nobleman. "They both died. That... set me on a different path, which is why I serve His Holiness and the Church. Temporal matters possess very little interest for me now."

Séverin studied the serious young man for a moment and came to a decision.

"We both possess the same ambition: to destroy this monster and its terrible master. I propose we work in concert. Together, we will be far stronger. And a *loup-garou* is no easy foe."

"Agreed," said Karnstein, extending his hand and gripping the swordmaster's palm in a strong grip. "Where do we begin?"

Séverin shook Karnstein's hand in return.

"The second most dangerous place in Paris, of course. Have you ever been beneath the Earth?"

CHAPTER VIII

Paris, September 1795

The Court of Miracles was a Parisian legend. To most it was nothing more than a story to tell naughty children, "Be good or the monsters of the Court of Miracles will take you tonight," and other such fables. Even the officials of Paris denied the existence of such a place. This was unsurprising. Government officials who attempted to war with a hidden underclass often found themselves treated like madmen, or dead by unknown hands. Far better to allow such beings to exist beneath the surface, invisible and forgotten. Myths within the modern world.

The Court of Miracles had become public knowledge thanks to the Sun King, Louis XIV. Paris had grown exponentially under the great king, causing an explosion in the number of poor in the city. A man, only known as the King of Beggars, had emerged and created a guild of the lowest of the low. He sat upon a battered tin and wooden throne in a ruined convent known as the *Filles-Dieu*. He protected his brothers and sisters like a feudal baron. The name of his group had come from the many false cripples under his auspices. The jest was that each night, blind and crippled men, women and children, all came before the King of Beggars. And miraculously their many infirmities would vanish in his presence.

Who was the King of Beggars? None knew. Some said he was a dispossessed son of a baron, an opponent of one of the leading Cardinals who sat at the right hand of the King. Others that he was an actor, a puppeteer who used his skills to teach beggars to become more bedraggled before the monied masses. Only the city of Paris knew the answer, and she held her secrets fiercely.

Fifty years ago, the original Court had been razed to the ground. Health concerns, such as the flourishing rat population, had been the excuse. But most knew the truth. Ending the power of the King of Beggars was the ultimate aim. For a brief time, the city fathers had been successful. But eventually a new King arose and his Court became hidden from view. The Court of Miracles still existed, but hidden from view or knowledge.

Séverin had met the previous King, a giant who called himself Cardinal Salmon. Salmon was a full head above the tall Séverin and far broader in shoulders and arms. He possessed a round belly like a cannon ball and a huge, thick, blue-black beard that was perpetually stained with food and wine. He laughed louder than any, fought with the power of a mad bear, and protected his people with the fury of a lion. A great man. Had he lived in more ancient times, he might have been a barbarian king, with an axe in one hand and a flagon of beer in the other.

He was also a learned man, despite his airs of foolish barbarity. The name was the clue. Most believed the pseudonym, "Cardinal Salmon," was simply to mock the tenets of faith. Appropriating the title of a prince of the Church was a clear method of demonstrating contempt, no? But a few, the ones who read deeper into the bible, understood differently.

Salmon was a name, an ancient Hebrew man who played an important, if somewhat unknown, role in the history of the people of the bible. Salmon was the great-great-grandfather of David, the righteous warrior king of distant days. And King David was the earliest ancestor of Jesus-Christ, the savior of all according to the New Testament.

In essence, Cardinal Salmon was declaring himself the father of a new line of saviors. Either this was the height of heresy, or a hope for a new future. Séverin believed the latter and hoped that the new King of Beggars would follow the beliefs of his predecessor. His name, Antipope, suggested demonic connections. However, Séverin knew the true master of darkness, the Devil's representative on Earth, possessed a different name. No, an Antipope was the title given historically when there were opposing claims to the pontiff's position. To be Pope was to be a king above those ruling countries, at least in theory. Many kings sought to control the position and attempted to force their choices into the Chair of St. Peter. When multiple claims occurred, there could be only one victor in the political struggle. The losers in these battles were deemed "Antipopes" by the Church and forever listed so in the annals of history.

That left the question, who was this new "Antipope?" Did he see himself as a fallen power in exile? A pretender to a greater throne? Or was he simply a man who heard a clever title and decided to use it as an alias to hide himself from the Parisian authorities? Séverin would discover soon enough.

The neighborhood of Les Halles was where Paris' fresh food markets were located, but all around it had sprung a maze of small, brick buildings, all closely packed, decrepit houses and sordid hovels. The area was filled with dubious types, so-called actresses, and writers of odd, outlandish pamphlets and tracts. Shockingly enough, there were a sparse number of prostitutes in the area. For some reason, the men, women, boys and girls, who plied the flesh trade felt a vaguely disturbing sensation. A sense of unease entered them the longer they roamed the narrow streets in the shadow of the Châtelet. Within a short time, they would venture elsewhere, the shadow of doom lessened in neighboring districts.

There was a nearly riotous quality to the area, Séverin noted. The air smelled of a mixture of dung and smoke, filth and grease, cheap perfumes and warm chestnuts. The people moved about in an almost challenging manner. Artists seemed to be seeking their subjects with a predatory gleam within their eyes. Bearded men and women in odd costumes argued in cafés about subjects so esoteric it appeared they didn't even completely comprehend the topics in question. And book sellers in small shadowy shops and almost hidden stalls sold tomes which produced an air of eldritch agitation among the examiners.

Séverin noted all odd occurrences, mentally placing them within his memory for future use. His pale eyes roved the buildings and citizens, finally noticing several beggars entering the same street. That alley had no official name, except at the point where it cut through the Rue Saint-Denis. There, a placard identified it as the Rue du Haut-Moulin—but everywhere else, it was popularly known as the Rue Morgue.

The first building in the Rue Morgue was a sleazy café whose sign bore the bold pun[6]: *Estaminet de l'Epi-Scié*. This establishment, which had an infamous reputation, was frequently raided by the Police. The Rue Morgue was a dark opening between the *Estaminet* and a house of ill repute filled with men and women. All the

---

[6] *épi scié*: lit. a sawed-off ear of wheat; *épicier* (homonym): grocer; the former being an allusion to a guillotined body.

men and quite a few women were smoking long, wooden pipes and the odor emerging from the doorway was noxious and sickening.

Standing before the passage were two men, neither hiding the fact that they were the guardians of this entry way. They were an odd sight, vastly different, yet both possessing the dead-eyed look of men used to a violent, harsh life. The first was tall, skeletally thin, and possessed a long, thin nose that resembled a proboscis of a mosquito. A brush of a mustache peaked out beneath the huge nostrils, only coming into view when he turned his head. His clothes were cheap, tattered and drooped on his emaciated frame and made him look a sad, bedraggled figure.

The second was far shorter, just above his companion's waist. He possessed a thick, huge, bushy, white mustache that spread wide across his round face. The facial growth was far too large for such a tiny man, but he could be seen stroking the extended whiskers fondly as Séverin approached. The man was otherwise hairless, not even possessing eyebrows on his billiard ball-shaped skull. His clothes were pricey, if old and slightly dilapidated from regular and, no doubt, long use. He resembled an aristocrat who'd lost his entire fortune, a tatterdemalion dandy attempting to keeping up appearances for his friends and fellows.

Both were armed with truncheons held loosely in their right hands. Also long, well-worn handles of knives protruded from their belts. They were conducting a conversation while scanning the streets, viewing every form of life that passed their way.

"I do believe that is true, my dear Cabot! The fellow smacks of one willing to poison a good horse to win a wager!" said the shorter one in a booming voice.

His tones were the careful intonations of an actor, one attempting to hide his accent and sound like one born to a noble class. The result was comic, a lampooning of the wealthy. But doubtfully the tiny man was unaware that his attempt was ridiculous at best.

"Didn't you do the same thing, Geof? I thought you gave that drug to the horse last year at the Christmas races to cause it to stop and piss every few steps," replied the taller man in a rougher voice, though with smooth tones that were easy upon the ears.

That one wasn't hiding his low birth, but his method of speaking was silky and seductive. He was probably an expert at wooing people to assist him in his ridiculous schemes. Séverin knew the type all too well. His father and younger brother had lived that lifestyle.

The tiny man named Geof stroked his mustache and stomped a foot.

"Drugging is not poisoning, Cabot! The animal lived and won last season's spring race! That scoundrel would murder the poor beast!"

The taller man named Cabot watched Séverin approach. He smiled, showing rows of yellow-stained teeth.

"Hello, my friend! I think you've come to the wrong location. Louise the exotic dancer has her place two streets over. Look for a wooden staircase."

Séverin stopped, unsurprised to see Geof grip his club tighter.

"I'm looking for the Antipope. Jonas and Silas One Peg told me to seek him here."

The pair exchanged a look, neither man demonstrating much emotion. They appeared to be conducting a silent conversation. This only occurred between close comrades, individuals who had served alongside each other in dangerous situations for a long time. The possibility of grievous injury or death appeared to forge a bond between individuals, ones that crossed classes or even personal likes.

Finally, the exchange was complete; Cabot placed his fingers in his lips. He blew a loud, discordant note that vibrated across the rickety walls of the tenements. A small boy appeared at his elbow a few seconds later. He possessed the same muddy brown hair as Cabot, as well as a similarly prominent nose. His clothes were old, but well-cared for, and there was a clean, healthy look to his eyes and face.

"Cicéron," Cabot stooped down to speak to the lad, "tell Jonas a man is here to see him. Fast, now!"

The boy named Cicéron fled into the alley and vanished from view. His footsteps could be heard for several seconds, but soon became lost amidst the noise of the street.

"You do understand, Citizen," said Geof, looking up to the taller Séverin, "we do not mean to be rude, but there are strangers who wish ill upon our company. Care, care and consideration, must rule us all."

"Yes."

Séverin didn't say anything more; he merely watched the pair and waited. Neither appeared concerned by his lack of discomfort. They resumed their conversation about race horses as if he were not present. They were a very self-possessed pair of scoundrels.

Almost half an hour passed before the boy returned. He was carrying a long gray cat, which stared at Séverin with narrow amber eyes. A moment later, both strode off, vanishing into the growing crowds.

Popping out of the stygian darkness of the alley appeared another man. Almost as tall as Cabot, but blockier built. He possessed hard, taunt muscles and hairy hands, which appeared to be covered by a layer of black soot. A brown leather patch covered his left eye and his head was topped by a thick mane of red hair. He smiled broadly upon seeing Séverin, showing a flash of square white teeth with large spaces between the ivories.

"Maestro Séverin!" he pronounced, his voice a surprisingly light and musical bass. "You don't remember me?"

Séverin smiled slightly and bowed.

"I do, Monsieur Jonas. You were accused of being part of a seditious plot, but I happened to see you brawling near my fencing academy that very afternoon, and testified accordingly."

Jonas bowed back.

"You saved me from a trip to the guillotine that day. Everyone charged was executed, even though most were innocent. But an informer had framed us and the Committee trusted that foul creature over good men and women. But I rattle on. How might I help you?"

"I need to speak to your, er, superior."

Séverin knew that secrecy was important among the beggars, which was why he had hesitated over naming their king, the Antipope, aloud.

"I was warned that you might pay us a call. You've just won me a *sou*. Another fellow believed you'd rat us out to the Directory, but I told him you were no sneak, whispering lies in the darkness. Our, er, superior—I like that term!—has agreed to meet you, but you must be blindfolded first. You may not learn our secrets, as you are not of our friendly gathering of fellows. And you must give all your weapons to me. I shall remain at your side at all times."

Jonas spoke very matter-of-factly, as if he was merely conducting a conversation with an old friend. This was wisdom and experience on the beggar's part. Had they held their discussion in hushed voices, stealing glances about for eavesdroppers, the entire neighborhood would have become interested. Instead, they were ignored, viewed as nothing of interest by the odd individuals of the district.

Séverin removed his sword belt, handing it over to Jonas. The latter accepted the weapons without changing expression. On the other hand, Cabot and Geof appeared startled.

"Is that wise, Citizen? A gentleman such as you should not find himself at the mercy of men of disreputable character."

Geof's dulcet tones sounded pompous, but there appeared to be some concern in his watery eyes.

"He's right," said Cabot, nodding his head.

The enormous nose bobbed up and down, resembling a wand in the hand of a street conjurer rather than a facial orifice.

"Truly?"

Séverin raised both hands as if in terror. Then his arms flashed out, snatching the daggers from both men's belts. The weapons were suddenly pointing at their eyes, mere inches away. Cabot and Geof were frozen in place, their expressions transforming from shock to open-mouthed terror.

"Cabot, Geof," said Jonas, "this is Maestro Séverin. He owns a fencing school. I've seen him hold off a crowd of wreckers with only a broom. Except for the Leviathan, there's no one among us who can endanger the Maestro—unless he allows it."

Jonas didn't hide his amusement at the discomfort of Cabot and Geof. He cackled with laughter at the looks on their faces.

Séverin withdrew the daggers, spun them once in hand, and bowed. He returned the weapons to their places in both men's belts and stepped back.

"I do humbly thank you for your concern, Citizens. I bid you both a very good night."

Cabot and Geof, both still staring with wide, goggling eyes, stepped aside and watched as Jonas and Séverin vanished into the alley. Finally, Cabot spotted a man and pointed his proboscis that way.

"Isn't that Henri? The one who always claims that horses from Flanders will always lose to ones from Badenburg?"

Cabot squinted, his eyes examining the man in the gloom. Geof glanced up and chuckled:

"It is at that, Cabot. Then he lost all his earnings betting against Fleur de Lys in the Stakes in June."

Cabot slapped his knee in amusement.

"Is that when his women chucked him out the second story window into the pig sty?"

Geof shook his head.

"No. That was because she caught him attempting to woo her younger sister. Losing the rent caused her to blacken both of his eyes and make him work for a month with the night soil collectors."

Their conversation continued for a while, their fears of the pale gaze and steady hands of Jean-Pierre Séverin soon relegated to the attic of their memory. Their attention upon humanity was limited to horse races. Other topics were not to be remembered for long.

The alley was unlit, a stygian wall which caused every shape to appear larger and more sinister. It was as if the illumination from the city lights could not reach this one location. To many brave men and women, this alley would feel like an oppressive assault upon their minds and spirit. That, Séverin knew, was the main purpose of this location. This inky darkness was a form of defense against the many who would seek to assail and assault the weak and strong who were members of the legendary Court of Miracles.

Though there were strong and dangerous men like Jonas, Cabot and Geof, they were in the minority. Most of the members of the guild were weak, infirmed, injured and lost. They clung to their organization in order to survive, fearful of a world which viewed them as a lifeform lower than the beasts of burden. To most of society, the beggars were a larger form of rat, vermin to be ignored or destroyed. The guild was their refuge, a sanctuary against the harsh treatment among so-called "good" people.

A hand on his arm stopped Séverin. The palm was as hard as a piece of old leather, a powerful mitt capable of crushing anything softer than iron. Yet the grasp was merely a simple barrier in the swordmaster's path. No violence appeared to be forthcoming.

"I am about to place a bag over your head. It's a tad rough, but it is clean. I will then place a line of rope in your hand. Hold on to it and you'll be led. By me and some others. It will be a long period before you get to the one you came to see. We take careful steps to guard our mysteries from outsiders. If that's no good, you can leave now. You wouldn't be the first"

Jonas had used the same calm tone, his words demonstrating no concern or even interest. There was a flatness about the man's manner. It was as if most human emotions were missing from his psyche. What could cause such a loss? Séverin wondered. But he knew Jonas would not provide any answers. If the beggar even understood the transformation of his spirit, such knowledge would be held tight to his person.

"Agreed," said Séverin.

He felt the sack slip over his head. But the gloom of the alley was such that there was no actual change in his eyes. A line of thick rope was pressed into his right hand and he was gently led inside one of the nearby buildings.

There began to oddest journey of Séverin's life—a a trip through many places beneath and above the surface of Paris. Completely blind, he walked into his self-inflicted darkness for two, possibly more, hours.

Sounds and scents assaulted him with every step. No words were spoken in the hours he was led through the land of the unfortunates. He did hear the cries of babies and the groans of the elderly; those were the only human noises which floated to his ears, other than the breathing of the three people who led him throughout his blind journey.

The first was clearly female, heavily-built, but moving with a powerful grace. The swish of her skirts floated to his ears, as well as her heaving gasps for air. The long walk was an exertion for this woman, a trial upon her body. But she complied, never even complaining as her knees creaked as they walked down a long ramp.

The second was a child, of sex unknown. Poor boys and girls wore pantaloons, usually made from cast-off rags. The child moved at a trot, very familiar with the locations in the underworld. The youth's silence was unnatural, with no hint of playfulness or fear. Just a steady pull upon the leading rope until the duty was discharged.

The third guide was Jonas, this much Séverin realized almost immediately. The man possessed a distinc-
tive odor, that of charcoal intermingled with blood. His
walk was light for a large man and he moved with the
self-assurance of a survivor who has battled against superior forces and came away the victor.

The trip, though blind, did come with other sensations. At first, Séverin walked across wood, rotted tim-
bers which yielded beneath his feet with an elasticity
which was unnerving. The air in that location was fresh,
but mingled with the refuse of the streets. Soon the atmosphere grew staler, thicker and heavy with dust and
decay. There was a tomb-like quality to this location, an
enclosed sense of oppression which was only relieved
when the wooden floor gave way to damp stone.

The stone level possessed many small puddles and a
smell filled with mildew, putrefaction, and human waste.
The skittering and scrambling of rats and other under-
ground creatures were audible, their musky stenches occasionally surfacing among the powerful scents filling
the heavy, humid air.

After over an hour in the stone passages, Jonas led
Séverin through a series of new plank floors and well-
packed dirt. In all these travels, at no time was he forced
to climb stairs or ladders. There were ramps, some sharp
inclines or declines, others more gradual. Surprising, but
also very interesting, at least to the swordmaster's mind.

"Close your eyes," Jonas said, stopping, his hard
hand brushing against Séverin's arm. "I'm going to re-
move the sack. You'll get blind. Open your eyes slow-
like, it'll be better."

Séverin complied, screwing his eyes closed and
slowly, gradually opening them to a harsh illumination.
He found himself in a long rectangular chamber, about

thirty feet in length and half that in width. Five men were in the room, Cabot and Geof among their number. Seated on a large wooden chair was a huge man. He was easily as tall as Séverin with enormous scarred fists and a huge, thickly, tangled beard. He looked like a younger version of Cardinal Salmon, the late King of the Beggars. But there was no merriment in his eyes. They were dark, harsh and unyielding.

"State your business, stranger," said the giant in a phlegmy, raspy voice, horrible on the ears.

"I wish to speak to the Antipope."

Séverin studied the man in the throne and began examining the rest of the company.

"That is me. Speak fast, for we, at the Court of Miracles, have no time for outsiders," the man replied in the same harsh tone.

Séverin met the man's eyes.

"You're no more the Antipope than I am. You're a bodyguard. Perhaps the most important one, but not the leader."

The man in the chair was about to protest, when a voice emerged from behind Séverin.

"How did you know?"

"I knew Cardinal Salmon. He wanted his people to rise, not remain the same. That man is a brawler, a fighter who still has blood on his knuckles. A leader who walks around with the bodily fluids of another on their hands would not understand the implication of the name Antipope. My guess is that he is the first bodyguard. Probably a very effective protector, but not imaginative," Séverin explained, without turning around, not wishing to turn his back on the rough company standing before him.

The false king turned bright red with each statement. He rose as the men began to giggle, each hushing when he glared in their direction. He stepped towards Séverin, but looked beyond the swordmaster. With a dip of his head, he subsided and stepped back, standing beside the battered throne.

"Do you know where you are, Jean-Pierre Séverin?"

The voice behind Séverin was soft, with the careful intonation of one hiding their true voice.

"A sub-basement of the building where I started."

Séverin kept his expression carefully neutral. He even refrained from chuckling at the shocked expressions that crossed the faces of Jonas, Geof, Cabot and their fellows.

A soft footfall approached, its sound a mere whisper that only the keenest senses could register. Stepping before Séverin was a woman. She was tall, able to look at the swordmaster eye to eye. Her hair was dark auburn, her face triangular with high cheekbones and almond-shaped green eyes. She was dressed all in black, her figure and long legs mere wisps of shadows that danced before Séverin's eyes.

"How did you know?"

The woman walked past Séverin and settled in the chair. She crossed her legs and the men around her all appeared to tense.

"My location? I was taken down a series of ramps. I assume the Beggars Guild built those structures to assist those whose legs do not work. From there through tunnels, old and new, and into the sewers. We never crossed the stream and turned back the way we came. The trip was a large circle. I then noticed clay dust on the pant legs of several of your men. The same composition as the house where I started. I thought I heard the sounds of arguing as we went one level lower. The men at your side were assembled at the last minute and shared the dust on their legs and, and at least two, on their arms. Based on my observation of Geof, he would not stand for such a stain upon his clothing for long. Therefore he was summoned just as I returned and did not have time to clean his trousers." Séverin paused and added, "I assume I am now addressing the Antipope?"

The woman nodded once.

"You are. And you would not learn this much if your reputation had not preceded you. Cardinal Salmon spoke well of you. As did Jonas and several others. What is it you wish to know, Citizen Séverin?"

Séverin opened his mouth to speak, but a sound filled the air. An unmistakable clamor that sent chills down his spine. The men surrounding the Antipope all leapt and started. Only their leader sat serenely on her throne, her eyes still upon Séverin.

A scream of terror followed a heartbeat later, followed by a second howl. The cacophony was one that filled all of mankind with terror. A primal eruption from the early days when primitive man lived in caves and every day was a struggle to survive. These primeval nightmares still resided within the deepest recesses of the mind.

The sound was the howl of a wolf…

CHAPTER IX

Paris, November 1804

Karnstein waited until they were in the street and walking down a busy boulevard. He spoke with the light tone of one discussing the weather with a friend. This as another hint to Séverin that there was more to this young man then met the eye.

"Where are we going? I know you stated 'beneath the Earth,' but please be less cryptic."

Karnstein didn't glance at Séverin. Instead his eyes searched the street, examining all the citizens in their path.

"I meant that mostly as a jest," replied the Morgue director. "But I will explain. You do know that Paris is a very ancient city?"

Séverin bowed his head briefly to a beggar, giving the man a coin. He never lost stride, the action appeared very practiced.

"Yes. I read about the Parisii tribe residing in the vicinity. I believe they were conquered by the Romans. But I will admit my knowledge was gathered mostly from some barely remembered readings of Caesar's *Commentarii de Bello Gallico*. My lessons in that area were, er, interrupted."

Karnstein's impassive face paled slightly as he walked, his eyes still roving.

"No matter. You would not discover what I'm going to tell you in common books. In brief, much before the time of the Gauls and the Celts, Paris was the site of an ancient empire. The denizens of this dark empire, the name of which is a curse and must never be spoken aloud, were worshippers of dark gods and demons. These lands possessed brass towers built through the blood of thousands of slaves. There are many tales of their fall. But their empire eventually became part of the dust of centuries, happily forgotten by all but a few."

Séverin knew he sounded like a schoolmaster lecturing a pupil, but this was information Karnstein might wish to know for the future.

"I accept that as a possibility. What is the point of this information?"

A trace of impatience had entered Karnstein's voice, but his habit of watching people had not ceased.

"When hunting evil, it is good to start in the place where it flourishes best. A gathering of dark magic worshippers controls one section of the remaining tunnels. We must ensure they're uninvolved in this affair. But the risks are great. They are very dangerous."

Séverin studied the young Baron Karnstein. He was unsurprised by the man's lack of reaction. There was something unique about Franz von Karnstein, but the swordmaster could not place the indefinable quality of the Austrian noble turned exorcist.

"Will we need to bring anything? Water? A lantern?" asked Karnstein, gesturing to vendors as they passed.

"No water. The liquid would be corrupted. And no lanterns. There are pockets of gas beneath the Earth that would explode upon contact with a flame. We will eat and drink before we travel below and I have a method of illuminating our path."

Séverin turned into a back alley and stepped into a small stall. He came out a moment later with a loaf of bread, some cheese and a bottle in hand.

Accepting a large chunk of the bread and some cheese, Karnstein ate as they walked through a series of narrow streets. The closeness of the houses and the dilapidated conditions of the low buildings exuded an air of archaic neglect. This was the Faubourg Saint-Antoine, a region of the city forgotten by most, a region where the poor resided, but not the destitute. These were the homes of the unskilled workers. These were the men who carried building material for craftsmen, dug ditches for the night soil collectors, cleaned the steps of the wealthy, or performed small jobs for the lesser traders. They were a hard-working people, but forgotten by society. Not ignored, like the impoverished, but treated in the same manner as one would apply to a useful beast of burden. A sad way of life, but one that is all too prevalent in modern society.

"Finish your food. We will be walking into the depths for well over an hour. The path is steep, but easy to take. Conserve your strength. And follow me the entire time. It is quite easy to become lost. There are many ancient mines, some more ancient than time is understood. And I am not sure what resides in those tunnels. I believe many dangerous creatures that still thrive down there. Best to avoid placing us in further peril."

Séverin watched as Karnstein finished the remains of his food and drank deeply from the bottle.

"Understood," replied Karnstein, checking the saber strapped to his belt, before adding, "Any further information I should know?"

Séverin shook his head.

"Just a final warning: we are about to enter a nest of human vipers. They are very dangerous. But if they are not involved, they may provide us with a direction in which to search—if we survive the encounter. You may have to take the life of another human. Or battle an inhuman fiend. If that is too difficult for you, please say so now. There is no shame in avoiding this battle."

"Shall we proceed?" said Karnstein, impassive,

Séverin smiled, a rare expression of happiness across his usually dour face.

"Follow me."

Séverin opened a small doorway in the side of a building and ducked inside. The interior was gloomy, a shadowy murk that was not exactly pure darkness, but a mix of shadows and light. A puff of gray dust swirled at the edge of the doorway, causing Karnstein to cover his mouth and close his eyes and he followed the tall swordmaster.

"We begin," said Séverin, pulling out a flat rock from his jacket.

A soft glow emerged from the stone, stronger than a candle. Before them lay a stone staircase, which spiraled deep into the Earth. There was no end in sight.

CHAPTER X

Paris, September 1795

"My weapons. Give them to me now," said Séverin, stepping towards the Antipope.

He knew that howl, recognized it all too well. There was a reason he was known as *Gâteloup*, the Spoiler of Wolves. Jean-Pierre Séverin would not fall victim to the creatures he had defeated in the past.

The Antipope was on her feet and issued an order:

"Cabot. Return the man's weapons at once."

Then, she turned towards the swordmaster:

"Do you know what we face?"

"Yes. A *loup-garou*. More than one. But you knew that as well, didn't you?"

Séverin took his weapons from the tall beggar.

All of the men were arming themselves, their arms varying from man to man. Geof pulled two expensive-looking flintlock pistols made from dark wood. Cabot vanished and appeared a moment later in possession of a long, thin rapier. A giant called Léon pulled a hammer as large as his torso. The mallet was made of dark, stained wood and rusting black iron. The other men retrieved old swords and long sticks. They wielded these weapons with obvious skill, their hands steady, their nerves calm. These men were street brawlers, experienced killers who protected the weaker charges of their guild. Few in Paris were as ready for violence as the Antipope's followers.

"Yes. The sound is unmistakable," said the Anti-pope, tossing aside the long thin sword on her belt.

She retrieved a heavy cavalry saber from behind her throne. A heavy flintlock was in her other hand. Both weapons were French military items, well-cared for and blooded in battle.

"Good," said Séverin. "If we work together, we may be able to defeat these monsters. My greater concern is for their master."

Séverin listened as the screams from above receded. The scratch of talons across brick and wood drifted to his ears.

"Listen to me," said the Antipope, not bothering to raise her voice.

All the men ceased whispering and moving about the basement.

"The creatures we are to face are inhuman. They're fast and possess claws and teeth capable of tearing a man apart in seconds. But they can be killed."

"How?" asked Geof, stroking his long mustache unconsciously.

It was his one demonstration of fear.

"They heal quickly, but not immediately," explained the Antipope. "Grievous injury to the head will kill them. Attacking their limbs is useless. A *loup-garou* with no arms or legs is still ferocious and terribly lethal."

Séverin looked up and the ceiling as a small cloud of dust drifted down.

"If we live," he said, "you must tell me how you know those unusual facts."

The Antipope ignored the question and looked back at her people.

"We work as teams. Léon, you are with me and our guest. The rest of you form up with Cabot and Luc. Prepare. We will shortly battle for our lives."

The men moved into two packs and the gargantuan Léon stepped between Séverin and the Antipope.

The clamor increased with each second. A moment later, a small portion of timber tumbled from above, landing with a clatter where Séverin stood earlier. The scratching grew in volume and a panting snarl filled the air.

Suddenly, there was a tearing sound and the ceiling exploded open. Plaster, wood and stone flew in every direction. Séverin and the beggar's guild members covered their faces. There were several yelps in pain as the splinters tore into exposed limbs. Two figures dropped into the room, towering forms that crouched on the floor without moving.

"Kill them, my pretties! Tear them all apart!" a man's voice called from above.

The voice possessed the slow drawl of the noble class. This was a manner of speech all but wiped out by Robespierre and his Reign of Terror. Thousands of men and women who had spoken in such a manner had fallen victim to the mock trials of the Committee of Public Safety. The people who had escaped that short period of horror and death avoided Paris, fearful that the Directory would follow the same bloody path.

Two creatures crouching in the shadows rose. They stood taller than anyone in the room, their heads close to the ruined roof. Their black furred skulls were a perverse mixture of human and wolf, complete with very human-looking eyes and snouts filled with massive rows of serrated fangs. Their shoulders were wider than two men. Huge dark talons flashed in the spare light, their sharp edges stained with blood and other unknown bodily fluids.

The first *loup-garou* stepped forward and lifted his head back. The howl that ripped from his twisted snout was a harsh growl filled with malice and blood lust. The cry of these inhuman fiends was an assault upon the spirit of all present. Yet, none fled in fear, but all stood resolute in the face of evil.

The gigantic Léon stepped forward, a high-pitched screech emerging from his lips. He swung his massive hammer towards the head of the *loup-garou* on his left. The massive mallet whistled as it sliced through the air. Mere inches before the creature's skull, a titanic taloned palm caught the hammer, stopping the weapon's lethal descent. The *loup-garou* pulled the hammer towards him, dragging Léon close. Then, with a slash of his other hand, he removed the huge bodyguard's head from his shoulders. A spray of blood covered the werewolf's fur, a stain of red upon the shadowy dark pelt.

"Wait for them to approach. Charging these brutes is an easy path to a bad end."

Séverin spoke with the same tone he used when instructing students in the very basics of the art of the sword. There was no room for discussion or contemplation, merely acceptance of these truths.

The two *loups-garous*, seemingly comprehending the swordmaster's words, hung back. They panted with naked blood lust and rivulets of drool fell from their thin red lips.

"Geof," said the Antipope raising her firearm. "The one on the right, if you please."

The Antipope and Geof fired their flintlock pistols at the same moment. The explosion of the powder echoed and a long tongue of flame emerged from each barrel. Both werewolves stumbled back, loud shrieks emerging from them as they crashed to the ground.

But just as the beggars were about to cheer, both monstrosities leaped back to their feet. With a scream of rage, they charged forward.

In an instant, they were within the group of humans. Each werewolf snatched up a man, pulled them close and bit down with their oversized fangs. Their claws sliced at their victim's bodies, tearing the beggars into pieces in seconds.

It was the tall, rakishly thin Cabot who acted first. He lunged forward and stabbed the *loup-garou* in the creature's side. The beast dropped the corpse in its grasp and spun in his direction. It raised a hand to slice the beggar open as Cabot struggled to free his weapon. Just as it was about to strike, Geof raised his other pistol and shot the werewolf in the side of the head. The creature screamed and lashed out, slicing the man next to Cabot in half. The monster dropped to its knees, snarling as his massive maw tore another man's leg in half. The beggar, a wide-shouldered man whom Séverin recognized as a professional bully, cried out in agony as a fountain of blood shot across the floor.

On the other side of the room, a cat and mouse game was being played. Séverin and the Antipope were ducking and weaving, their movements athletic and resembling a dance. Yet it was a lethal jig, their weapons slicing and pricking the *loup-garou*. The beast snarled and slashed, talons and teeth slicing the air as the pair avoided each potentially lethal blow. Blood from numerous cuts upon the hirsute flesh of the werewolf sprouted, but the beast was not slowed by the loss of it and the growing number of his wounds.

Séverin ducked a pair of swinging arms and stepped in close. He stabbed upward with his small sword, thrusting through the monster's jaw and into the *loup-*

garou's brain. The monster issued a strangled cry and fell back. The werewolf clawed at the weapon, his motions frantic, yet growing weaker with each passing second.

The Antipope was a heartbeat behind Séverin, her heavy saber slashing across the back of the fiend's neck. The backbone snapped with a loud crunch and the *loup-garou* collapsed to the ground, hitting the floor with a dull thud.

The remaining beggars surrounded the other fallen *loup-garou*, their weapons striking down and tearing the monster into pieces. They ceased when the beast was reduced to little more than a large mound of meat and blood. The remains were unrecognizable, little more than torn gristle covered in unrecognizable fluids.

"Enough," said the Antipope, stepping closer to her men.

They all froze and turned in her direction, their eyes wild as they comprehended the full horror of the situation.

"The monster... it killed Léon and Joseph and..."

Geof's voice was flat, lifeless and dull as he recited the names of the dead scattered across the hall.

"Cabot, you and Geof search the upper levels," barked the Antipope. "If anything lives, rescue them. Then bring down the building. The deaths can be attributed to the collapse. Meet us at Salmon's third home."

The men moved, some like sleepwalkers, others were spurred to fast action. But within a few seconds, they were all scurrying out of the sub-basement, abandoning the dead. After they had gone, she turned towards Séverin and said:

"You. Follow me. We have a great deal to discuss."

Séverin watched as she stepped around a pair of barrels and revealed a hidden tunnel.

"Do I require another bag on my head?"

"I think we can dispense with such foolishness" replied the Antipope, shaking her head. "Just keep our mysteries and we'll keep yours. Agreed?"

"Agreed," said Séverin.

He followed the leader of the Beggars' Guild down a narrow passageway. He didn't know where they were headed, but he did sense that the Antipope and her guild were his allies in the new struggle against darkness.

CHAPTER XI

Paris, November 1804

The stone steps into the depths of the Earth gave way a short while later to a rocky walkway. The floor of the decline was carved out of the earth by the tread of feet through more millennia than the memory of mankind could remember. There were no visible supports along the walls and ceiling. The ancient builders of these tunnels had used methods unheard of, even by the advanced sciences of the 19th century. There was an unnatural smoothness to the walls and roof, a glass-like quality to the igneous base.

An hour's walk later, the tunnel began to change. The progression was slow, almost imperceptible. The walls and ceiling gradually roughened, with the occasional stone arch appearing to support the coarse surroundings. The floor became grayer, a dead dust trampled down by innumerable feet over untold centuries. An ambience of antediluvian disintegration could be felt by both men as they progressed downward. All who had seen these passages created were now naught but dust. A powerful sense of history was present, of lost knowledge and forgotten times.

As the tunnels became less precise, smaller openings to the left and right appeared. Some were tiny—a mouse could barely have squeezed into such passages. But others were nearly human-sized. Séverin and Karnstein could traverse any if they crouched low. The plutonian murk within the tunnels was profound. It was like viewing a wall of pure darkness that resisted even the power of Séverin's glowstone.

"What lays down these other passages?" Karnstein asked, looking at each tunnel, small and large, with open wariness.

"I only know a few," shrugged the Morgue Director. "These ancient tunnels were converted into mines by the Celts, and later improved and expanded by the Franks. A few were made into ossuaries, but that is all I know. The path to the ancient temple is the one I use exclusively. Best to be wary about exploring the other regions."

Karnstein absorbed the information and continued to scan the openings in the walls and ceiling as they marched deeper into the catacombs. He detected an echo just beneath the tread of their feet. It was a scratching, skittering sound that ceased whenever they paused. Karnstein wished he could ignore the hellish jangle, knowing that concentrating on such a terrible cacophony was the surest way to madness, but the horrible hushed clamor was always present, just beneath the edge of their movement.

It was then that the young Austrian began to notice an even more blood-chilling spectacle. As they walked, the light of Séverin's luminescent stone was reflected by *something* inside the seemingly impenetrable gloom. Just on the edge of their vision, sometimes motionless, sometimes pulling away, never approaching closer. Sometimes tiny, barely visible to the naked eye; other times, larger, as big as a man's fist. But always present.

It took Karnstein a few moments to realize the truth of these ever-changing visions on the edge of his perception. They were eyes. Some were the tiny red reflections of rats, an ever present, always expected, subterranean dweller. But others were yellow, with multi-faceted jeweled orbs. Insect eyes, though the sheer size of the owners of such orbs was inconceivable. Others were a sinister bloody red, eyes that reflected a predatory soul awaiting a helpless moment to attack and feed.

"This is truly a place of the damned," Karnstein said as he gripped his saber tighter.

The light of the glowstone suddenly revealed a waist-high pile of human skulls, the bones brown and white. The pile of human remains stretched deep into the distance, lost into the void. Squatting on the top of the pile was a vaguely human form, but the differences between this being and an ordinary man were stark. The creature's head was oblong in shape, hairless, and covered in pale, gray skin that appeared to glisten with some barely visible form of mucus. The body was tiny, about the size of a toddler, with clearly defined sinews that appeared more feline than human. His eyes were oversized and bulging, like some undersea creature dragged from the bottom of the ocean by an unlucky fisherman. They glowed a sickly green in the stark light as it stared at the two men passing. Black talons twinkled across each long, spindly finger, the digits caked with brown stains.

Just as fast as this spectacle caught Karnstein's eyes, it vanished into the darkness. A soft rasp of talons across the bones was audible, but quickly passed as both men stepped deeper into the dark. But the sight would remain with Karnstein, as terrible a vision as the one that had always haunted his waking and sleeping mind.

"Ah," said Séverin, stopping in his tracks as a soft yellow light appeared in the distance, "we have reached our destination. The room is circular, with a stone altar to the left of where we will be entering. Be very careful.

These people are not to be trifled with in any way. They practice very dark magic."

Karnstein nodded, but his face remained blank. He watched as Séverin wrapped the glowing stone inside a cloth and replaced it within his jacket. The swordmaster then drew his small sword and led the way towards the distant illumination.

Voices echoed down the tunnel, slowly becoming clearer as they approached. A deep basso tone was the most audible, followed by a murmuring chorus. Soon all of the words were easy to discern, even from a distance.

"Do you hear what they are saying?" asked Séverin.

His walk was slower, but almost completely silent. He moved with the sinewy grace of a jungle cat stalking its prey.

"Yes. The Lord's Prayer backwards. Typical," replied Karnstein in a voice tight with rage.

"Yes. Some Devil worshippers cling to their traditions. Draw your sword, my friend. They will not be happy when we interrupt their unholy rites."

Séverin's free hand gripped a vial of holy water. He remembered the first time he and his teacher had battled one of the evil cults using this ancient locale for their Satanic spells. The battle had been terrible and fierce, but they had prevailed and sent the Fallen back to Perdition.

"No need. I have other weapons."

Karnstein's assurance surprised Séverin. The young Austrian spoke like one far more acquainted with the darkness than his years would suggest. There was a mystery there, a tale hidden beneath the calm exterior of the Austrian Exorcist.

"As you will," said Séverin. "Let's hope we can accomplish our aims with a minimum of violence."

The Morgue director led Karnstein down the passage and into an arched opening.

Ancient scroll work covered two obsidian columns. Images of massive fanged serpents encircling the globe, swallowing the sun. Oddly shaped pictograms were visible, stamped out in gold. The images were disturbing to the eye. Both men looked away, focusing instead on the strange ceremony unfolding in the large, round room.

About twenty people were present, their bodies and heads hidden beneath heavy black woolen robes. All were kneeling in supplication, their heads bowed, their hands pointed downward. It was a clear intentional mockery of the position taken by Christians praying in their churches. A massive brass and wood crucifix was propped against the distant wall, turned upside down so the image of Jesus was reversed. The face of the Messiah had been despoiled, caked with excrement and other unidentifiable fluids. The lips, eyelids, and cheeks of the image were painted, causing the Son of God to resemble a painted tart.

Near the desecrated cross lay a stone slab, a solid rock jutting from the floor of the chamber. It was of the same jet stone as the columns, but the images appeared faded, almost unidentifiable to the eyes. Laying across this altar was a nude woman, her long blond hair artfully arranged to fall like a golden shower down the edge of the black rock. She was young, perhaps eighteen, with large, round breasts and the milk-pale skin only the wealthy were able to maintain. She writhed and moaned upon the stone slab in obviously false ecstasy. Another mockery of the sanctity of the Christian religious ceremonies.

At the naked woman's side stood a boy, about her age. His hair and skin were the same tone and texture and he too was naked. He watched the girl with hungry eyes, a thin rivulet of drool slowly dribbling from the corner of his mouth.

And behind them both was the one Séverin immediately classified as the high priest of this unholy order. He was taller than the boy, with dark-brown hair which fell to his shoulders and a well-trimmed rounded beard and mustache. His hands were small, soft, and pink; his arms, which protruded from under his heavy black robes, were pale and devoid of muscle tones. Séverin suspected that, beneath the black wool, was a fleshy, flabby, frame, the indolent figure of a man who had never worked a day in his life.

Pulling his eyes away from the rites, Séverin scanned the room again. A pair of stone braziers, both built in the wall with a small onyx-type stone, belched a thin cloud of blue smoke. The scent emerging from both was heady and noxious. These were herbs meant to weaken the wills of those present. A typical tactic of followers of the left-hand path.

On the far-right wall were a series of wooden tables, all recently lugged down to these dark depths. Upon the boards were heaps of sumptuous foods, bottles of expensive wine and expensive little cakes, usually reserved for the wealthiest families of Europe. A feast worthy of Lucullus, fare fit for the table of the deceased king and queen of France.

"Oh dear," Séverin sighed. "If we intervene now, they'll attack us en masse. Poor odds and it won't accomplish our needs. We'll have to suffer through waiting for their disgusting rites to be complete."

"It will not be my first time viewing such activities. But I agree with your view. Before the final ceremonies, they will be quite weakened by their behavior. Our safety will be in somewhat less peril."

Karnstein's voice was flat, but Séverin detected a slight sarcastic barb within the words. The young Austrian Exorcist understood the danger fully. They were outnumbered by a horde of Devil worshippers. And they were about to demand information from them regarding evil events in Paris. A perilous place to stand, physically and metaphorically.

A moment later, the prayer ceased and the kneeling worshippers stood up. A cry emerged from somewhere within their throng and they whirled around. Not towards Séverin and Karnstein, but towards the banquet on the far end of the chamber.

With a howl, closer to that of a predator attacking weaker prey, they charged the table and began to gorge themselves. No words were spoken as the men and women threw off their hoods and fell upon the feast. They snatched the food and bottles of wine with greedy hands and stuffed their mouths full. Half-consumed food fragments full upon the floor and walls, ground into the stone by bare feet. The ravenous assault was closer to a feeding frenzy by a pack of blood-crazed animals than that of a gathering of humans.

"They try very hard to behave in opposition to accepted religious practices," said Séverin's in a voice that was little more than a murmur as he viewed the disgusting display.

"The teachings they follow set a simple path for them," replied Karnstein with the assurance of an expert. "One designed for damnation. But they fail to realize it because they're little more than sheep. Their true master leads them to sell their souls and become little more than puppets for powers beyond their imagining."

He sounded, to the ears of the highly experienced Séverin, like Grost, or the other men and women who had taught the swordmaster the truth of what lay in the shadows.

They watched as Bacchanalian banquet continued. Food and drink were consumed with fervor, a furious attack made upon every morsel and drink. The bottles were smashed and the plates holding the fare were shattered and tossed into the growing piles of rubbish. Men and women vomited out the contents of their stomach, only to fall back on the feast and begin ravenously consuming once again.

Soon, nothing was left to eat, drink or smash. The multitude of worshippers then screamed and howled, shrieked and screeched. They began grabbing each other, lifting robes to reveal pale naked flesh. They fell upon each other. Their movements were sexual in origin, but possessing the same deranged ardor as that used upon the food and drink. Partners were indiscriminate, old coupled with young, female with male, male with male, female with female, and partnerships of threes, fours and fives operated for quick, intense moments. Then they broke apart, leaping upon others and continuing their random coupling.

There was no visible joy or pleasure on the part of the participants. This was little more than an exercise, an intense act that was physical and only sexual in the biological view. Though resembling something out of the worst tales of the court of Caligula, there was no passion present. The members of this dark church were acting upon orders, nothing else.

"Another method of demonstrating derision upon the church," Séverin noted.

He was not revolted by the acts unfolding before his eyes. He knew this was little more than a method of control upon the congregation by the master of the left-hand path.

"Not merely the Roman Church," said Karnstein. "Think far older. These actions were used by the cults of Astarte in ancient days. And by the followers of Bacchus and Artemis in Greek and Roman days. And there are hints of far older origins. The young Emperor Elagabalus also attempted to enact similar changes upon the Romans over one thousand years ago."

Séverin pursed his lips in thought.

"You appear better informed upon this than many experts I've met in my lifetime."

Karnstein appeared to relax and shook his head.

"Only upon dark worshipers and demons. There are many creatures of which I know little."

He smiled, a rare feat for a normally quite sober, solemn man. But this admission demonstrated much of the young Austrian's true nature.

"Their sexual congress appears complete. Shall were interrupt them now?" asked Karnstein as he glanced at the cultists composing themselves and beginning to resume their places before the altar.

"Yes."

Séverin did not wish to see what followed. He knew the disgusting final act of this ceremony and never wished to view it again.

The boy and the girl, who were probably brother and sister, would mate before the Satanists. The high priest would then rape one, or both, and kill them. Their bodies would then become vessels for some unknown being from beyond. Demons, elementals, or some other sinister creatures, would inhabit the bodies and become a plague upon mankind. They would bring about suffering on an untold level, their every act meant to despoil good and damn as many souls as possible in their short lifetime.

"Allow me."

Karnstein pulled a small pistol from his cloak. It was a tiny flintlock pistol, no larger than his hand. The barrel of the weapon was oversized, larger than the rest of the gun.

He raised the weapon and fired. An enormous boom shattered the silence as a two-foot-long tongue of flame emerged from the barrel. The desecrated image of Jesus Christ on the cross exploded, showering the room with tiny fragments of stone. The Exorcist then dropped the gun to the ground. Séverin noticed the barrel was warped and smoking, the wooden stock scorched and blackened.

Several yelps of terror emerged from the pack of dark cultists. A few cowered, most merely turned towards Séverin and Karnstein. Their reactions were dulled by the food, drink, and rampant sex. Angry looks and a few fists were raised, but otherwise the throng remained still.

The girl on the altar ceased her false display of sexual frenzy and sat up, looking at both men. She did not cover her nudity, but watched them with large, frank, assessing eyes. The boy turned his head their direction, but otherwise appeared disinterested by the display. His large light eyes blinked slowly, but there was no sign of any form of reaction of the current events.

The high priest was momentarily startled by the gunshot. He jumped and shook for a moment, looking around every direction. Upon spotting Karnstein and Séverin in the doorway, he regained his composure. Pulling himself upright, he twisted his round adipose face into a sneer of amused disgust and stared their direction.

"You dare? Do you know who we are? Do you? You have delivered yourself into the hands of darkness. You shall find we are not forgiving to little people!"

He spoke in a heavy, well-educated and noble-sounding voice. His delivery was like that of a professor on a lectern, with the basso tones of a man used to being listened to by those whom he considered his underlings.

"The hands of darkness?" replied Karnstein contemptuously. "Why is it that you Devil worshipers always use such exalted titles? Is it your need to puff your tragically weak selves? Attempting to hide that you're little more than a sad little slave, a worm beneath the cloven hooves of a being that views you as little more than a puppet for his dark will?"

His contempt was like a physical assault upon the congregation of Satanists. A few stared at him with open mouths, shocked, astonished that anyone would be so bold as to speak in such a manner to their order.

Séverin, for his part, was also taken aback by the young man's boldness. Baron Karnstein, though clearly knowledgeable and dedicated, appeared to be an analytical sort of man, not one filled with the hot-headed foolishness of youth. Yet, here he was, mocking and taunting a room full of devil worshippers, without demonstrating a trace of fear.

"Who are you?" asked the high priest, his voice dropping to a low hiss.

The sibilant, serpentine sound struck them like a physical force. There was power in these words, a command filled with power. But neither Séverin nor Karnstein appeared moved by this hidden assault. Séverin knew of such tricks of old, and was well beyond falling for such parlor games. As for Karnstein, he merely seemed amused, though that emotion was mixed with unhidden disgust.

"Don't you know? Can't you use your mighty powers to tear the truth from my very mind?" Karnstein chuckled, rolling his eyes. "Maybe now these poor deluded fools will see you for the charlatan you truly are, false priest."

It was now the high priest's turn to laugh.

"You wish to learn my power, fool? I am a graduate of the Scholomance! I was one of the Devil's chosen messengers upon this world! I shall serve in his court as a prince!"

Séverin was unsurprised to see the members of this Satanic congregation shrink back in fear. The high priest's invocation of the unholy academy was a source of terror to these worshippers of evil. To them, a man or woman who had attended the Scholomance was Lucifer's trained creature, a demon among mankind. They dreaded such beings, but were hopeful to follow in their footsteps to fulfill their dark dreams and desires.

The Morgue Director was doubly surprised by his companion's reaction. The young Austrian stared at the high priest for a heartbeat, then burst out with loud, derisive laughter. The followers of the left-hand path were all stunned by this sight and sound. No man had ever reacted in such a manner before their terrible magus.

"You are no Solomari," Karnstein snapped, his face still twisted in a mirthless rictus.

His invoking the secret name of a graduate of the dark magic academy was a greater astonishment than the mirth of the tall, young Austrian with the light eyes.

"I am! I am one of the ten chosen to attend the hidden school of darkness," the high priest shrieked. "I was taken to a place deep in the mountains. And by a clear lake with no bottom, I was taught magic by Lucifer himself. Nine of us were chosen to spread evil in the world. The tenth rode away on a dragon to serve as the Devil's servant!"

He spoke in the manner of a man reading a psalm from the holy bible. There was a majesty to him as he spoke, one that caused many to ignore his sweaty, blubbery face and corpulent form.

Karnstein clapped his hands slowly. The mockery of his motions was impressive, an act worthy of a street performer. But his amusement was apparent to all observing—and his disgust.

"Very well said," he said. "You tell the tale in an impressive manner. That is the legend as spoken by the peasants of Transylvania, and even as far as my home in Styria. But that's nonsense. The true Scholomance is beneath the Earth in a tower built upside down by a dark magician. Ten scholars of darkness are chosen, very true. But one, the least powerful, is sacrificed to the Dark One by the other nine. I am told the death is long and lingering."

Karnstein's bared teeth and flashing eyes caused the Satanists to shiver with fear.

"How do you know this?" asked the naked girl on the altar, studying Karnstein with frank appraising eyes.

"How?" Karnstein's voice dropped to a low angry hiss. "That is because I am Baron Franz von Karnstein of Styria. And I know more of the Scholomance than the fat fool before my eyes!"

His finger pointed at the high priest, the hand of an inquisitor or a judge accusing a thief.

"You are no graduate of the Scholomance, or the Deep School, or any of the dark academies," he continued. "You are a dark priest. What caused you to fall? The inability to be chaste? A desire for wealth and luxuries? No matter. You were a priest of Rome. Probably a second or third son, forced to take orders. But you discovered a grimoire or three, and learned how to invoke the power of darkness. Your kind are not the kings of evil; you're its servants. Little more than slaves with delusions of grandeur."

The high priest's face turned white and he pointed a finger back at Karnstein.

"Kill him! He screamed. "Tear him apart in the name of the Unholy One, The Fallen One, Lucifer Morningstar!"

Several of the cultists stepped forward, their hands raised with fury. However, the clear majority didn't move, unwilling to advance upon one who had bearded their leader. But this was not the vision that caused Séverin and Karnstein to pause.

The naked boy at the altar was the first to move. Stepping forward, his body began to glow with a red light. His face remained expressionless, but his eyes transformed. First, they became black, then pools of bright red flames. The boy raised his hands and wicked black talons glinted in the spare light. He then grinned and his mouth stretched far too wide for his small face. The enormous maw was filled with serrated fangs more suited to a jungle beast than a man.

"Demon," said Séverin, unsurprised, as he struck the first charging cultist.

The demon was pushing through the crowd and the smell of brimstone filled the air.

CHAPTER XII

September 1795, Paris

"Two of my best men! Two! Gone!"

Jean-Joseph Grenier hammered his fist on the wooden table over and over as he ranted. He was a man of medium height with thick light brown hair and a triangular-shaped face, which flushed red as he shouted.

"Your best? I think not," said the man seated behind the table.

He appeared unconcerned, almost bored, despite Grenier's fury and spoke with the slow drawl of one born to ancient nobility.

"Do not take that tone with me, Saint-Evremonde. I agreed to your assistance in our endeavors, but I am the leader here, not you!"

Grenier continued to pound on the table in an attempt to emphasize his words. But he was unsuited for the role. The fourth son of a penniless baron, he had been entrusted to the Royal military as a child. A captain in the cavalry who had spent more time in the office than in the saddle, Jean-Joseph Grenier had fled the Revolution, then served the returning Bourbon King Louis XVIII as a liaison with other Royalist forces. Promoted to Colonel, he had been ordered to assist in the destruction of the now-weakened Parisian forces.

"Do not speak to me as if we were equals, Colonel Grenier," said the Nobleman, bristling. "My family stretches back to the days of Charles Martel. Yours amounts to little more than jumped up merchants. One of your ancestors was a peasant who was a bed-warmer of Louis XIII. You will address me as 'Monsieur le Marquis' or Monseigneur.' Nothing else is acceptable."

The lazy way Philippe de Marguetel de Saint-Denis, Marquis de Saint-Evremonde, spoke was irritating to listen. The Royalists in the Paris cell all despised the man. But worst of all for Grenier, being of noble birth and the last of his line, the Marquis was heir to his father's title. And the Saint-Evremondes were related by blood to the royal line and quite willing to speak on the subject at length.

"Yes, blood line is important, Monsieur le Marquis, but nevertheless, I am the leader of this cell. We agreed to help you because our late sainted King was said to believe you were a warlock. He wished you burned for that…"

Grenier tried to hint at the perilous place the nobleman was in now, but Saint-Evremonde appeared unmoved.

"He tried to have me executed," said the Marquis, "but I am not so easily destroyed. Our great and mighty King, Henry IV, first of the House of Bourbon, once remarked as such. An excellent king. Far wiser than his descendents."

Saint-Evremonde often spoke this way, invoking the names of long-dead kings or queens. It was only his calm self-assurance and skills that kept anyone from calling him a bald-faced liar.

"Why do you speak ill of our sainted Louis XVI?"

Grenier could not hide his glee that the Marquis had been cursed by the executed monarch who all Royalists viewed as a martyr.[7] The Royalists used the late King

---

[7] Louis XVI was guillotined on 21 January 1793.

and his lovely murdered Queen as symbols against the Republicans. They were a frightful example of how anyone could be killed under this new and terrible order which sought to equalize all social ranks.

"Sainted?" sneered the Marquis. "The man was a fat, stupid, ill-bred, impudent, indecisive, impotent waste of flesh. His queen was an unlettered creature with the worst breeding imaginable. She was an Austrian. Louis would have been happier as a carpenter and Marie-Antoinette as a milk maid. The reason for the Revolution is that they failed to listen to my suggestions. Had they done so, Louis XVI would have been considered the most powerful monarch since the Sun King."

The Marquis did not bother to hide his contempt and Grenier was surprised to see several men nodding in agreement.

"I give orders here!" reiterated the Colonel. "And we do not speak ill of the sainted monarchs in my presence! I have received information from my superiors. It is time to rise up, my noble lords! Like those foolish Republicans years ago, we will charge the lines and arrest the rulers of Paris!"

Grenier waved the intelligence report in his hands and was delighted to hear the cheers of his men.

"You will waste most of your men in a foolish attack reminiscent of the doomed tactics of the ancient Gauls. A rout will follow, exactly like at Agincourt, and once again, the flower of France, all those gathered here, will die like dogs."

The Marquis de Saint-Evremonde caused all, even Grenier, to pause. His tales of battles since ancient days had earned him respect, because the man did seem to know a great deal about killing his fellow man.

"Now, we outnumber them by an order of six of our warriors to one of their farmers," retorted Grenier. "That traitor, Baron de Menou, commands the forces protecting the Directory. Our cell is meant to charge the lines and destroy what few forces they have ready. Then, an army of Royalists will attack and arrest the false rulers. By the end of October, a new king will sit on the throne. And we will be his dukes and barons!"

Grenier looked around, expecting cheers and a rousing roar from the men. Instead, he was met by a stony silence.

"Colonel, may I speak?" asked Captain Alfred Hermilly, stepping forward.

He was a young man, but a dashing, excellent soldier from a good family of squires from Calais. Short, squat and powerful, with the face of an angry bulldog, Hermilly was a born infantryman. He could march all day besides his men, and shoot and fight with impressive expertise that had earned him the respect of all who served with him.

"Of course! Speak, Captain," said Grenier.

He trusted Hermilly far more than the Marquis.

The Captain stood beside Saint-Evremonde and gave the man a small bow.

"I think Monsieur le Marquis is right. If we go charging into the lines, weak as you say they are, none of us will survive to even start the work needed to help the army. There are only about a hundred of us, Colonel. How many are in the Paris garrison?"

Grenier suppressed a snarl of annoyance. Even staunch Hermilly was behaving like a servant before the Marquis. But to show his anger now would lose him the remaining respect of the men present.

"Five thousand. Though perhaps only half will be on duty when our part begins," he replied, knowing full well that he was sealing the doom of his plans.

But winning the battle was all that was important now. They could not live another year under the rule of common shopkeepers and academics.

Hermilly raised a hand, signifying that Colonel Grenier had made his point.

"Two thousand or more, against our hundred."

"You shall not survive" interjected Saint-Evremonde. "Unless you do as I command."

The Marquis looked at Grenier. Their eyes locked and, for a moment, neither man moved. Grenier met the dark eyes of the noble braggart and was prepared to laugh in his face. Saint-Evremonde needed to be brought to heel, made a servant of the Royalist cause. If he was as powerful and ancient as he said, why was he not the ruler of France? Why was he seated with a cell of out-laws, planning on taking back Paris? If he was so dangerous, why was he not sweeping away the armies under General Hoche by his power alone?

But those feelings of contempt and disdain were swept away when he met the eyes of the Marquis. A wave of power seemed to wash over Jean-Joseph Grenier—an overwhelming sensation. He felt like an insect being studied under a glass. Grenier knew, in an instant, that he was nothing before this nobleman. His earlier behavior was that of a child, a naughty infant. The Marquis de Saint- Evremonde was greater than he, an exalted being to be revered and obeyed.

"Monsieur le Marquis," said Grenier, his tone that of a child apologizing to a terrifying school master. "You know best. Please. Give us orders and we shall obey."

Saint-Evremonde rose and smiled. His teeth were large and appeared rather sharp. The smile vanished as fast as it had appeared and a somber expression crossed his handsome face.

"We have enemies in this city. That is a fact. Some of you shall be sent out to confront these inconveniences. The rest of you, I shall prepare. We shall charge the lines, as the Colonel wished, but I shall grant you powers to make you greater than any man alive. You are no longer a cell of soldiers seeking to overturn the Directory. You are my wolves, hunting our enemies. And you shall rend them limb from limb and feast upon their bones!"

A cheer and a howl went up among the men. And Jean-Joseph Grenier's was the loudest of all. They were the wolves of the Marquis de Saint-Evremonde, and soon they would feast.

CHAPTER XIII

Paris, September 1795

The Antipope led Séverin through a quick series of passages and up onto a busy street far from the district they just left. They entered a brick building, a well-kept dwelling one would have associated with a merchant or a successful lawyer, near the Rue Quincampoix. They were met by an attractive young woman in a maid's uniform and a pair of barely concealed daggers.

"Madame," said the maid, curtseying and showing a great deal of her tanned legs in the process.

She stared at Séverin with assessing eyes. Her tiny pink tongue protruded between her teeth, touching lightly across her generous red lips.

"Lisebette, can you tell cook to prepare two meals? And bring the good wine. Monsieur Séverin and I have a great deal to discuss."

The Antipope walked past the young girl, leading the tall swordmaster into a Spartan dining chamber.

"Cook got into the beer barrel and is more soused than a clergyman," said Lisebette. "I'll get the wine and ask Antoine next door to make you some chicken."

The girl didn't wait for an answer, but vanished down the hall and out-of-sight.

The dining room was rectangular with dark wood covering the unadorned walls. A small brass candelabrum was in the center of the long wooden table. The table and chairs were a matching set, old in appearance but utilitarian. These could be the furnishings of a tavern, a military barrack, or a monastery. They were austere, functional and lacking in artistry. This was, in Séverin's eyes, the way of the future. Great artificers and houses of such would exist for the wealthier classes, but the common people were rapidly asserting their independence. This would eventually cause the rise of simple items, mass-produced. A loss of originality, but also a freer future for mankind. At least, so he hoped.

"Your guard?" asked Séverin as he sat in the offered seat, across from the Antipope.

He was unsurprised that she placed a long knife on the table, next to her right hand. A carefully protective move.

The Antipope nodded once, a quick, energetic move.

"Well-spotted. Most are fooled by her womanly assets. That's why she's one of the most effective assassins in Paris. And a thief almost as effective as myself."

"An assassin? I thought Cardinal Salmon was against all such violent activities."

Séverin remembered how the massive man would assault any of his people who behaved in such a terrible manner. The giant would roar and snarl at any of his people who acted violently, unless they were attacked first.

"The meek shall inherit the Earth," Salmon had roared as he had shaken two men like rats. Their feet weren't even touching the ground as they struggled in vain in his mighty grasp. "I am meek, am I not? Meek! Meek, I say! Am I not meek?"

"Yes," the two men had managed to squeak, and were dropped to the ground by the titan known as Cardinal Salmon.

"You shall both be servants, feeding our neediest until you learn to curb your violence."

Cardinal Salmon had kicked both men in the rear and sent them sprawling into the muck. He then had rested on his battered wooden throne, downed a quaff of ale and belched. The sound had been like the rumble of an earthquake, causing everyone present to roar with laughter.

In the present, the Antipope chuckled briefly and leaned back in her chair.

"Salmon openly despised violence. Not that he was above using it to enforce his position. But he always had killers ready to confront menaces. We were kept very much in the dark. My killers are all girls and women. All badly abused by the world. We usually work as a team. Dark thieves in the night. But at times, we use our skills to end the lives of the wealthy or powerful. The ones who kill the weak for pleasure."

"That makes a degree of sense," said Séverin. "Am I right in assuming that you have these houses and the like because of your thievery?"

The Morgue Director knew he was on dangerous ground. Criminals often liked to keep their secrets. But he also felt that, thanks to their earlier battle with the *loups-garous*, he was able to broach so delicate a subject.

The Antipope studied Séverin for a moment and then appeared to make an internal decision.

"You are right. Any money earned by the beggars is placed in a general fund. I use it to buy food, medicines and places to live for the poor. What we get is never close to enough, but we do what we can."

"I think Salmon would approve."

Séverin wasn't sure if that was true, but it felt like the correct thing to say.

"Thank you."

The Antipope didn't say anything else. She watched as Lisebette returned and placed a dusty bottle on the table with two pewter mugs. The young woman skipped from view, a lively step that was filled with youthful energy.

A silence fell between the two, but not an uncomfortable one. Séverin poured liberal portions in each mug and tasted the wine. It was dry, but good quality. The type he preferred, though less watered than he would have liked. He had adopted the habit of watering his wine in the same manner as the great emperor and philosopher, Marcus Aurelius. The great man had been cautious in his drinking, according to Séverin's readings. But more importantly, one of his quotes was of great help during times of terrible tragedy. Séverin had a copy of his words framed and placed on the wall besides his small and lonely bed:

When you arise in the morning, think of what a precious privilege it is to be alive, to breathe, to think, to enjoy, to love.

But civility prevented him from asking for water. He would drink slowly to keep a clear head. The wine was refreshing, at least, especially after such a terrible battle.

The Antipope broke the extended silence. She downed her drink and met his gaze.

"You had a clear reason for seeking my help?" she inquired.

"Yes," replied Séverin, pouring her another full cup. "I want to know if there is a cell of Royalists attempting to revolt."

The Antipope shrugged.

"Yes, several. Most will talk until the day Christ rises from the Earth and the Last Judgment begins. I could also list three groups of Jacobins who wish to lead anyone with more than two *sous* to the guillotine."

Séverin leaned on the table, attempting to get a little closer to the enigmatic Queen of the Beggars.

"I'm not an informer. I'm searching for the man behind those monsters we just faced."

"Why?"

The Antipope also leaned closer. She looked curious, studying him carefully.

"This is what I do," replied Séverin. "I seek out such evils and prevent them from harming anyone."

Séverin sensed that honesty was the best direction with this enigmatic woman. She possessed a calm, controlled confidence that was impressive, and would not, could not, be challenged easily.

"You're the Morgue Director, and a former fencing master," she shot back. But then tilted her head in thought, "But they do call you the *spoiler of wolves*."

"Correct."

Séverin sat back and waited.

"Based on your actions and knowledge today, I presume this means you've faced similar and worse menaces in the past..."

The Antipope wasn't actually asking a question, but airing a thought.

"Also correct."

Séverin knew he didn't need to confirm her statement, but in saying the words, he would be granting the Antipope his word that there was purely a supernatural reason for his initiative.

This was a critical moment, one which both parties present understood on a deeper level. Though the Queen of Beggars possessed massive stores of information, her knowledge was not for sale. Many leaders, noble, royal, or common-born, had attempted to force this wisdom from the grasp of the legendary Court of Miracles. Such as the archdeacon at the time of King Louis XI, the so-called "spider-king." Apparently his predecessor had died due to some involvement by the Court of Miracles. The man, a silly little person of good birth named Châteaupers, had attempted to control the Beggar King. He had failed and was later accused of treason, arrested and executed. According to legend, Châteaupers' own brother had been forced to arrest and imprison him in order to prove his loyalty to the monstrous, manipulative, monarch of France.

But he hadn't been the first. Less than fifty years earlier, the grounds that the Court had occupied had been destroyed. The reason was for health; the ancient location was a rat-infested slum which spread disease throughout Paris. But the Ministry of Police had been behind the action in an attempt to curb the power of the Beggar King. In truth, the opposite had occurred. The new king had used to destruction of their home as a method of forging closer ties between his people and the poor of Paris.

The final attempt had taken place during the brief reign of the Jacobin Club. Their leader, the rapacious Maximilien Robespierre, had wished to know every secret in Paris, possibly all of France. He had possessed a spy, known only as the Shrike, who had ferreted out that the Beggars' Guild knew all the secrets of France. Robespierre had launched several assaults upon the Court of Miracles, attempting to seize the King and his people. But all he had managed to do was lose some poorly-trained soldiers and arrest a few aged cripples, unable to flee from the battles. According to legend, the king, Cardinal Salmon, had refused to provide any information to the enemies of the Jacobins when those terrible men had fallen from power. His reasoning was that the mysteries his people learned were not for outsiders. Even enemies like the ones who sat on the Committee for Public Safety.

"What will you do with this information?" the Antipope asked, pouring herself another full mug of wine.

However, she did not lift it to drink. Instead she kept scrutinizing Séverin's face.

"Seek out the one who's using monsters. Who controls the country is not my concern. Politicians come and go like the seasons, but if a man using monsters attempts to destroy the current rulers, then all life is in danger. Can you imagine an army of *loups-garous* in battle? They would destroy any forces in their path. Then they would begin to feed upon the general populace. Within days, Paris would be reduced to an abattoir. Mankind would be cattle. And all other animals would be exterminated. This city, and the rest of the country, would become a desert, devoid of life. All that would exist would be blood, bones and dust."

Séverin rarely spoke at such length, but the idea that someone might create an army of such monsters was terrifying. And that someone might be a *vampire*.

Loups-garous possessed no real self-control. They were creatures of pure appetite, feeding regularly upon the innards of any living being. The larger, the better. Only a vampiric master possessed the authority and influence to curb their need to feast. But a herd of monsters would eventually tax even his power. And slowly, the werewolves would begin gorging unchecked. Then, all life on the planet would be at risk.

"If they attack the Directory, what then?" asked the Antipope.

She broke eye-contact and downed her wine. Lisebette appeared at that moment and laid out a meal of a cold roast chicken before leaving the room without a backward glance.

"I'll make certain they're defeated by the Parisian defense forces," replied Séverin. "These beasts are not unstoppable with proper planning. A military genius I am acquainted with is up to such a challenge. And I will attempt to destroy their vampiric master."

Séverin didn't hide his concerns. He could not merely kill the vampire and be done with it. That would leave the werewolves uncontrolled and result in an even greater loss of life. Nor could he passively wait for the monsters to attack Paris. Each day this evil was unchecked would result in greater loss of life.

The Antipope pulled a leg off the chicken and took a dainty bite.

"What if your friends in the Directory wish to know how you learned such information?"

"I will lie. They will not learn your involvement. I made the same pact with Cardinal Salmon."

Séverin also pulled a small piece off the chicken and took a bite. Though unheated, the bird was tasty and well-cooked, with just a hint of unusual spices to make it tastier.

"I will assemble a list," the Antipope said finally. "One of my people will give it to you. Someone you recognize. Is it acceptable?"

Séverin nodded.

"Excellent. Then, no more business. We will eat and you can tell me how you earned that nickname, *spoiler of wolves*."

The Antipope leaned back in her chair as Séverin began to weave a tale of torment and terror in the Gévaudan region of France.

CHAPTER XIV

Paris, November 1804

"Demon," Karnstein confirmed.

Before he could say more, he was knocked from his feet by a tall woman with golden blond hair. She'd been memorable during the orgy, possessing impressive physical assets that had caught his eye despite the disgusting situation.

A fat man and an old woman joined the attractive devil worshipper as they kicked the fallen Austrian nobleman. He attempted to rise and fight back, but was tripped and trapped by the assault. If the cultists had not been weakened by the gorging and debauchery, and the fact that they wore no shoes, he might have been severely beaten.

Meanwhile, Séverin struck a charging pair with the flat of his small sword. He drew his saber and dropped three more with bruises and light cuts. Clear for the moment, he stepped over to the three attacking the fallen Karnstein and slammed each upon the skull with the flat of his sword. Killing these followers of the left-hand path would be easy, but it may complicate the situation in the moments to come. And there was still the demon coming in their direction.

Helping Karnstein to his feet, Séverin was gratified to observe that the younger man, though bruised, was otherwise uninjured. He swept the feet out from another cultist and took a step back. The smell of brimstone was rising and the chamber was growing warmer by the second. Sheathing his saber, Séverin reached into his belt pouch for his vial of holy water. The blessed liquid would not kill the demon within the boy, but it would injure it and force it into retreat.

Karnstein stepped in front of Séverin, blocking his view of the approaching demon. Though brave, this was foolhardy at best. Demons were not so easily defeated as human cultists. And the young Exorcist appeared unable to deal with that lesser danger.

"Karnstein, step aside" urged Séverin. "I have a means of causing the fiend to flee."

The Morgue Director had the holy water in hands and removed the cork stopper on the bottle.

Karnstein did not look back, but in fact took two steps forward. Séverin's eyes widened as he saw the possessed man further transformed in the short time. The youth now stood taller, almost as tall as the swordmaster. His skin was bright red and a pair of wicked looking horns protruded from his elongated, horse-like skull. The beautiful boy was gone; a monstrosity stood in his place.

"Karnstein! Back away! It will destroy you!"

Séverin rarely raised his voice or called out in fear. But he didn't want Karnstein's bravado to cause his death. Not when the young man appeared to be on a very decent and much needed firmer path in this world.

"I think not," said Karnstein.

The Exorcist stepped closer and he began to speak. His words were of a guttural, odd tongue and a white light seemed to exude from his tall form.

"DALKHU TARU SERU ESERU ETUTU INA ETUTI ASBU DARISAM!" emerged from Karnstein's lips.

Just for a split second, a symbol of white and silver light appeared between the Exorcist and the demon. It was a seven-pointed star in a hexagram, with odd symbols surrounding it. A flash briefly blinded everyone present, and a loud, guttural screech filled the air.

It took a moment for Séverin's and the cultists' eyes to adjust back to the current light. What they viewed then caused a collective gasp of fear. Séverin blinked several times in surprise, unable to believe his own eyes.

The boy, once possessed by the demon, now lay stretched out upon the ground. The demonic transformations were gone and a ragged hole where his heart once had been was exposed. The body was beginning to rot, collapsing upon itself and aging before their eyes.

Séverin knew what this meant. The boy was long dead. He had been sacrificed by the high priest to some nameless demon in the distant past. The body only existed as a puppet to the demonic spirit, a fleshy glove that was propped up by a fiendish, alien will. With the expulsion of the monster within, time had caught up to the body and soon nothing would remain but desiccated flesh and bones.

How did Karnstein managed to dispel so dangerous a demon with one short phrase? The common time for an exorcism was six hours, just to complete the full rites. And often, according to Séverin's information, the priests performed the ceremony three or more times. This was unheard of, a completely unexpected event.

The cultists were equally dumbfounded. They stared at the fallen boy in drop-mouthed shock, which quickly morphed into stark, open terror. They fell back, almost trampling each other to get to the far walls. The only ones frozen in place were the high priest and the naked girl.

"Who... what... how...?"

The high priest looked both enraged and frightened. His formerly controlled voice cracked as he stammered and stared.

"Oh, do shut up," said the girl, shooting a look of naked disgust at the high priest.

She turned back to Karnstein.

"What you just did should not be possible," she stated. "What are you?"

"I am Franz von Karnstein, Baron of Karnstein and Vordenburg, heir to Count Karnstein. I am an exorcist in the service of His Holiness Pope Pius VII. And I have seen and battled evils that would send your paltry coven of craven *debauchés* screaming in terror into the night. Now, you will answer our questions."

Karnstein's voice was a low, rough, snarl, spoken through clenched teeth. His Austrian accent added a sinister edge to his implied threats. He looked, even to Séverin's cynical sight, more substantial than anyone present. As if his will had caused all nearby to retreat and become shadows.

"And you'll leave us in peace?" asked the girl.

She stood and wrapped herself in a diaphanous gown that made her appear even more naked rather than clothed. Her long, smooth legs peeked out and her jutting breasts appeared larger and more sensual than when she stood before them naked.

"We'll leave you to your damnation" replied the Exorcist. "For now, at least. We have a greater mission this day. But peace? No, not ever. When our mission is complete, I will remember your unholy rites."

Karnstein ignored the high priest. Apparently, they'd been wrong. This girl, who appeared to be the

121

victim at first sight, was more important than they had realized.

The girl waved a hand in a gesture of reluctant surrender.

"Ask then and be damned with you," she said.

Séverin stepped forward, sensing Karnstein's growing fury. A cooler head was needed.

"There is a vampire in Paris," he stated.

The girl chuckled and sat down on the altar, crossing her long, perfect legs in a casual manner.

"Only one?" she smirked. "My, oh, my... How frightful."

Séverin touched Karnstein's arm to prevent the coming storm. The girl's mocking tone was intended to put them off-balance.

"There is only one of importance. He can create *loups-garous* and use them as slaves. Where is he?"

The girl stared at Séverin, her large dark eyes unreadable. Finally, she appeared to make a decision.

"Why do you wish to find him? She inquired. "He cannot be killed. I'm not sure he can even be injured."

"You fear him?"

Séverin sensed an opening, a chance to get some assistance from these servants of darkness.

The girl threw back her head and laughed. But the sound possessed no mirth. This was a laughter born in fear, an inborn response to something so alarming that a shriek of fear wasn't even possible.

"Fear him? Of course, we do. A being immune to our spells, unable to die from a stake to the heart, or a fiery torch thrust into his face. We tried to beg for his help, but he and his pet destroyed our members. All he promised was to return and make us his inhuman, mindless slaves one day."

The girl leaned forward towards Séverin as she spoke. Her voice rose and cracked, her terror even more evident now.

"Give us his location," asked the Morgue Director, "and we will destroy him. Once and forever."

Séverin sheathed his small sword and crossed his arms across his chest.

The girl frowned and seemed to weigh her choices. She then nodded once.

"So be it. A messenger will provide you with all we know. Then our alliance with you both is over. Kill this vampire and we will be glad, but not grateful. That is not the way of the true King of the Earth."

Karnstein snorted. He appeared more amused and contemptuous than enraged now.

"Ah yes, the virtue of selfishness," he smiled. "Always the main point of any follower of Lucifer Morningstar. Speak to a Satanist and you're ultimately confronting a spoiled child. A well-fed brat who wishes a greater portion of the world. And all for no other reason than because they don't wish to work for anything in life."

The girl stood, hands on her hips, her face a mask of fury. She no longer looked pretty. Instead, with her hair wild and tangled, she resembled one of the gorgons of myth. If she could have transformed Karnstein into a stone statue, she would have done so at that moment without consideration.

"Some of us have other motives. Like overturning a social order that places us as lower than cattle!" he uttered, her voice filled with a rage, the likes of which Séverin had rarely heard in one so young.

"And you'll do that by murdering innocent children? And having their bodies possessed by demons?"

Karnstein looked ready to explode once again. Séverin placed a hand on the young Austrian's shoulder. They didn't have time for this debate.

The young woman smiled, suddenly looking very attractive once again.

She uttered:

"LO NOR-QUASAHI TORZUL. ADPHAHT AMMA DONASDOGAMATASTOS CHISO IALPON BALTOH."

The words were harsh upon the ear. The cultists cringed with each syllable. Séverin disliked the sound, but had heard this language before from the mouths of both good and evil beings. This was the language of Heaven and Hell, Above and Below. Called Enochian by a madman named John Dee, this was a purer form of the tongue than he'd ever heard spoken by mankind.

Before he could ask, Karnstein responded:

"APACHANA YORB AVAVAGO G-MACALZA BABALON BABALOND"

Karnstein practically spat the words back and the cultists, if possible, fell back even further from his presence. The girl on the dais flushed, and pointed a long finger at the door.

"Leave! Leave before I raise Lord Lucifer himself to destroy you and all life on Earth!"

"Send the information quickly," said Séverin.

He did not ask, but made the words more of a warning. He then waved Karnstein to follow him and they left the unholy temple. There was a great deal they needed to discuss before they confronted the immortal monster haunting Paris.

CHAPTER XV

Paris, September 1795

The Marquis de Saint-Evremonde watched as Colonel Grenier shrieked and writhed upon the stone floor of the basement.

The first transformation was supposedly one of the most painfully horrific experiences one could undergo. The "torments of the damned," it was deemed by one of his past servants. Saint-Evremonde saw no reason to disagree with that poetic phrasing. Based on his observation, the agony was all-encompassing. It often shattered the psyche and mind of the victim, which was quite delightful to the ancient vampire. Pain was food for his admittedly black soul.

It had always been this way for the Marquis. Even back when he had served the magnificent king, Philippe IV, also known as the Fair. Ah, Philippe, beautiful of face and blackest of hearts, one of the most rapacious and evil men who had ever lived. And Saint-Evremonde, then a mere knight in his court, had worshipped him. Philippe had considered himself nothing less than divine, and all who failed to comprehend this fell. He and Saint-Evremonde had been close friends, boyhood compatriots learning under the very strict Guillaume d'Ercuis. That old man was a monster who beat them for the slightest failure, but they had flourished thanks to his teachings.

Though there were many moments filled with blood and terror in Saint-Evremonde's memory, the time in King Philippe's court was like an epicurean feast for one of his disposition. His love of violence, torture and death made him one of the King's personal knights, his favorite *homme de main*.

"You are my attack dog, my dear Saint-Evremonde," Philippe had told him as he had elevated the young knight to the post of Marquis and Grand Huntsman of France. "Like a greyhound, you will chase and pull down my foes."

"Yes, Your Majesty!" Saint-Evremonde had beamed, on his knees, relishing the thought of their next crusade against the King's enemies.

That was the time when the King had cleverly got the English to yield their lands in France. Philippe had told the stupid English king, Edward the long-legged, that the lands would be returned. A truly amusing lie. The minute the lands were back in the Fair One's hands, Edward's supporters had been robbed and turned out by Saint-Evremonde's forces.

Then, there were the Jews. Saint-Evremonde had little interest in them as a people. He had enough money and they didn't mix with society. Aliens in the lands of France—but useful ones. However the King had needed gold. To borrow coin would have been ruinous for the realm, which was why he had outlawed the Jews. This allowed Saint-Evremonde a chance to murder, rob, and rape, sometimes in that order, the women and children being exiled from France. It was a wonderful time. Hearing the shrieks of the prisoners, begging for the lives and promising all their gold, was like listening to the sweetest music.

But truly, the most wonderful duty he had performed for King Philippe was still felt by the whole of Europe to this day. This was none other than the destruction of the holy order of the Knights Templars, the wealthiest order in the whole world, bankers of supreme skill and possessing their own army. This had not merely been a move to ensure that Philippe's royal coffers would be perpetually filled. Oh, that was important! But not the true motivating factor. It had been a means of allowing the ruler of France to assert greater control over the Papacy in his own country. The Templars had been too strong; destroying them made the Crown supreme, in spiritual as well as temporal rule.

It hadn't been hard either. Some well-crafted falsified evidence of heresy and Philippe the Fair had struck. The Templars had been arrested, their lands and holdings seized, their Grandmaster burned as a heretic. Philippe the Fair had become the mightiest monarch in Christendom, and all the world lived in fear at his very name. A wonderful result.

Or so it seemed at the time.

Philippe's puppet Pope, Clement V, had died mere weeks later. And then Philippe, too, had died, of a stupid accident while hunting. Most had believed this had been happenstance, a bad roll of the knucklebones, but in secret, they had whispered that the actual cause was the curse of the innocent Templars.

Saint-Evremonde knew the truth, for he had been the third victim. The day Philippe had died, his boon companion and trained killer had also fallen. But thanks to the dark powers, the Marquis had risen again. He was still a murderous lover of horror and pain, but without Philippe's guidance and control, he had become a plague upon the world.

As a "distant relative" of the renowned Marquis de Saint-Evremonde, he had eventually returned to the court of King Jean II, a.k.a. The Good. A fool, one more interested in creating awards for his favorites and slipping beneath the petticoats of his queen and mistresses. It had been simplicity itself to betray him and allow him to fall into the hands of the English. A joyful time to be a vampire. The black death had allowed Saint-Evremonde the opportunity to feast and gain greater strength as a creature of blood and darkness.

Later, King Louis XI had proven to be an even more enjoyable monarch than Philippe had been, in so many ways. He had lived up to his nickname, the "Spider King." Louis's web was his spy network, a hidden group of men and women who sought to ensnare anyone who sought to deny the monstrous monarch's will. Saint-Evremonde had murdered his last living descendant, taken his place and joined Louis's faction. The slaughter of the king's enemy had been glorious, but it had had to be more circumspect, a good lesson for the now ancient vampire. Rampant murder was only effective on the battlefield. Cunning creatures survived longer.

The last French king Saint-Evremonde had truly served was the most dangerous and intelligent of them all, and the one who had known the vampire for what he really was—his true nature. François the First, man of letters, diplomatic genius, great warlord—and pervert. It had only been one month in the court when François had cornered him in his infamous maze.

"You're not human, are you, Marquis? Are you even a Saint-Evremonde? Before you answer, know this: I have the headsman nearby. I can summon him here. I'm not sure which fate you would earn. Burning? The axe? Or something more ancient and crude? Or you can tell me the truth. And be warned: I will know if you lie, creature."

François's voice had been like an oily whisper, a loving caress that hid a razor within its folds. His every word, every gesture, suggested all of humanity was his victim. His plaything. Fail to amuse this dread king and one might become subject to the tortures unheard of by mortal man.

"I am a Saint-Evremonde, sire," the ancient vampire had confessed, not bothering to hide his terrible teeth and talons. "I served your predecessors, Philippe the Fair and Louis the Spider, just as I can now serve you."

And use him King François did over the years. Saint-Evremonde became his secret assassin, hunting hound and destroyer of all Hapsburg influences in the realm. In payment, the King had gifted Saint-Evremonde with wealth, and access to all the pleasures of the court. For François had enjoyed sampling the delights of sex with women of all ages. Their favorite, for a time, had been an English beauty named Mary, whom the Marquis had nicknamed, "the English mare." But even those pleasures had eventually become tiresome.

It was then that the Marquis de Saint-Evremonde had examined his extended life and found it wanting. He was over two hundred years old and what had he accomplished? Delightful pain, torture, rape and pleasures, but nothing else. Being a vampire had granted him powers greater than any normal man, but what had he learned about his nature? His abilities?

After King François I had died, a skeletal ruin of a man, riddled with pox, Saint-Evremonde had decided to explore—not the world, for who cared about how other people lived—but his powers. Allowing some distant relative to inherit his titles, the Marquis had moved south and studied a host of mystic tomes he had hoarded over the years.

The vast majority of these had been little better than the ranting and ravings of madmen and beings with minds he could not begin to comprehend. But within this vast mountain of dross, there had been tiny truths he could discern. The hidden veracities of the cosmos were unimportant to Saint-Evremonde. His only concern had been his own powers—and how to truly live forever.

The magic itself had never worked. He had not been able to control the minds of others, or absorb his victims into his own body and release them as his slaves. His tongue did not extend and allow him another form of attack. And obviously, the tales in the books about vampires able to transform into rats, bats or wolves had just been another pathetic peasant superstition. Still, he had learned how to move his heart to another part of his body to prevent being killed by his enemies. He could speak in the minds of the weak-willed, if not influence or control them in any way. But the shock was often enough to terrorize the foolish into total compliance. Also, he could create and control the beast the peasants called the *loup-garou*.

This last power had been the most satisfying. All his life, both natural and undead, had been dedicated to the hunt. As the Grand Huntsman of France under two different kings, Saint-Evremonde had taken great pleasure in the thrill of the chase. There was little more satisfying then the search for a prey and the kill. Both Philippe and François had allowed him the most enjoyable hunts of all—humans.

Both sovereigns had arrested numerous criminals for treason and other crimes against the crown. The nobles were allowed trials and death through various means, but peasants had possessed no true rights. They were property and could be disposed of by any means necessary or expedient. A hunt through the streets of Paris, or on some noble holding, was greater than the killing of some half-starved wolf or boar.

The Marquis had experimented with his power to control the beasts over the years. In the early days, it had been difficult to control even one of these creatures. Saint-Evremonde had created and abandoned dozens of the pathetic monsters, which had all been hunted down by peasants and clergy. But that had been unimportant; they were merely humans after all. He was something far greater, a being on an exalted plane beyond the ken of the mortal mind.

By the time his control had been perfected, there had been nobody worthy of his assistance. The Bourbon Kings were weak-willed and easily led. Louis XIII had been under the control of the devious Cardinal de Richelieu, and that holy man had been as intelligent as François and as dangerous as the Spider King. No, it has been best to stay away from court then.

After Louis XIII's death, Saint-Evremonde had attempted to exert influence upon the new monarch, but Louis XIV had quickly seen though his guise and had ordered his army to hunt him down and bring back his head. The undead Marquis had barely escaped, only returning to society in time to see the execution of Louis XVI.

This new France was a puzzle even greater than the worst written human skin books on summoning demons from his collection. Peasants ruling the city? Condemning men and women whose ancestors' blood made them greater than the rest. How was this possible? The Republican values were pure insanity. Society existed because the noble ruled over the weak-blooded masses.

Which was why the Marquis de Saint-Evremonde was a Royalist, determined to return society back to a time he understood. He would ally himself with the nearly useless Bourbons, prop them up with his skills, while remain a power hidden behind the scenes. He possessed the dangerous edge of his beloved Philippe IV, the Machiavellian manipulation of Louis XI, and the genius and daring of François I. France and the rest of Europe would soon be his plaything, his food. The Marquis would be the eternal master of all life. It would be glorious.

But first, there was the Directory to eliminate. Grenier's transformation was almost complete. Now, for the remainder of the cell. It would not be long now before his hunting hounds tore apart the peasants and Paris would fall under his thumb.

CHAPTER XVI

Paris, November 1804

The return trip to the surface was uneventful and mostly silent. Both men were tired and Séverin had a great deal to say, but did not want to do it within this series of stygian shafts beneath Paris.

They emerged in the same location and, after a short walk, collapsed in a small inn located near the demolition site of the Bastille. The tavern was a ramshackle ruin, a smoky, shabby shelter with tasteless food and watered wine. But it would do for the moment. The depressing atmosphere would allow them some degree of privacy.

"Cost you extra if you want the chicken on the spit," said the tavern-owner, his eyes examining their every possession.

He was a skinny young man named Thénardier, half as high as Séverin and Karnstein and he looked as if he was about to cough a mouthful of phlegm in their faces. His wife was a buxom, blond woman, with large hands and the rapacious eyes of a sewer rat.

"I'll pay extra for that if you open a new bottle in front of me at the table," replied Séverin, placing a pair of coins on the table, but keeping one hand over the money.

He waited until the fresh food and wine were provided and lifted his palm. Thénardier was content that he'd gotten him to overpay, but only a little. That man would never be completely happy with anything in life.

The innkeeper left the two men, seeking another victim to be robbed. His sense of survival told him the two tall men, although tired, were more dangerous than they seemed. For one thing, they both appeared to be armed. Best to overcharge them and move on to weaker targets.

"You have questions," said Karnstein, almost amused, between bites of the tasteless meat.

He waved the leg languidly and added:

"Ask away. I won't attempt to lie to you. I suspect you would be able to discern any attempted falsehood."

"How long were you a student at the Scholomance?" asked Séverin, not bothering to waste time, but going straight to the heart of the issue.

Though Karnstein was obviously on the side of good, mystics who used the left-hand path of magic, even in the service of good, soon fell into dark practices.

There was a belief by students of magic that there was no true morality in occult practices, that everything was merely the use of energy, without any connections to morality. Séverin knew that this was a fallacy, a foolish attempt to justify their behavior, because the use of dark power invariably corrupted their users in the end. Men and women who took up the practice of witchcraft or sorcery desiring to help the world, slowly discovered the expedience of transforming people, places and objects to their whim. In time, it became easier to simply control the people and environment. Free will in others becomes anathema, a sin. Practitioners concluded that their learning placed them on a higher plane of thought, one beyond ordinary mortal ken. They were exalted beings, the only ones capable of keeping all life on a correct path in life. These foolish thoughts then led to a

greater evil than the one they had desired to fight initial-
ly. A terrible circle, a pathway to utter damnation.

Karnstein placed his chicken leg down on his plate.
His pale eyes locked with Séverin's and he answered in
a deceptively mild tone of voice:

"I have never been a student of the Scholomance,
the Deep School, the Dark Academy, the teaching con-
servatory of the Brotherhood of the Ram, or any other
school or tutelage in magic."

"Yet you performed magic."

"I did no such thing."

Karnstein placed both hands on the table, but the
hands were balled in fists so tight, the knuckles were
white.

"Allow me to point out that you defeated a demon
with one brief set of words in an ancient tongue," observed Séverin, holding up one finger. "One I could not
identify, and I do speak one of the oldest languages on
Earth, Aramaic."

"The language was Sumerian. Far more ancient."

Karnstein's voice was still mild, but a storm was
growing in his eyes, one that Séverin had viewed many
times in his long life.

"You expelled a demon with that phrase in Sumerian," continued the Morgue Director, holding up a second
finger. "The shortest exorcism in my experience lasts six
hours. Your act took under ten seconds. This is unheard
of, an action nothing short of a miracle."

"No miracle, merely... unique. As I told you, I possess other methods of fighting evil."

Karnstein's body was tense now, the storm in his
eyes growing.

"And you engaged that young Satanist woman in
what I believe to be Enochian," added Séverin. "The

language of the thaumaturgistic scholar; or, simply put, the words of a warlock."

By now, the Morgue Director was holding up three fingers—a trident, the Devil's pitchfork so to speak.

Now it was Karnstein's turn to be surprised:

"You speak Enochian?"

Séverin shook his head.

"I have the notes of a dictionary from a mad scholar named John Dee. And he wrote that this was the method to invoke the power of angels. But other treatises on Dee's foolish works declare that only the fallen angels respond to such demands for power. And no magic is darker than that of Lucifer and his fallen flock."

"On that much we agree. But Enochian is not merely for power. It is a method for angels, light and dark, to communicate with mankind. Any other method would result in the destruction of our body and minds. The fact that a Satanist spoke Enochian so clearly concerns me greatly."

Karnstein appeared to relax a tiny degree as he spoke.

"The fact that either of you spoke the tongue of higher spirits concerns me even more" said Séverin. "What was said?"

He remembered the words clearly, but to translate the brief conversation would take hours, possibly even days. Enochian's many variations and odd intonations made all efforts arduous.

Karnstein considered the request and appeared to decide in Séverin's favor.

"The woman said an ancient evil pledge. The followers of the Devil behaved as if it was a prophecy, but they fooled themselves again. Her words were, 'The first sons of pleasure rise. Unspeakable curses and hellfire

burn the righteous.' Understand, this is a rough translation. The meanings are far deeper."

"And your reply?" asked Séverin.

"I replied with a simple insult. My words were,
'The slimy things made of dust roar like thunder in the
presence of the wicked and harlots.' You can comprehend why she was so enraged."

Karnstein did not seem amused by his jest. Instead
he merely shrugged. Séverin, on the other hand, threw
back his head and howled with laughter. The patrons of
the inn turned briefly at the sounds of mirth. But, within
a moment, they turned back to their own food, drink or
hushed conversation. They did not, could not, realize
how unusual such a reaction was from the normally dour
Jean-Pierre Séverin.

"That was delightful, young man," said the Morgue
Director. "And I can believe every word of it. That
woman's fury could only be caused by such a response.
But I did see a mystic symbol when you spoke those
words: a star in a circle with mystic sigils. Agrippa referred to that representation as a pentagram."

Séverin drew a similar sign in the condensation
from the wine bottle on the table.

Karnstein scrubbed out the image and wiped a bit
more water onto the scarred, pitted rickety wooden table.
The mark was like the one etched in water by Séverin.
But there were differences. The star was more exact and
he used small dots in place of the occult emblems.

"That was what you viewed?"

Karnstein looked up and caught Séverin's nod.

"That is no pentagram. It is the Seal of Solomon. A
holy lustrum. Not magic. Holy."

Séverin sipped his wine for a moment and contemplated the statements of the Austrian exorcist. Pope Pius

VII, though raised to the upper echelons of power by his relative, the late Pope Pius VI, was reputedly a shrewd man and a firm believer in the religion he led. This man was no Borgia, sitting his bloated fundament on the throne, little better than a petty feudal baron. But would he recognize the difference between a holy miracle or a magic ceremony? Doubtful. Few men or women in the world understood the perils of manipulating the powers of the universe. The one detail in Karnstein's favor was that the Holy Inquisition wasn't investigating him and his place among the lesser order of exorcists.

"If I may?" said Séverin. "You know far more about seminaries devoted to the left-hand path of magic. That is uncommon, to say the least. In fact, there are some who battle monsters and Satanists who would find your knowledge to be very alarming."

Karnstein rolled his eyes and seemed almost amused. Almost.

"The very fact that I am a Karnstein of Styria would make most of them attempt to take my life."

"I can't deny that fact. In fact, I'm forced to inquire further. You said that you never attended the Scholomance and several other such conservatoires. But your family is legendary for their presence among the darkness. I doubt even the order of exorcists would know the name of the Brotherhood of the Ram, not to mention speak Enochian with fluency. Who are you *really*, Franz von Karnstein?"

Séverin knew the rules of polite society prevented such open inquires, but he'd never been subject to such limitations in the past.

"That is quite a tale—one that would take far too long to tell in one sitting. But I will tell you one part of the chronicle that is my varied life. It begins in Karnstein Castle in my home in Styria…"

CHAPTER XVII

Paris, October 1795

Séverin's day and nights became a simple routine. Rise before dawn, walk for three to four hours. Eat a simple meal. Then train. Sword, dagger, maul, hands and feet. Each morning the weapon changed. He needed to be ready and at the height of his skills. Then a brief meal followed by studying in his library.

His collection of books, inherited from Grost and other teachers, was considerable and impressive. His DaVinci's Latin copy of the *Necronomicon* was in good condition. And the notes from Dee's translation of a similar text allowed him to confirm mistranslations. Also in his collection a copy of the manuscript of *Unholy Followers of Darkness* by the Templar Brian de Royalton, only slightly singed. The author himself was the first of his order to be condemned by the Church as a heretic. The manuscript had been prime evidence used to destroy the powerful men known as the Knights Templar, but the text had been, according the legend, smuggled away by a monk who was fascinated by the dark cults and terrible practices discussed by the author. Rumor had it this monk, a man named Brother Simon, had vanished from the world shortly after distributing three copies he made personally, using his own blood.

Séverin's manuscript was said to be a reproduction of one of those unholy versions. It had last been in the possession of the infamous necromancer, Giles de Rais, the profane madman responsible for hundreds of souls sacrificed to his dark demonic master. The work was horrible, tales of alien cults whose monstrous practices would cause even the worst murderers in Paris to blanch in revulsion.

And this was just one tome in Séverin's collection—and far from the worst. Were the Church to see some of these books, the swordmaster would probably be condemned as a warlock, and burned at the stake.

Séverin spent the early evening walking and running. One of his swordmasters, a former master of arms called Bertrand des Amis, always stressed a simple dictum. If you did not possess the endurance to survive an extended battle, you would fall, no matter how effective your technique.

"One of my closest compatriots, a man I viewed as a brother, fought the Vicomte de Valmont for ten minutes. He defeated that noble fiend and then his heart failed. A bitter end. He loved to drink and eat too well."

Bertrand des Amis had repeated that story often as he forced Séverin to run the hills behind his training hall.

Then to sleep. And repeat the next day. And the next. The number became a blur as his concentration remained absolute upon his goal. To face a vampire in an even slightly weakened state, mind, body of spirit, would result in a terrible death—or worse.

He kept to that routine remained for some time. Leading a solitary life allowed him to maintain an existence best suited for a warrior-monk of the Crusades. And, in a true sense, this was the purpose of his Spartan life. Even while married, Séverin always viewed luxury and easy living as a method of weakening one's body and spirit. Simplicity was a far easier method of life.

The great Marcus Aurelius had said it best: *Very little is needed to make a happy life; it is all within yourself, in your way of thinking.*

But as he returned from his latest walk, Séverin knew the routine was about to end. A new aspect was about to enter his life. Someone was within his apartments—an intruder. There was no sound, no evidence or their entry, but he knew this to be true. Séverin's instincts were at their height. And like all swordmasters, his sense of anticipation of assault approached the superhuman.

Pulling out the Florencian dagger from his side, he also removed the sheath. Opening the door, he stepped into the room, keeping his eyes forward. Looking as if he was about to walk further, he lifted one foot in the air. Then he exploded into action.

Kicking the door closed with the lifted foot, he threw the dagger sheath behind him and into the rafters above his head. As expected, the hard leather struck a body. Séverin's eyes shifted upwards and he crouched in a fighting stance.

A small form, clothed entirely in black, dropped to the floor. Barely a sound was heard as the latter landed and drew a pair of stilettos. The man in black moved with the light, languid motions of an experienced fighter. The attacker's hands moved in a circular motion, an almost hypnotic action, which caused the knives to flash as they passed through the light.

Suddenly, the man in black slashed for Séverin's eyes. A traditional move, attack the eyes while the other hand stabs the stomach. Even a glancing hit in either location weakened the victim and could result in a painful demise.

But Séverin was an expert. He had trained under the legendary Giorgio Borgia de Medici. Giorgio was the last chief assassin of the House of Medici, known by the terrible title of "Master of Sleep." The elderly cutthroat had taken Séverin as a pupil, passing on his stygian secrets before retiring to a small villa in the countryside. And this was the first assault the old murderer had taught him to repel.

"Killers. They get too used to the easy methods. Eyes and insides. Most do that first. Like taking the same way home each night. Easier to live by living without thinking. Only fools and horses live that way. You a fool or a horse, boy?"

Giorgio had emphasized his words by prodding Séverin with the ash can he always had in hand.

"No, master."

Séverin was young, but still knew the proper form of address of the ancient monster.

"Then don't even try the easy steps. Use that thing between your ears. Smart fighters grow old. Impulsive idiots feed fishes. Now, from the start. Attack!"

Giorgio had rapped the cane against the ground to emphasize his words. And the lesson had never left Séverin.

Now, seeing old Giorgio's words proving correct, Séverin was ready. He ducked beneath the slash to his eyes. At the same time, his dagger slashed downward. Not point first, but with the rounded handle in the lead. The heavy circular metal struck the attacker's wrist, causing their hand to open involuntarily. The knife in that hand clattered to the ground. Séverin kicked it behind him and mentally mapped the location in his head. You never knew when a weapon might be needed in a fight.

The attacker, whose face was hidden, circled to Séverin's left, still moving with the same slow, hypnotic rhythm. Suddenly, he reversed his grip and threw the knife straight at Séverin's neck. At the same time, his foot fired up, aiming for the swordmaster's groin.

Another classic trick from street fighting. Séverin knew the attacker's shoe also possessed a protruding razor. The blade was tiny, probably no more than an inch, but the damage such a weapon could do to a sensitive region like the male testes was immense. One hit could reduce even the most dangerous killer to a mewling, whimpering, simpering infant. And death could easily result, unless immediate medical care was available.

But Séverin was ready for such an assault. Slapping the tossed dagger aside, he kicked his attacker's thigh. The kicking leg was propelled backwards and the leg's owner toppled to the floor with an audible crash.

"Stay down," ordered Séverin, drawing his small-sword and pointing the tip at the fallen man.

"I surrender."

A musical voice laughed and raised a pair of dark gloved hands.

"No wonder she likes you," said the would-be assassin.

"Lisebette? Why are you trying to kill me?" asked Séverin as the young woman revealed her pretty face.

Lisebette's jet black hair tumbled across her shoulders as she pulled the scarf off her head.

"To test you, of course," she replied.

Her face transformed from delighted laughter to a cold, controlled, fury. She was now not unlike a stone statue, rather than a living, breathing, beautiful woman.

"Explain," said Séverin.

He did not lower his sword. He felt the chill he always experienced when confronting a being such as Lisebette. They lacked the basic humanity, the soul that exists within every man, woman, and child. Some event in their lives had caused them to reject the compassion that resides within the psyche of mankind. This had transformed them into beings capable of terrible acts of cruelty. Whether it be torturing the weak for some odd perverted pleasure, or killing individuals for cash, something was missing from these once-humans.

Séverin had experienced such beings in the past. As a swordmaster, he confronted many who took up the art of the blade to indulge their sadistic caprices. They often became professional duelists, killers for hire. For a high fee, they acted as "champion" in contests of honor. And often they extended the battle with their hapless opponent by slicing them apart slowly, deliberately.

As a true weapons master, Jean-Pierre Séverin despised such creatures. He battled them and defeated them quickly, destroying them in the same manner as one would use to execute a mad dog. Later, training in other weapons, he had confronted assassins and street toughs with similar attitudes. Usually, they were experienced adults. This was the first time he had observed such a lack of soul in a person barely old enough to be called an adult.

Lisebette's face didn't change, but a note of challenge entered her tone.

"The woman you know as the Antipope is my world. She trusts you. She thinks you're worthy—and dangerous. I was told you were a swordmaster, but I've killed plenty of men with blades. They're so used to rules and such, that killing them is easy. She said you were better than that. I needed to know for sure."

"And what if I'd failed? Got cut or killed by one of your attacks?"

Séverin found Lisebette's reasoning bizarre to say the least. But he also knew she was dangerously deranged. The young woman shrugged and smiled, showing her clean white teeth.

"Then, she'd know you were just another poseur, and you'd be forgotten. Now, are you going to take me?"

Séverin's face creased in a frown.

"Take you?"

Lisebette nodded and ran a hand down her neck and exposed her prominent chest.

"Drop your britches and have me here. You won, so you can use me all night. The winner gets his spoils."

Séverin's face turned as impassive as Lisebette's a moment earlier.

"Cover up and get out" he said. "Now!"

Lisebette ran a pink tongue across her large, red lips.

"Don't you think I'm pretty? Or if you like boys, you can take me from the back. I won't mind. I'll even talk like a lad."

Séverin stepped around Lisebette and opened the door.

"Leave. If you stay another moment, I will throw you out the window and into the street."

Lisebette stood up, her blank countenance returning instantly.

"Final test passed. You *are* impressive. No wonder Salmon said you were something else."

Séverin rolled his eyes.

"You thought I was stupid enough to fall for that trap? Give me some credit."

Lisebette shrugged again.

"Men, and many women, will lose all thoughts when I smile and act all innocent and obliging. I put on the maid's costume and they pant after me like dogs after a bitch. Usually, I cut off their privates before I slice their throats. It's easy."

Séverin didn't lower his sword.

"I've been doing this longer than you, girl. And I've met a hundred just like you. They all come to a bad end."

Lisebette chuckled as she pulled a roll of paper from her bosom.

"I was headed to Hell anyway, swordmaster Séverin. I weren't meant for anything else. I might as well make the trip worth it. Here. From the Antipope. The information you asked her to get you. I'll tell her you are as good as she says."

Séverin extended his sword and used the blade to accept the note. He wasn't about to allow this crazed killer too close.

"Thank you," he stated.

Lisebette nodded, covering her hair and face again before walking out the door with a second glance.

"If you need someone killed, call me anytime. I don't come cheap, but I'm the best in Paris."

"I'll remember that assertion," said Séverin, closing and bolting the door behind her.

He was grateful to get the young murderess out of his home.

Keeping the blade in hand, he opened the paper. A single address was listed in a neat, feminine handwriting. The location was in Boulogne-sur-Seine. A medium-sized house, occupied by the Royalists. It was a place to start. Possibly the only chance he had of stopping the monster who wished to transform Paris into an abattoir.

Without a backwards glance, Séverin opened a large chest at the far end of the room. His equipment was within, cleaned, honed and ready for battle. Saying a brief prayer in his mind, he stripped and began to dress in the clothing within the trunk.

As he did so, a second prayer came to mind and he began to recite it aloud. Grost and Kronos had said this one often, and it applied this day:

"God of power and mercy, maker and love of peace, to know you is to live, and to serve you is to reign. Through the intercession of St. Michael the arch-angel, be our protection in battle against all evil. Help me overcome war and violence, and establish your law of love and justice. Grant this through Christ our Lord. Amen."

CHAPTER XVIII

Styria, 1784

"Franz! Franz! Come here, if you please!"

Lena Vordenburg-Karnstein, Baroness and mistress of Karnstein Castle, was not often given to raising her voice. In fact, she was rarely given to involving herself with anything other than her paintings, books, and other amusements. Her actual involvement with her son consisted of one weekly discussion before church on Sunday, as the carriage drove them to services. Afterwards, she insisted on silence and they would proceed to opposite wings of the castle. Therefore, this call was unprecedented.

Though young, Franz von Karnstein knew to straighten his clothing and check his hair as he walked towards the sound of his mother's voice. There were several mirrors along the way to his mother's sitting room. She liked mirrors, spending much time gazing into them and admiring her long blond hair and milky pale skin.

Franz did not resemble his mother, other than possessing a similar complexion. He resembled his father Peter Joseph, dark haired, dark eyes and a handsome, if dangerous, face, though less dissolute thanks to his youth. Peter Joseph Karnstein was a general in the Emperor's forces and only returned once or twice a year to check on his estate. For even though a young child, Franz knew he was little more than a object for his father. Proof to his uncle the Count Karnstein and his distant relative, the Emperor, that the rumors of his unsavory tastes were nothing more than gossip told by enemies.

To his mother, Franz was a disturbance, an inconvenience she was forced to endure. Franz was her link to the eventual title of Countess Karnstein. The day old Count Karnstein died, she would become one of the most powerful women in the Empire. Only a few Archduchesses in the Emperor's Court would be more important than her, and they didn't count since they would be married off one day to some foreigner. Until that time, she would endure the company of her son—though in a limited manner.

Walking into the sitting room, Franz stopped several steps away from the large, thick rug which covered most the stone floor. The carpet was from Russia, a gift from the Vordenburg family after her marriage to Baron Karnstein. Franz knew his mother guarded the rug with a bizarre fervor. Her protectiveness of this piece of fabric was greater than that of her own flesh and blood. Best to simply never tread upon her beloved article.

"Yes, mother?" he inquired in a moderate tone, barely above a whisper.

His mother flew into a rage whenever his voice was little more than this volume. She had "sensitive" ears, according to her rants on the subject.

"Come and meet your cousin," said Lena. "She introduced me to your father and is one of my oldest friends."

Lena Karnstein was smiling, an expression she rarely allowed unless it was to herself in a mirror, or when one of their tenants remarked upon her loveliness.

The information about this cousin was confusing to Franz. Almost as puzzling as seeing his mother smiling and happy. She often told him how she had been introduced to the Count during a ball celebrating a famous victory by the Duke of Styria. Franz was never sure in which war it had been fought, or even if that was the true reason for the party. But the main point of the ball was to ensure that his father would choose a noble-born wife and sired a son.

That aside, Franz never remembered his mother mentioning any close friends or other relatives. She had been raised in her family's manor house with only her father, brother, maid and governess. Her learning had come from her governess, a former school teacher and Italian artist and model. By the time she had been old enough to attend the Emperor or the Count's courts, she had viewed other women as competition, or helpers in her quest for a higher social status.

"This is the young baron? He looks like a Karnstein."

The woman standing beside his mother stared across the room at Franz. She was tall, at least a head taller than Franz's mother, with golden blond hair that shimmered in the firelight. Her eyes were wide, deep blue, and seemed to resemble pools of liquid. Her mouth was a crimson cupid's bow, twisted in a smile that was more smirk than happy grin.

"This is he," his Mother replied, nodding as Franz bowed their direction. "My son, this is your cousin, Mircalla Karnstein. Mircalla, this is my child, Franz von Karnstein."

Mircalla curtsied deeply, the irony of paying homage to a child obvious in her actions.

"My lord Baron. I am so very honored."

"Your pardon," said Franz, bowing again, but meeting the newcomer's gaze. "I am not a baron."

151

Hiding her smile behind a hand, Mircalla pretended to look embarrassed, but it was clear she was enjoying Franz's ignorance.

"Oh my, I am so sorry! Does the child not know the sad events of the past month?"

Her words had been spoken in a tone of false sympathy, but her barely hidden smile was malicious, mocking and filled with sadistic glee.

Lena Vordenburg-Karnstein shook her head and composed her face to look suitably solemn. An act, at least in Franz's young eyes. She was disinterested in the details as they affected her child.

"I've not had time," she said. "It is so very hard and my grief is so profound."

Franz, even in his youth, found the statement to be ludicrous and filled with falsehood. But to remark so would only result in difficulties. Baroness Lena possessed a vicious streak when crossed. Biting words or ordering her servants to inflict pain were her favorite weapons of terror. Best to merely look blank and wait for the sad news.

"Shall I?"

Mircalla didn't wait for a response but stepped in Franz's direction. Her stride was lithe, youthful and full of barely contained energy. She halted an arm's length away and smirked.

"I am sorry to tell you this…" she began.

Franz didn't hide a quick look of derision. His cousin's manner was happy, amused and enjoying the potential of pain. But he also knew better than to maintain the expression for more than a heartbeat.

Mircalla caught the look and narrowed her eyes.

"…but your family has suffered sad losses," she continued. "Your father passed away six weeks ago. He was thrown from his horse. And a week later, your grandfather, uncle and cousins of the Vordenburg family were killed in a fire. So very sad."

"You are now the Baron of both regions, my son," added Lena. "The Vordenburgs possess a goodly bit of land, but little money. The Karnsteins are far wealthier."

She didn't attempt to continue her pretend grief. Her thought was upon the power she would hold. As the new Baron's mother, she controlled almost as much influence as that of the Count of Styria.

Mircalla swept Franz into her arms and hugged him, the very picture of a relative comforting a grieving child. But her embrace was cold, unfeeling, a sham for Lena and any observing servants.

"I am so very sorry, dear cousin," she said. "So very sorry for your loss."

Franz allowed Mircalla to hold him for a few seconds and then pulled away. He asked and backed out of the sitting room:

"If I may be excused?"

Not waiting for an answer, Franz turned on his heel and fled to his wing of the castle. Hot tears filled his eyes, but he did not sob. Air seemed rush from his lungs and he gasped, attempting to breathe. Locking the door to his bed chamber, Franz collapsed to the unyielding, cold, stone slab floor and wept.

His pain was not for his dead father. Peter Joseph Karnstein had been a cold, distant man. Their occasional moments together had been uncomfortable. Peter Joseph had spoken to his son with the same tone he'd used for his hunting hounds. To him, dogs and son were untidy creatures who needed to be controlled before they made a mess. Occasionally, usually after winning a large wager, he sent gifts that were completely inappropriate for a child. In Franz's room was a cavalry saber, a set of handmade dueling pistols from London, a book of erotic poetry in Italian, and a set of dice.

No, his mourning was reserved entirely for the Vordenburg side of his family. His grandfather, Franz, was a jolly, good man who treated his tenants well and ensured that none in his region ever went hungry. A former soldier, he told wonderful stories of battle and the history of the Vordenburgs. And he laughed all the time. Every time his Karnstein grandson travelled to their region in Styria, it was a true pleasure. Hunting, games, lessons and, most enjoyably, Grandfather Franz's tales of adventure and mysteries.

Grandfather Franz's son, also named Franz, was a less ebullient man, more stern and dour, but a good person nevertheless. He gave his Karnstein nephew lessons in sword fighting, the bible and the proper treatment of all men, women, children, and animals. He was respected by all and viewed as a future leader of Styria. He and his children were good, kind, people and Franz von Karnstein wept for their loss. They were his family, the people he was related to and loved best in the world. Even his child's mind dreamed of the day he would be allowed to see them more often.

But that day would never come now. Franz wanted to curse God, but his uncle had always taught him that to do so was the path to darkness. His favorite quote was from Job 27:3-4, *As long as my breath is in me, and the Spirit of God is in my nostrils, my lips will not speak falsehood, and my tongue will not utter deceit.*

Those words now rung hollow in Franz's mind, but he could not, would not, violate his beloved uncle's beliefs. Instead, he cried himself to sleep, prayed for the souls of his lost family.

Little did he know that the memories and decency of the Vordenburgs would serve him well in the dark days coming...

CHAPTER XIX

Paris, October 1795

Boulogne-sur-Seine was a better hamlet than those sectors of Paris that Séverin had visited recently. Many craftsmen and skilled workers resided there. The nearby forest gave the village a peaceful atmosphere, despite its growing population and craft halls. The location he had come to investigate was a four-story mansion, supposedly owned by a merchant who spent most of his time in Bordeaux.

The truth was easy to ascertain after some discreet inquiries at the local inn. The mansion was owned a member of the Royalist faction and was used as a refuge for a cell of Royalists. In the days of the Jacobin Terror, its occupants would have been in deadly danger. Every informant in Boulogne would have ratted them out, using them as coin to please the madmen who had sent thousands to the guillotine. But in these far more peaceful times, the Directory had no wish to return to the days of past bloodbaths. A cell of Royalist was an almost common sight now. In fact, Séverin had heard tell of another group plotting to seize power in a bookseller shop in Passy. He also knew they would argue about how to act from now until doomsday. Even the police found them ridiculous.

But according to his information he'd received from the Antipope, these Royalists were not the theoretical type. They were connected to Comte d'Artois and his armies, currently in the field battling General Hoche. Or at least, so the news sheets sold in the streets said in loud dramatic type. Most doubted the Royalists possessed the skills required to defeat Hoche. Séverin agreed, having met the man and knowing he was one of the few rivals Napoléon Bonaparte possessed in the military. Both men were geniuses, but he knew it would be his protégé who would rise up some day to occupy the supreme position within France.

"Does not look prepossessing, right?"

The Antipope suddenly stepped into view besides Séverin. Her flame-colored hair was hidden beneath a thick black woolen scarf. She was dressed in a skin-tight black leather suit with knee-high Hessian boots. A pair of small swords were strapped to her waist and Séverin spotted at least two daggers in her boots.

"Not as such," Séverin agreed, unsurprised by her presence.

Her people had been assaulted by creatures born from within this very house. The losses meant she had a score to settle with these Royalists. Otherwise, she would not be viewed as the King of Beggars and protector of the weak.

Cabot and Geof stepped onto the other side of Séverin. The latter was bristling with pistols, causing him to jangle when he walked. A massive blunderbuss was in his small hands. Cabot's motions were silent; he was a human shadow with an uncommonly long proboscis. A long rapier was strapped to his waist as well as a small sword, club and a well-used dagger.

"Good evening, my good Citizen," said Geof, giving Séverin a sketch of a bow. "Your skill with the sword caused me to recall the tales of the legendary Monsieur de Bergerac, the greatest duelist in France. He once slew a relative of mine over an actor."

"Evening, Citizens."

Cabot's words were more grunt. He looked bored and focused his attention upon the building.

"Cabot and Geof insisted on skipping an evening of cards to assist us in making these creatures pay," explained the Antipope. "Do you have a plan? Or will you merely rush in and attack everyone?"

Séverin shook his head.

"The house is empty—or mostly so. Possibly there are a few left behind, but the conspirators have gone."

"How, if I may ask, do you know, Monsieur?" asked Geof, his mustache rising in annoyance. "We observed you approach. Watched as you stood in view and stared. I heard nothing, nothing at all!"

"Silent as a church on a Tuesday," added Cabot, pulling out a pair of dice and rattling them in his hand.

He looked down, nodded and rolled them again into his other hand.

"That's the point," the Antipope said, nodding to Séverin. "A building filled with *loups-garous* would be a raucous, bloody horror. Even a powerful vampire couldn't keep them silent for long—or unfed."

"But one or more may be left within," said Séverin. "I thought I heard sounds in the silence. Oh, and Mademoiselle Lisebette? Your foot scraped against a cobble before your compatriots approached. Please step into view."

The swordmaster did not like the idea of the attractive your assassin lurking at his rear.

Lisebette appeared at the Antipope's elbow. She shot Séverin a look of hatred and fury before transforming her face into a bright smile.

"You are clever, swordmaster. Possibly too clever."

"There is no such thing," replied Séverin, looking to the Antipope. "I will not order you or your people. But I do believe we should stay in a group."

The Antipope nodded.

"Lisebette, you will scout ahead," she ordered. "Do not engage. Remember, they are as keen as dogs. Geof, you will lead us. Fire only when I order it. Then, Maestro Séverin, Cabot and I will cover the rear."

Lisebette pulled her face covering up in response and headed for the door. She examined it for a moment, then removed a thin wire from her belt. She slid it between the frame and the door and slowly moved it up and down, left and right. A few seconds later, the door opened, a bare few inches. A distant yellow light peeked through the crack, but no sounds were audible within.

"Go," said the Antipope, her voice barely audible.

She drew a smallsword and placed her hand on a dagger as Lisebette slipped inside the building.

Geof stepped behind Lisebette, his blunderbuss in his hands. He was whispering to himself, a mere murmur in their ears. Was it a prayer, a verbal regret for choosing to take this path? None could tell and he didn't appear interested in explaining.

The stench wafting from inside the house struck them with the force of a hammer. A putrid scent, bursting with horrific markers of the abominations that had occurred within these walls. Old spilled blood, rotted meat and other unidentifiable fluids were just part of the odors that caused all present to gag and recoil. Underlying those smells were fevered animal musk, the redolence of maddened dogs. This was a site of nightmares, a location forever tainted by the inhuman acts of its inhabitants.

They moved in a line, their steps filled with trepidation. Though every member of the group was hardened by life, used to the horrors of night, they still felt revulsion by the disgusting odors. The further they crept, the more horrors were revealed. Rotted pieces of carrion littered the floor along with piles of dried feces. The walls were stained with urine, the ammonia smell mingling with the other stenches in the air.

Lisebette stopped near a door and signaled everyone to stop. She leaned closer and listened. Then, turning on her heel, she waved a hand across her throat and leaped up. Grabbing a rafter, she vanished from view, mingling with the shadows.

Just as the young assassin vanished from the view, the door exploded outward. Splinters flew about the corridor as a *loup-garou* burst into view. It was huge, at least eight feet tall, possibly more, with a massive gray-furred canine head. The creature's maw was packed with enormous fangs and the monstrous hirsute phalanges ended in wicked black talons. The beast panted and snarled as it rushed towards Séverin and his group. Its crimson eyes were visible even at a distance, and within those orbs lay madness and bloodlust.

Geof fired his massive blunderbuss, the retort echoing in the hall. The balls struck the werewolf's body, causing it to stumble back and howl in agony. But the beast sprang forward, enormous claws raking across the walls as it reached for the tiny gun-wielding beggar. Séverin stepped next to Geof and lunged forward, his smallsword piercing the monster's chest. The Antipope stepped on the other side of the beggar and stabbed upward. The weapon pierced the *loup-garou*'s eye, thrusting into the brain. The werewolf shrieked and crashed to the ground, dead.

"That was easy enough," said Cabot, kicking the dead form while waving his rapier in the air.

"That was only the first one, idiot!"

Lisebette's voice floated down from the ceiling, causing the beggar to jump in surprise.

Three more werewolves emerged from the destroyed doorway, gray and black-furred beasts, each as massive as the one they'd just killed. A strident series of howls pierced the ears of the humans, as harsh and horrible a sound as any had ever heard in their lives. The monsters stumbled over each other in their rush to attack.

Geof's pistols barked, tongues of flame lighting the hall. The lead balls struck one of the werewolves in the chest, causing the creature to fall back behind the others. The other two snarled and snapped their immense jaws as they reached for the tiny beggar. He dropped the pair of muskets in his hands and fumbled with the next set, his terror causing his hands to shake and his body to quake.

"Look out, son," shouted Cabot as he pulled Geof back while slashing the air with his rapier.

His action was more born of enthusiasm than skill, but his hand was steady. The keen edge sliced one of the werewolf's hands. The blade caused a finger to drop to the ground with a wet plop. The lycanthrope shrieked in pain and pulled back. But the beast's red eyes narrowed and it growled deep within its massive chest. And then it leaped forward, incisors flashing in the spare light.

Cabot buried his rapier deep into the werewolf's chest. The colossal creature screeched and backhanded the lean beggar, causing him to tumble back and crash to the floor. He looked up, stunned and unable to move as the *loup-garou*'s claws reached for his chest, intent on tearing his body apart.

Just then, the monster's gigantic skull exploded, spraying blood and gore across the beggar's face and chest. Cabot scrambled backwards as beast crashed to the ground. The massive body came to rest where the beggar once lay. He stared at the dead monster, unable to form words. A small hand waved in front of his face and he spotted Geof.

"Get up, son," said the other beggar, smiling. "There's more fighting to do, and we still have to decide whether to travel to Normandy for the yearly race."

Despite his smaller size, Geof pulled the taller Cabot to his feet. His other hand held a smoking flintlock pistol. The gun was huge, despite being a hand-weapon; its barrel was almost as enormous as blunderbuss.

Cabot carefully pulled his rapier free of the dead werewolf.

"We go," he said, "even if the wife disagrees. I'll take the lumps. It's the stakes, son!"

The other uninjured *loup-garou* roared as the Antipope sliced its leg and shoulder with a pair of quick attacks. Séverin ducked a massive paw and buried a smallsword in the creature's arm pit. He released the weapon and stepped to the side, slashing the werewolf's other leg. The swordmaster wanted to attack the head, but the monster was moving too fast, too furiously, for an easy assault.

Nearby, the other *loup-garou* was slowly standing back up. The musket holes were closing and healing and the creature howled. The cry was half-lupine, half-human scream, a sound straight from the depths of Hell. Despite himself, Séverin shivered, but kept his focus upon the monstrosity attempting to tear off his head.

From the rafters, a figure dropped. Lisebette, forgotten by all, leaped upon the back of the third werewolf, burying a pair of long daggers into the shaggy back. The *loup-garou* shrieked in agony and spun around, but the young assassin hung on for dear life. Her hands gripped her daggers and her legs and boots tightened into the fleshy flanks of the monster. Sensing she only had seconds before the beast slammed her into a wall, Lisebette pulled out a long dagger and, with a two-handed grip, plunged the weapon deep into the elongated ear. The werewolf moaned as the blade sunk into the brain, killing him instantly.

Nearby the Antipope fell back, a harsh tear across her shoulder and chest. A welter of blood emerged and she gasped in pain. But a fierce determination burned in her eyes and she snarled and slashed the werewolf across the snout. The monster yowled in pain, a sound which turned into a scream as Séverin sliced deep into his neck. The *loup-garou* collapsed, sinking to floor and whimpering. The swordmaster whipped the other blade out of the beast's torso. With a harsh downward stab, he killed the creature, then pushed the corpse aside with his boot.

Stepping to Antipope's side, Séverin pulled off the neckerchief around his neck and pressed it against the bloody wound. The blood was flowing quickly and the attractive King of the Beggars gritted her teeth with pain. The cloth was soon soaked with blood and Séverin grabbed her head covering and added it to the bandage.

"She needs a doctor," he said. "One experienced with injuries. Quickly!"

Séverin didn't look behind him as he supported the Antipope with his powerful hands.

"Take me to Florimel," the Antipope said, looking at Geof, Cabot and Lisebette.

"She's a birthing woman!" exclaimed Cabot, taking his leader's arm.

His oddly shaped face was twisted with disgust as he helped her towards the door.

"She knows more about surgery than any fool graduate of a university," retorted Lisebette. "Geof, go get the wagon! Cabot, take her outside."

Her look was venomous and Geof recoiled, fleeing for the door.

"I'll be fine. I suffered worse in the past," muttered the Antipope, her face was covered with a thin layer of perspiration.

She spoke in harsh gasps. That was her only admission to the agony which was obviously tormenting her body.

Séverin made to follow, but Lisebette held up a hand to stop his progress.

"We only have room for four on the cart. But I warn you this, Jean-Pierre Séverin. If she dies this day, I will kill you."

"You may try, but you will fail, Lisebette."

Séverin understood that the young woman was speaking from fear, but he also knew she was a dangerous murderer, who might act on her desire to kill him anyway.

One of the dangers of leading a life devoted to the sword was encountering others devoted to killing. A true swordmaster viewed death as possible in battle, but not his first choice. The height of a warrior's skills was to defeat your opponent without even harming them in a duel. But this was a higher comprehension of the art, one lost upon many who trained in swordsmanship. Take the Marquis de La Tour d'Azyr. A swordsman of spectacular skill, but a total sadist who used his expertise to bully the untrained into duels resulting in their death.

Lisebette, like De La Tour d'Azyr, was a sadist. They enjoyed the pain of others. This was why the attractive young woman had attacked him earlier. Why she had attempted to seduce him once her assault had failed. Her love of torture, pain and death was a sickness, a danger to all of mankind. Lisebette was a mad creature, in her own way as dangerous and terrible as the *loups-garous* who littered the floor at their feet. But she could hide the monster within behind her pretty face and bright smile—but that smile was the toothy grin of a predator. Lisebette would smirk as she slit the throat of a child. She would laugh as she poisoned a pregnant woman. No being, saintly or evil, was above her love of blood and death.

Lisebette fired Séverin an angry look before turning on her heels and fleeing the building. The cart, rushing away at great speed, soon vanished in the distance and Séverin turned back to the building. He said a brief prayer of deliverance for the attractive, amazing woman who used the alias, the Antipope.

"Praise the Lord, my soul, and forget not all his benefits who forgives all your sins and heals all your diseases, who redeems your life from the pit and crowns you with love and compassion. Amen."

He then ran a hand across his face and frowned. The vampiric master of this cell of monsters had fled with his creatures, but he had been wise enough to guess that others would find this location. That would explain why he left these three behind. But that was also a mistake.

"This monster expends his *loups-garous* without thought. They were not his people. Which suggests he was not close to them prior to their transformation. This is axiomatic. As Aristotle once said, 'He who sees things grow from the beginning will have the best view of them.' This demon sees his creatures as cannon fodder, not compatriots. Meaning he was not the original leader."

Séverin spoke these words out aloud, knowing the only ones who could hear his musings were the deceased werewolves. Cleaning his blades on the fur of a fallen *loup-garou*, the sword master continued:

"As this is a cell of Royalists, the leader would be wary of informants. Therefore, he would hide all correspondence in a secret location. Which means the information I need may still be somewhere in this house. But where to search? The cleanest rooms first. The vampire would symbolically take the leader's quarters and keep his shape-shifting beasts in the lower chambers..."

With that plan in mind, Séverin sheathed one of his swords and stepped over the dead werewolves. There were many rooms to search, and he sensed that he had little time. Crossing himself, he began to seek only rooms unfouled by the former inhabitants. This would not be a simple task...

CHAPTER XX

Styria, 1784

Life in the Karnstein Castle changed over the next month. Franz's mother and his cousin Mircalla immediately transferred the elderly and established servants to the lesser castles owned by the family. A new class of servants appeared. They were younger, far more attractive, and possessed the rapacious look of born bandits. They were servile to Mircalla and merely obedient to Lena—when their lovely mistress allowed it. Lena was little more than a servant herself, giving her Karnstein cousin the master bedroom and moving into a small room nearby.

Franz was treated better than he had been in years, especially by Mircalla. She hugged him regularly and seemed to delight in stroking his dark hair. There was a possessive nature to her behavior. In his mind, she ministered him in the same manner as one would act towards a beloved pet. He was her toy, her amusement and, he believed, she had deeper plans in mind for him. Because, despite his young age, Franz von Karnstein, recognized falsehoods with an inbred instinct. Mircalla wanted something from him.

Perhaps this comprehension came from spending time with his imperfect mother. Franz knew Lena Vordenburg-Karnstein was a power-seeker. She was bitter that, despite her impressive looks, she had been unable to marry an Archduke. She had settled for the heir of a Count, one of the oldest titles in all of Europe. Occasionally, in public and with other noble families present, Lena would demonstrate affection towards her only child. Her actions were impressive, but ultimately they were nothing but playacting. Three years earlier, Franz had attempted to approach his mother in the manner she treated him in public.

"Get your disgusting hands off me, you little pest!" she had shouted.

Then, she had slapped him across the face and screamed for a footman.

The servant, an older, but large former soldier named Leo, had appeared a moment later. He stared at them with impassive eyes.

"Yes, My Lady?"

"Take this brat to the stables and lash him until he bleeds!"

Lena had pushed Franz into Leo's massive hands and turned her back.

Leo, a simple creature, had dragged Franz off, ignoring his tears and wails. He had tied the child's hands to a post, pulled down his tiny britches, and struck him four times with a piece of rope. Spotting blood at last, he had nodded, untied Franz and led him back inside.

Lena had been waiting to inspect the wounds, which she fid, briefly.

"Move him into the old Baron's wing" she had said at last. "He is to eat his meals in that area from now on."

And that had been the last time Franz spent any time with his mother. Like a child burned by fire, he had never treated her like a parent again. She was the authoritarian figure who lived in the main part of the castle. He had learned to ignore the loss. Tutors in reading, music, science and religion had kept his time engaged, as well as regular trips to see his Vordenburg relatives.

Possibly, the knowledge of Mircalla's falsehoods derived from an inner source. Franz was clever, far more intelligent than his years suggested. His religion, history, and sword instructor, Father Sandor, had informed his as much in his gruff manner several times.

"You'll do, boy. You'll do," the huge priest had said, which, given the man's nature, was like hearing a lengthy sonnet of love from another man.

In any event, Franz was unmoved by his cousin's constant affection. He maintained his distance and ate in his own chambers. But he also knew that more information was needed. Which was why, he changed one habit and allowed Mircalla to see him off to bed. The contact and his seeming vulnerability might grant him further information.

"Do you like to read?" asked Mircalla, looking at the book on his nightstand.

It was a French translation of the epic poem, *Cantar de Mio Cid* which Father Sandor had given him as a Christmas gift.

"Yes," replied Franz, knowing that short answers were always best.

Mircalla didn't seem to listen to anything he said for long.

"It may be time to send you to a special school," she said. "We Karnsteins often attend an academy for an elite few. I think you will be the next."

She brushed back his hair and blew out the candle before leaving his bedroom.

The next night, Franz made it a point to be found reading a work by the legendary swordsman writer, Cyrano de Bergerac. She smiled seeing this, her lovely face demonstrating delight; but her eyes were cold, assessing, and rapacious. At that moment, she resembled a wolf studying a weak animal rather than a beautiful woman.

"I am glad to see you reading widely," she said. "You read French. Latin, too? Ah, good. You'll need that at the Scholomance."

Mircalla kissed his forehead and stroked his head before leaving once again. And that was all the information Franz needed. One word: *Scholomance*.

Waiting an hour and feigning sleep, he was unsurprised to hear his door open and hear Mircalla's soft footfalls. She studied him for a moment before leaving once again.

Once she was away, Franz crept into the library two doors down from his bedroom. With a tiny candle, his search began. He wasn't sure what a *Scholomance* was, but doubted it was anything good. The way Mircalla had spoken the word, it was like a loving caress in verbal form, but something sinister was also present.

Sadly, the books were no help. Franz repeated his search for a full week without any success. His small library was filled with unusual books of all variety, but none possessed even a hint as to the existence of a school called the *Scholomance*. Finally, he decided to risk himself and ask Father Sandor.

Franz understood that speaking the word aloud might be a bad idea. He thought for a time and realized that there was an easy method. Father Sandor, though a brusque, hard man, was highly intelligent as well. And he knew more about intrigue than anyone else in Styria. The powerful priest had formerly served as confessor to the Emperor's court, a risky political position at best.

Three days later, Father Sandor was present in the castle. While Franz was writing an essay, the huge holy man paced, his mind elsewhere. Once the essay had been completed, Franz wrote one more page and placed it in the middle of the stack. Then he picked up his bible and read, knowing the Father would review his work within the hour.

Franz was partway through the Gospel of Luke, specifically the genealogy of Jesus, when Father Sandor stopped reading. The priest muttered to himself and finally folded the pages and placed them in his pouch.

"Merely an adequate job, my boy," said the priest. "Your penmanship improves, but you must study further proper sentence structure. I will send you several books before Vespers. Read each and practice better composition."

And with that, Father Sandor was off.

Two hours later, a novice arrived, handing a small stack of books to the new footman, Otto. Otto was almost as large as Father Sandor, though far more handsome. He possessed curly golden locks and a perfect skin that reminded Franz of the poems about Zeus's cupbearer, Ganymede. But Otto was a sneak and a thief who was perpetually looking for small items to pocket. Franz had caught him stealing three times and looked forward to a chance to make the older youth pay. Otto wished to be wealthy and powerful, but he was too short-sighted to think past earning a few coins by stealing anything shiny that caught his eye.

Mircalla had rescued him from a small town outside Vienna. Otto had lived as a professional thief, who spent all his earnings on tavern women and even the occasional wife or daughter of a merchant. But, one day, he had stolen from the wrong man. A doctor had caught him rifling through his bags and beaten him within an inch of his life. Then, he had turned the young thief over to his cousin, the town magistrate, who contemplated the removal of either an ear or the nose. Either would have spoiled Otto's good-looks and forced him on a better path. But Mircalla had intervened, paying everyone and whisking the handsome thief off as a servant.

Otto glanced through the books, finding nothing of value. They were old, dusty tomes, owned by the church. Best to just leave them alone. He handed them to Jana, the other servant brought in by Mircalla, and pointed a thumb towards the far wing of the castle.

"Give these to the brat," he ordered.

Otto was outwardly servile towards the young Baron, but when the child wasn't around, he was nasty and contemptuous.

Jana, a shapely red-headed woman given to wearing dresses that paraded her large bust and shapely rear, took the books and stuck her tongue out at the tall, handsome footman.

"Jana doesn't like to climb all those big stairs," she said. "Send one of the maids."

"I sent them home," replied Otto, shaking his head. "Some type of celebration in the village. You bring it."

Jana pouted for a moment but accepted the books. She turned on her heel and shook her rear once before heading towards Franz's wing. She was a bizarre creature, one of constantly changing moods and desires. Outwardly, she behaved like a naughty child, speaking of herself in third person and sucking on her thumb when talking to others. But she was also a born seductress, able to determine the best means of getting her desires from most men and women.

Beneath that act, however, was a born sadist. Mircalla had found Jana in Prague, one step ahead of her being hunted down by a growing crowd of murderous men and women. She had enjoyed seducing the wealthy and powerful and promising love and devotion. Then she destroyed that person and sold any gifts she had received in the process.

Her last victim had been a second son of a general. The boy, a student about to become a priest, had thrown aside his vows for the lovely young woman. He had given her gifts of horses, gowns and jewels. And then one day, he had found her door barred. Her servants had refused to admit him and he had received a short note telling him that Jana never wished to see him again. The young man, distraught, had cut his wrists in his bath, dying in the Roman fashion.

His father and older brother had attempted to have her brought up on charges, but they had been unable to do so. Consequently, they, along with a cadre of Jana's other former lovers, had decided to bring about justice by their own hands. The girl had been saved by Mircalla and had become devoted to her dark mistress since that day. However, her seductive sadist streak remained, just a little more hidden from view.

Jana walked into Franz's library, not bothering to knock. He was too young for her to try and ply her wiles upon him, which meant she barely acknowledged his existence. Dropping the books on the table by his side, she didn't bother to speak. Instead she knocked the pile over and into his lap, grinned and walked out.

Franz straightened the books out and stopped when he reached the third one. The title leaped out at him: *Myths and Legends of Ancient Dacia*. Saying a quick prayer of thanks to Father Sandor, Franz von Karnstein opened the book and started to read...

CHAPTER XXI

Paris, October 1795

"This cannot be the truth," Napoleon Bonaparte said after having studied the papers, reading each page with care.

"I assure you, it is nothing else," replied Jean-Pierre Séverin.

He had discovered the pouch filled with papers in a secret cache within a wooden floor of the house. The search had taken four hours. The noxious odor, if possible, had grown worse in time. Séverin, despite knowing that the stench would cling to his body, had decided the information was more important than General Bonaparte's sensibilities.

Happily, they were seated in a park, and Napoleon had carefully placed himself upwind. A long-time campaigner, the youthful general was used to similar horrific sensations. He had wrinkled his nose once, but continued reading the papers.

"How did the Royalists manage such a deception? An army of thirty thousand, preparing to attack in three days? That is unheard of, an action entirely unanticipated. I believe we only have a tenth as many troops in Paris."

Napoleon ran through the names and appeared to be absorbing each detail.

"That is far from all," said Séverin. "The reason I discovered these papers was related to my search for the monster killing our citizens. I determined the details.

Possibly one hundred such creatures will lead the assault upon the Directory."

Séverin hoped Napoleon would be as willing to listen to the horrific details as he was when this case had begun.

"What are we fighting?" asked the General. "Leave no details untold."

Napoleon sat back and crossed his arms across his chest. One gift he possessed was the ability to focus completely on the subject or situation at hand. This skill enabled him to view possible avenues of response clearly and react quickly.

Séverin explained the chain of events that had led him there, but did not reveal the names or identities of the Beggar King or her underlings. He caught Napoleon's frown of annoyance, but the General soon moved on to the more important details. The killing of the three *loups-garous* in the hallway caused him to narrow his eyes and concentrate even more deeply. When the story was complete, he did not move, but appeared lost in thought for several minutes.

"Interesting," he finally said. "Based on your narrative, these werewolves are very dangerous, but in a limited fashion. Their threat lies in close-quarter battle, but from a distance, they are as vulnerable as any bystander standing before a firing line. You spoke of one falling from one a shot from a large blunderbuss. Had you each carried such a weapon, the creatures would have been destroyed in one breath. Destruction at a distance. That way, our troops have nothing to fear..."

Napoleon stood up and shook Séverin's hand.

"What do you plan now?" asked the swordmaster, seeing his former student come alive before his eyes.

The depressed, saddened figure of a man from less than a month ago, was gone without a trace. Before him was the vibrant, imaginative, military genius who would one day rule all of France. Séverin knew that from their first meeting years before, and, if possible, that belief had only increased. Though a Republican, Séverin understood that Napoleon's destiny was to rule France. He would be called "Sire" one day, and never be forgotten by mankind.

"I will go to the Directory and speak to the members. No doubt they have discovered, or will soon discover, the danger. They know my skills and I will gather our forces in defense. I have a plan that will defeat the Royalists. But to do so, I will require complete freedom of action. Then, I will destroy these unholy demons, and none will know of this terrible act against mankind."

Napoleon stepped back, smiled and turned on his heels. His step was lively and passers-by stepped aside as he walked.

Séverin watched the little Corsican vanish from sight, relieved but also knowing that the General had missed an important point. There was the vampire to confront as well. Would guns or bayonets kill that monster? He doubted as much. Vampires were creatures devoted to their personal survival, and this one appeared particularly devious. Using *loups-garous* as a weapon demonstrated his reluctance to do battle directly. But he held no compunctions about destroying the lives of others by transforming them into his werewolf minions.

That, in and of itself, was the most telling point. Séverin had learned, thanks to his lessons at the feet of the legendary Professor Hieronymus Grost, that the behavior of a vampire was often the best method of comprehending their actions. Grost had often told him of a female vampire who had stolen the lives of poor, hapless girls. Her motive had been two-fold: first, to return to her youth and beauty; second, to return life to her husband, dead of the plague. The victims had been drained of their youth. All that had remained were ancient crones, where before they had been lovely, young, and full of life.

"You see, young man, vampires are quite dangerous to the untrained mind," had pontificated Grost, his twisted body being slowly lowered into a large chair.

Born a hunchback and ostracized by most people because of his odd looks, he had been a brilliant man with a kindly soul.

"I should think those creatures are dangerous to all life," had replied Séverin, pouring his teacher a glass of wine.

He had moved slowly, having trained all afternoon with Grost's compatriot, Captain Kronos, formerly of the Imperial Guard, who had been a weapons expert and the strong arm of the vampire-hunting duo.

"Quite true, a telling point," had said Grost, chuckling. "But when battling such creatures, their actions, towards victims and foe alike, enable one to better combat the creatures with greater precision."

"For example?"

Suddenly, Kronos had returned. Séverin had bowed to his instructor and waited until he'd taken a seat at the table.

The elderly soldier still moved like a young man. His blond hair was mostly white and the lines on his face gave him a harsh, unyielding, profile. Kronos spoke little, but with each word, said much.

Séverin had treasured his time with Grost, feeling like a favored pupil with a beloved master. But he had respected Kronos to an even greater degree. He was a great man, capable of changing the destiny of any he encountered.

"That tale we told you, of the vampire who stole youth?" Grost had continued. "She raised her husband from the dead. He was her only interest. That, and being young and pretty once again."

"Forgive me if I fail to understand your meaning," had replied Séverin, shaking his head.

Kronos had placed his booted feet up on the table and looked at the young Séverin, saying:

"I destroyed her husband first. Then, she was too distraught to be a danger."

"Kronos fought and killed her husband," had further explained Grost. "Once a great sword master, he'd lost some of his skills when he'd joined the undead. Perhaps he believed he no longer needed to avoid sword thrusts? No matter. When he fell, the wife all but threw herself on Kronos's blade to join him in death."

The light of understanding had then entered Séverin's tired mind.

"Yet she was the greater danger," he had observed. "A vampire witch, able to transform herself and bring her dead spouse back to life as one as well."

Grost had applauded.

"Learn to understand the mind of the vampire through their actions, young man. It is far better than roaming about the countryside hammering stakes into the hearts of the dead."

And that lesson had stayed with Séverin many years later. Even when fighting a particularly clever werewolf, the one who had earned him his nickname *Gâteloup*. Séverin had used his mind to win each battle. Oh, his skill at arms was a part of these battles as well, but

Grost, Kronos, and the three other teachers had taught him that expertise with one, and weakness in the other, would lead to his untimely end.

"Strong body, weak mind. Easy to outthink and trick. Strong mind, weak body. Easy to destroy," a Russian warrior had once told him as they rode upon the steppes in search of a warlock intent on bringing back an ancient empire of evil.

Using this philosophy, Séverin contemplated his strategy as he walked home, bathed and ate. A plan formed in his mind, one that would require exact timing. Act too soon, he would be torn to pieces. Act too late, Napoleon and his men would be destroyed.

"But it could work," he mused while he dressed.

He had some scouting to do this day…

CHAPTER XXII

Styria, 1784

The book told much, suggested more, and Franz von Karnstein understood he was on the precipice of something truly horrifying. Should he move in the wrong direction, he would fall into the metaphorical abyss. Either he would die, or be remade into a being of such monstrous evil that death would be preferable. For Mircalla's plans for him were now clear before his eyes. And it all came from her vain belief in her own genius and beauty. But one word, told to an intelligent, inquisitive child, would spell her doom.

That word was *Scholomance*. Franz knew there was some deeper significance to it, even though Mircalla has used it in an off-handed manner. But only a fool deluded by her unquestionable loveliness would not have recognized its importance.

Which was why Franz had penned a simple note, one he had passed to Father Sandor days after failing to discover the meaning of *Scholomance*. The good, gruff, priest was known to be an expert in the darker aspects of the world and, according to local gossip, had once destroyed a demon seeking to possess an Archduchess. Why he left the court to live as simple leader of a moderate-sized church in the country, unknown to all, was a mystery.

But, most importantly, Father Sandor was a good man. He fought against ignorance and prevented old women from being killed as witches because they used folk medicine. Or those dying youthful deaths from being treated as vampire victims and buried on unsanctified ground without prayers. He was not like Father Albrecht who lived near the Karnstein manor three days ride away. Father Albrecht always seemed convinced everyone was a witch, sent by Lucifer to destroy all goodness on Earth. Even Franz, despite his youth, could tell that priest was an ignorant idiot who caused more harm than good.

Franz's note had been simple. It read as follows:

Father,

My cousin, whom I do not trust, talks of sending me to a school called the Scholomance. *I cannot find any school of that name. Is it a terrible place? I have a feeling it is no common school. Please help me understand.*

Thanks to you and our Lord,

Franz Vordenburg-Karnstein

Happily the good Father understood this was no mere fear of a private school. The book of Dacian legends told the tales of this legendary academy of evil. The story sent chills down Franz's spine as he read the words, realizing his worst fears had been correct.

The Scholomance was, according to legend, the Devil's school of magic. Ten pupils were accepted and studied the deepest, darkest secrets Satan could impart to the minds of man. Nine of these students were sent out into the world, their duty being to spread evil upon the Earth. They became powerful warlocks, witches, warlords, and, most terrifyingly, vampires.

This was Mircalla's plans for Franz. Her words proved that the Scholomance was no mere myth, told by peasants to explain the nature of evil. This school was a reality, a dangerous domain dedicated to destruction of the light in the world. To attend this academy would re-make Franz von Karnstein into a creature of horror, a being only whispered about in hushed tones for fear he might hear the summons.

To most children, such a revelation would have struck terror in their hearts, but not Franz von Karnstein. Though raised by a mother who despised him, and a father who was never in his life, he did have some good in his upbringing. His Vordenburg relatives had taught him the notion of right and wrong. And he knew the horror of the vampires from his grandfather, Franz, because the majority of the old man's tales were stories of the Vordenburgs' battles against this dark menace. One quote his uncle used often summed up what must be done when confronted by the Devil's servants.

Therefore submit to God. Resist the Devil and he will flee from you. James 4:7.

But Franz also knew that he needed proof. Father Sandor was, no doubt at this very moment, seeking aid from the Bishop. But the Bishop would need permission to act from Count Karnstein. That would take some time, and Franz doubted he had much left, so he needed to find proof by himself.

Waiting an hour after Mircalla's check on his sleeping habits, Franz dressed quickly and crept from his wing. He had an inkling that his lovely cousin and her two handsome servants would be less circumspect if they believed he was asleep in the far wing of the castle.

Franz had learned from watching his mother that you could tell the most about a person when they didn't realize you were watching their behavior. Then the mask of civility was dropped and the true person behind was revealed.

In this case, he was right. They were all assembled in Lena's sitting-room. All four were naked and he could hear their laughter and howls once he'd entered that wing of the castle. The sight before his peeking eyes was astonishing, terrifying, and revealing in many ways.

Otto was flat on his back, with Jana happily bouncing up and down on his muscular form. Lena was kissing and biting Otto, her sharp incisors drawing blood, and she lapped it up like a greedy kitten with a saucer of milk. Mircalla was behind Jana, her pointed teeth alternating between biting the lovely maid's neck and breasts.

After a time, Mircalla stepped away from Jana and grabbed Lena. She pulled the baroness away from Otto and began kissing and licking her. Their blood-covered mouths and tongues came together for a time, and Lena moaned in Mircalla's embrace.

This was not particularly surprising to Franz. His father, during his rare visits, was often found mounting some peasant maid, hired because of her pretty face and pert bottom. Even old grandfather Franz had a "helper" named Alina who tended to his needs and shared his bed. Nor were women kissing shocking. Kissing was kissing, who cared about it anyway?

No, it was the blood and teeth. According to all the legends he'd read, vampires possessed the teeth of animals and feasted on blood. That Mircalla was a vampire was horrifying to discover. But finding that his mother, too, was one was horror personified. Though she was a spiteful, cruel, distant figure, she was still Franz's parent. To find that she'd given herself to the Devil caused him to feel almost as sad as when he'd found that his Vordenburg relatives had passed away.

"Dead at the hands of Mircalla, no doubt," he whispered after returning stealthily to his room.

Franz had just realized the truth. A chill ran down his spine and he sat heavily down on his bed. His young mind was spinning, terrified by the horrors before his mind's eye.

Mircalla's whole plan was revealed at that moment. Franz was meant to attend the Scholomance and return transformed as a vampire. Like her, he would be ageless, handsome and dangerous. Possibly, she meant to marry him and become the Countess Karnstein. Then their dark influence would spread from Styria onto the rest of the Empire. That plan might have worked, but the ghosts of the Vordenburg family seemed to stand by his side. They were helping him to see the truth—and map out a course to destroy this blight upon the Karnstein name forever.

"Thank you, father."

Franz spoke these words out loud as he found some of the gifts his dead parent had given him over the years. They would be his way to redemption.

The next day was bright and lovely and Franz was up before sunrise. He secreted one item in his mother's study before returning to bed. He slept for a time and was woken by Jana. The beautiful maid entered his room by banging to the door against the wall, placed breakfast on a table, and left without a word.

Franz ate sparingly. His stomach ached with the inner terror he felt about what he was about to do. But he didn't have a choice. To do otherwise would mean all his relatives had died for nothing. Kneeling before his bed, he said a prayer he had learned from Father Sandor:

"Saint Michael, Mighty Archangel, defend us in battle. Be our protection against the wickedness and snares of the Devil. May God rebuke him, we humbly pray; and do thou, O Prince of the Heavenly Host, by the power of God cast into Hell Satan and all the evil spirits who prowl throughout the world seeking the ruin of souls. Amen."

Then, he picked up the bag he used for traveling and headed into his mother's wing of the castle. Mircalla and Lena were in the sitting-room. They looked up at him with quizzical looks upon their lovely faces. Franz did not speak; he mere stepped deeper into the room and pulled the brass cross his grandfather Franz had given him as a present a while back. It was an old item, a relic a Vordenburg had earned during a war hundreds of years in the past.

Both women recoiled at the sight of the holy object. Their eyes grew wide and their faces fearful. Lena looked away, shielding herself with her gown. Mircalla raised her hand in defense, her sharp teeth revealed as she hissed at the child.

"Otto! Jana!" shrieked Lena as she shrank back even further.

Franz heard the drumming, thrumming, pound of feet approaching and reached into his bag. Otto appeared in the doorway, his face twisted with fury. He stepped towards Franz, not noticing the dueling pistol in the young man's hand. Franz squeezed the trigger and a loud explosion echoed in the room. Otto crashed to the floor, half his head missing. His blood began pooling upon Lena's beloved carpet.

Mircalla and Lena were still frozen by the cross and stared in shock at Franz plucked a second pistol from the bag. He pointed the weapon at the doorway and fired when Jana appeared. The seductive servant fell to the ground beside Otto, her face decimated by the heavy pistol ball.

Franz dropped the pistols back into the bag and pulled out a small pouch. This he opened with one hand and tossed it at the feet of his mother. The contents spilled across the floor and Lena stared down, unable to tear her eyes away.

"Lena, no! I command you!" said Mircalla with a ragged voice.

Lena Karnstein ignored her dark mistress and dropped to the ground. Her soft voice floated through the air.

"One, two, three..."

The contents of the pouch were tiny seeds. One lesson Franz had learned from his grandfather was that new vampires were unable to resist counting fallen items. The way to stop such a creature was to drop seeds or rice at their feet. Their hunt would cease as they dropped to their knees and counted each item. It was a mighty weakness.

Mircalla sneered at Lena and turned her haughty expression upon Franz.

"Guns will not kill me, little boy. And soon you will tire. Then I will bite you and tear your heart from your chest. And your last memory will be watching me and your mother feasting upon the blood and meat."

Franz did not answer. He merely stooped down and pulled an object out from beneath a large couch. This was the article he placed in the room before daybreak. Another gift from his dead father. A cavalry saber. The blade gleamed in the sunlight as Franz stepped close to Mircalla.

"No! No!" Mircalla screamed as she tried to back away.

She struck the wooden wall and shrank downward, pulling herself into a ball.

"Yes. This is for my Vordenburg family. And even for my father," spat Franz.

He swung the heavy blade downward. The steel sheared through Mircalla's neck. Her head fell away from her body and a fountain of dark blood spread across the stone floor.

Stepping around the corpse of his vampiric cousin, Franz stepped next to his kneeling mother. She was still counting, her soft voice rhythmic as she separated the seeds.

"...fifty-three, fifty-four..."

Lena never looked up as Franz raised the sword in two hands.

"I'm sorry, mother."

Franz's voice shook as he swung the blade down hard and fast. A spray of blood spattered across his face and his mother's head rolled next to that of Mircalla.

The next day, Father Sandor arrived. He was not alone, but with the Bishop's personal retinue as well as a host of guards on loan from Count Karnstein. He found Franz von Karnstein on the steps of the castle, the dried blood still on his face. He was clutching the cross in his two hands and mumbling a prayer as the men approached.

Grabbing the child by the shoulders, Father Sandor forced him to look straight into his eyes. Seeing the light of reason still present, he asked him in a soft voice:

"What happened, boy? Are you injured?"

Franz merely stood and pointed towards the castle. Father Sandor and the other adults followed him through the extensive corridors and into the main wing. The scent of blood and rot was rising and Franz pointed past the bodies of Otto and Jana.

There, they found two headless corpses. Both were desiccated bones and dust, their heads mere grinning skulls with enormous fangs visible. The bodies were clothed in new, fresh clothes, spattered with fresh blood.

"What happened here, boy?" Father Sandor asked as the Bishop's people examined the bones and whispered the word "vampire" under their breath.

"Cousin Mircalla was a vampire. She made mother into a vampire. I… sent them away… they're gone… were already gone." Franz mumbled.

Then, he seemed to pull his shattered spirit together. He looked at Father Sandor and the Bishop's representative and spoke in a more even tone:

"I killed my mama. She was a vampire too."

And then he burst into tears.

CHAPTER XXIII

Paris, November 1804

Séverin sat back in his chair, barely able to comprehend the story Franz von Karnstein had just told him. The young man had narrated his tale in an almost clinical fashion, but the emotion beneath his words was powerful, almost heart-breaking. This cold, dangerous, and mysterious man had executed his own mother while still a child. Could anything on Earth be so rending?

"That is a sad tale," said Séverin, unable to think of much else to comment upon. "But, in the case of Mircalla Karnstein, impressive. She was, based on your description, quite old."

To mention his feelings regarding Franz's mother and her grisly fate might open up old wounds, and he did not wish to harm this man.

Franz nodded and took another drink.

"Father Sandor and Deacon John believed her to originally be Lady Mircalla Karnstein, widow of the Hungarian warlord who died at the Battle of Kressenbrunn," he stated. "That would have made her at least five hundred years-old by the time she came to my home."

Séverin was impressed, despite himself. Vampires of that age, even ones who were brought back years later, were often very difficult to destroy. The fact that Franz had accomplished such a feat at such a youthful age was a feat of herculean proportions.

"Is that how you gained your magic?" asked Séverin, also intrigued by the unusual exorcism he had witnessed at the Satanic ceremony.

In the company of most people, he would have merely hinted at his interest. But the Morgue Director, always a good judge of character, knew that these hints would be ignored. Best to border on rude behavior and signal his interest.

Franz von Karnstein shook his head.

"I practice no magic, Monsieur. None at all. I quote from Deuteronomy 18:9-12: *When you enter the land which the Lord your God gives you, you shall not learn to imitate the detestable things of those nations. There shall not be found among you anyone who makes his son or his daughter pass through the fire, one who uses divination, one who practices witchcraft, or one who interprets omens, or a sorcerer, or one who casts a spell, or a medium, or a spiritist, or one who calls up the dead. For whoever does these things is detestable to the Lord; and because of these detestable things the Lord your God will drive them out before you.*"

Séverin was unsurprised by the young Karnstein's response, though somewhat intrigued. What he did was a form or exorcism, but so vastly different from all accepted ritual that it was almost alien in nature. Yet, Franz von Karnstein rejected the idea of magic or witchcraft out-of-hand. It was odd.

Surprisingly, Franz smiled and shook his head again.

"Allow me to assure you this much, Monsieur. I practice no magic. I am not a *dhampir* or any other mixed-breed creature of dark power. I carry no holy objects and I am not descended from the blood of the angelic hosts. I am a Vordenburg and a Karnstein by birth.

We are said to be originally Dacians and Thracians. The first Karnsteins were warlords of their tribes and mingled with the Celts. Noble blood earned through battle. And I would add one simple fact that proves I am none of the creatures of the night you fear."

"And that is?" asked Séverin, intrigued, despite himself.

"I am a member of the Order of Exorcists and a personal advisor to His Holiness Pope Pius VII. Do you believe the officials of the Inquisition or the soldiers of the Swiss Guard would allow a weaver of spells within the presence of the Holy Father? Or a being related by blood to monsters?"

Franz downed his wine, shook the bottle and heard no sound.

"You do have a point," said Séverin.

He had to acknowledge that much, for the moment. He did have trouble seeing the crazed, evil-hunting maniacs of the Inquisition allowing a sorcerer to exist in the Church, let alone in the presence of the Pope. But still, the odd exorcism vexed him to no end.

"But you are still disturbed by my actions?"

Karnstein didn't appear unduly concerned or even ruffled by Séverin's attitude.

"Truly, yes, I am. They are somewhat unprecedented."

Séverin searched the cold, calm, countenance of the Austrian for something, anything to relieve this mystery, but Franz von Karnstein merely smiled.

"Unprecedented? No, not at all. Very unusual? Yes. Only three others have been like me since the time of the Kings of Israel. More I cannot say."

"Cannot? Or will not?" replied Séverin, decided to test the water.

"Both. My apologies, but I must now change the subject. Do you know this vampire? The one you claim is a danger to all of Paris?"

Now it was Karnstein's turn to study the face of the older swordmaster and try and discern the truth.

"Yes. I first faced him ten years ago, on the 13 of Vendémiaire. It was a terrible affair." Séverin shuddered at the memory. "He is very old, and far deadlier than Mircalla Karnstein. And he is a master of the *loup-garou*."

"Mircalla was far from the most dangerous being I've faced," said Karnstein, tracing the talon scar on his face unconsciously. "Though I believe this foe is more insidious and deadly than any I've met in my short career as an exorcist."

"You are correct. I wish I had time to train you properly. Your... abilities are unusual, but your fighting skills are still weak. However, I doubt we will have the time. Will your extraordinary skills work on a vampire? Or a *loup-garou*?"

Séverin stood and indicated to Karnstein to follow him from the road house. It was time to prepare. Soon the Satanists would give them a possible direction to attack and they needed to act immediately.

"I do not know," replied the exorcist. "Vampires are so dangerous. Their existence cannot be properly comprehended. A vampire whose powers derived from the bite of another? No, very doubtful. They are almost like plague victims. Their powers are weaker, though still deadly. Like a feebler form of a disease, infecting their body and soul. Most become mindless leeches. They perpetually seek to feed upon the blood of anything living. And later, they will enjoy the blood of the dead as well. Their humanity is lost by then."

Before Séverin could speak, Franz von Karnstein continued to muse out loud:

"A vampire created by training at the Scholomance or such dark domains? I know not. And there are other sources that cause the transformation. But even if I am able to act, there is a difficulty. I must have several seconds to invoke the might of Heaven to expel the monster. I doubt that will be possible."

Karnstein followed Séverin outside and pulled his cloak tighter about his body. A chill was in the air, though his action might be based in anticipation of the coming struggle.

Séverin ignored the cold and led the young nobleman towards his fencing academy.

"There may be a way," he said. "Follow me and I will consider this puzzle."

They headed off in silence, but they were being observed from a distance by another player in this grand game…

CHAPTER XXIV

Paris, October 1795

The Marquis de Saint-Evremonde disliked the forest. Man was not meant to live in a place of trees and beasts. To spend nights sleeping in one was nearly unbearable. Nature, though rhapsodized by poets and other useless fools, was disgusting. Trees dropped sticky sap that got in your hair and ruined clothing. Animals were perpetually hooting and making other bizarre sounds. And the stench was simply disgusting.

Back in the days when he was a living man, Saint-Evremonde only enjoyed only one aspect of the natural world: hilling the creatures which inhabited said kingdom. Whether they hid in the forests, fields or the homes of useless peasants, there was always something wonderful to hunt down and destroy. Back when he served his beloved king Philippe, the hunts were such a delight. Stags, bears, boars, English prisoners—the sport was always a joy for them both.

But he, like beautiful Philippe, despised the forest in every other way. There was an ancient majesty to such locations. A primeval spirit existed in the rocks and ancient gnarled branches of the huge trees. It dwarfed all of mankind, reducing them to lesser beings on the face of the Earth. They were little more than fleas scurrying over a being of antediluvian age and unspeakable strength.

And that simply would not, could not, be allowed, or be accepted. Was not Man the highest being in all of

Creation? Did not the Creator design humanity in his own image? Could one possible compare a boar or a bush to Philippe the Fair and his dogsbody, Saint-Evremonde? No. The wooded places upon the Earth were there to be used or ignored. Nothing else.

Yet, on this night, the Marquis squatted upon a fallen tree in the woods just on the outskirts of Paris. He did not do so by choice, but because he knew he had to move his hunting hounds for fear of discovery. Their previous hiding place, a series of buildings, could not remain unobtrusive any longer. The stench of the dead, needed to feed his *loups-garous*, was becoming overwhelming. Soon the effluvium of putrid flesh would overwhelm even the heartiest of souls in the district. It was time to move, yet remain entirely free from the prying eyes of the Parisians.

The woods were a perfect, if disgusting, choice. Before, there had been two encampments of people, all ragged specimens of humanity. Saint-Evremonde's werewolves fell upon these tramps and fools and killed them all, to the last child. They also slaughtered their goats, mules and few horses. The scraps would hold them until the time of the attack. Then they could feast upon all the soldiers and republicans within the Capital.

But in choosing this location, Saint-Evremonde had been forced to relive memories he had carefully chosen to ignore until now. The ones he treasured, his days with Philippe, killing and replacing his distant relations, manipulating the royal court and more; those he recalled with happiness and keen relish. Those were the times of joy, pain to many, blood and death. He, as an exalted being above all, was his bliss. And the pain that brought about… Well, that was spice to the proverbial meat.

But the wooded places of the world intruded on his many pleasures. The natural world's primeval essence invaded his mind, causing the most painful time to appear. Because, despite his great age in the minds of men, he was little more than a wisp, a speck of time in these eldritch sites. Saint-Evremonde vainly fought each time he was obliged to linger within the woods. And that caused him to hate nature even more, if possible.

But remember he did, time flooding back into his undead intellect, a parasitical assault he could never prevent, or fight. It was one of the most distinct moments of his life, one that defined him irrevocably.

The day of his death. The moment where the fragment of humanity within Saint-Evremonde had been torn away forever.

It had happened a mere week after his beloved Philippe had died—a black day for him. The world had been a sadder place, a diminished domicile fit only for the weak. Louis, Philippe's son, was so much less than his father. Philippe had been a game player, a man who treated all of Europe as his chess board. Only Edward of England had been a worthy opponent, and even the great "Longshanks" himself could not match the Fair One's genius.

King Louis X, Philippe's son, had loved hitting a ball with a racket and chasing it. A waste of time, a pastime for merchants and weaklings. That had summed up his character well enough. He would never have succeeded in such grand schemes as the destruction of a body as powerful as the Templars. No, Louis X would struggle and argue and complain. And then he would die. Or be killed by a more suitable candidate.

Which was why Philippe's favorite, the Marquis de Saint-Evremonde, had stayed away from the court for a week after his mentor had died. He had moved to a manor house in the countryside, alone but for a few trusted servants. His wife and family had been sent far away. He had had no interest in them—never had, in fact. Marriage and children had been a necessary evil; the family line had to continue. But he didn't have to pretend to care about the broodmare who had borne his young, or the children themselves. He had sent his wishes to his family, enough money for them to live on, and promptly ignored their existence afterward.

He had wished for nothing more but to be well away from court or obligation. His manor, on the edge of the Forest of Compiègne, has not been large, but as a Grand Huntsman of France, he had the right to hunt in these ancient woods. This had been a rare privilege, as these grounds were traditionally held by the Kings of France. According to legend, the long-haired Merovingian rulers had practiced dark rites derived from their barbaric Frankish origins. The truth was not known, but Charles Martel and his Carolingian descendants had done their best to eliminate all who had once dwelled in these deep woods.

No matter. To Saint-Evremonde, the lands had been a perfect place to find solitude. Louis X, the useless king, would not visit them, engaged as he was in his new court. And few others possessed the right to even walk upon these grounds. The Marquis would be alone and left in peace.

The servants of this manor had known their master well and served his wishes quickly with bowed heads and hushed voices. None had tried to earn his favor, knowing the wrong word could result in, at best, a stinging slap. Or one might never be seen, or spoken of, again. This manor house had been a somber, fearful place where the sun's rays never seemed to brighten and the land appeared perpetually in a gray pall.

Saint-Evremonde had not seemed to notice any of this. He had risen with the sun and hunted in the deep woods. His servants were always nearby, acting as beaters when ordered, standing silent otherwise. Afternoons had been spent practicing sword, mace, and bow, keeping his edge. Then, there had been time for another short hunt, feast on the kills, and to bed.

It had been a simple life for a nobleman, but one which Saint-Evremonde had chosen. He had never been one for court politics and intrigue. Seduction of women was boring; best to take a peasant girl or a pretty boy and use them for a time, then discard them. If they were no good, or threatened to tell others, a cut of the knife and they were left for the beasts or fishes. Not that those impulses had overcome him too often. It was rare for Saint-Evremonde to desire anything more than the hunt.

The hunt was his true joy. Even an unsuccessful one was true pleasure. The chase, on foot or horseback, of an elusive creature or a fast peasant had caused Saint-Evremonde to feel alive. His whole body had felt more awake, more aware of his surroundings. The taste of anticipated blood, the tangy coppery sensation, was always lingering in his mouth as he had flown through the forest. Other than his moments with his beloved Philippe, the hunt was the only time when Saint-Evremonde truly felt alive.

And so it was ironic that it had been an early morning hunt that had brought about the end of his life. The day had been astonishingly bright, with few clouds in the sky and no anticipation of rain. The dew had glistened off the grass and trees, sending a kaleidoscope of rainbows chasing across the sunny woods. A perfect day to hunt.

Saint-Evremonde was on foot. There was a greater thrill chasing down a stag with only your bow and no help from a horse or beaters. His servants had stood in a clearing near the start of the trail, a mile or more back. If their master killed his beast, their job would be to locate the beast and carry it back to the manor house. This was a chancy thing, predators of the woods would converge on the dead animal, looking to feast upon its remains. Also, failing to locate the prey could result in a furious, and usually violent, retribution by the Marquis. But this had been the method he preferred. Having a host of servants about spoiled the chase, scared away the game. And that simply would not do.

Which was why nobody was about when the four masked men had burst from the brush.

They had stepped into view, their faces covered by black hoods. Two had held small, ancient swords. The third had been tightly gripping a flanged mace. And the fourth, a sharp axe. Both swordsmen had been in front; the axe-man and the mace-holder to the rear.

"Get out of my way, scum."

Saint-Evremonde's voice had been a typical harsh snarl

He then fired an arrow into the chest of one of the swordsmen. The man had shrieked and fallen.

Saint-Evremonde had spun around, letting go of a second arrow. That shaft had pierced the masked face of the axe-man. He had fallen with a gurgling, strangled moan.

But the remaining swordsman and the mace-holder had charged him. Saint-Evremonde was now forced to rely on his long hunting blade.

Knowing the woods well, he had plunged into a barely visible trail on his left. The path, little more than a run for small animals, had been one that he'd rarely trodden, but it would do for now. If he could get a little more distance, both attackers would fall by the shafts of his arrows. He merely needed to get some distance. Then these men, and the ones who had sent them to kill him, would discover the folly of crossing the Grand Huntsman of France.

Just as that thought crossed his mind, he had felt a harsh blow to his back. The Marquis had stumbled and caught himself upon the thick bough of a tree. He had gasped in pain, finding himself barely able to breathe. Glancing back, from the corner of his eye, he had spotted the feathered end of an arrow.

The cowards had had a hidden bowman!

Pushing away from the tree, Saint-Evremonde had carried on. Each breath had been painful to draw, yet he would not give up. A second arrow missed him, striking a boulder and shattering before his stumbling, shuffling feet. Apparently, their archer was not nearly as expert as their noble quarry. The thought had made Saint-Evremonde chuckle lightly.

Now, it felt as if his boots had been filled with lead weights. Every step, each stride, had been a trial. Yet he would not yield. He was no wounded animal, laying down and willingly accepting the merciful end from a hunter. He was the Marquis de Saint-Evremonde, Grand Huntsman of France, companion to God's own ruler upon the Earth, King Philippe IV of France. He would kill all who attempted to slay him by a craven ambuscade. Then he would find their masters and make them wish they had been drowned by their peasant mothers at birth.

Just then, his right leg had exploded with pain. Despite himself, he had yelped in pain and fallen. The agony had increased a thousandfold as he had crashed to the ground. Saint-Evremonde didn't need to look to know what had occurred. The archer had fired a shaft into his leg. A crippling shot, meant to slow his attempt at fleeing.

But it had not been enough. A Saint-Evremonde never gave up. He had pulled himself to his feet by the strength of his arms alone. By then, his bow had been cracked and unstrung, but it had served him well enough as a cane. Shambling and lumbering, he had moved behind a large, ancient tree. It had been enormous, stretching above the small path, looming above him like a giant from ancient myth.

Suddenly, the path had been cast in shadows, sunlight only peeking through the enormous boughs. The trees here were larger, antediluvian oaks and other unidentifiable plant growths. The ground had appeared almost scorched, a gray powder rather than the rich dark earth of the woods. And the sounds of birds and other insects had diminished, hushed and fading as Saint-Evremonde had lurched away from his faceless assailants. It had been even harder to breathe in this place, as if the air had been thinner, absorbed by the primeval plants which had seemed to press in upon his failing form.

The woods, though nearly silent, had appeared even more alive to the Marquis. It was as if each tall tree, each silvery stone, he had passed had stared at him, had judged him unworthy of their presence. The spirits of the wild were here, and men were unwelcome invaders. Or perhaps that had been merely a fevered dream from loss of blood? No matter. Saint-Evremonde had slid around a large root and had used a skeletal bush for support. The touch of the wood had felt odd, off-putting. Instead of a natural growth, it was as if he had been clutching the finger bones of a fallen foe. Recoiling, he had fallen backwards and landed in a tiny grove, a circular break in the desolate forest.

To his surprise, he had discovered a small altar of stone in the center of this empty area. A flat white stone, clearly carved with fading symbols. No natural formation, the etchings in the rock were too detailed, but almost impossible to distinguish. But what little he observed had filled him with a sense of disquiet, even dread, greater than the woods he had just escaped.

Above the altar, carved out of a fossilized tree, had been a statue. The image was several feet tall, a brown figure covered in a pale, hooded robe. A face had peeked from under the heavy cowl; it was hidden beneath a yellow mask. Oddly shaped eyes were immediately visible, more reptilian than human.

Saint-Evremonde had realized this was a hidden temple to the blood-seeking ancient deities who had controlled the destinies of the kings of the Franks. The name of the being worshipped in this forsaken spot had been lost in time, forgotten by the rise of new gods and new ways of worship. But there was power here. Sleeping power in these pale stones and crumbling idol. The power of the god, or possibly demon, who resided there had not been destroyed when the long-haired kings had been replaced by their distant relatives of the line of Charles the Hammer. The mystic might of those times had been waiting to rise again, and return to the gory, hoary, veneration of ancient, forgotten times.

Pulling himself up to a kneeling position, Saint-Evremonde had coughed. A spray of blood had fallen across the top of the altar. The viscous red fluid had seemed to sink into the pale rock, vanishing from view in seconds. Looking up at the ancient image, he had suddenly felt a cold wave of fear. This had once been a being of terrible power, a creature disremembered by mankind. Possibly for the good of all. Was it right to invoke this horrific creature?

The answer had come to him immediately. Of course it was! He was Philippe de Marguetel de Saint-Denis, Marquis de Saint-Evremonde! He was a being far superior to any god or monster of ancient days. He would use the power of this lost being and destroy his enemies. If the world suffered, so be it.

"Whoever you are, whatever you are," he had uttered in a hoarse croak, barely above a whisper, "give me the power to destroy my enemies. Give it to me!"

There had been no movement on the altar and the statue had remained a fixed figure, but the air had seemed to take on an electric quality. It had felt as if a great storm had appeared just overheard and its lightning was about the strike this very spot. A heavy thrum of power had seemed to fill Saint-Evremonde's ears. Something was about to happen...

And something had!

Three men had pushed into the clearing, their faces still covered by black hoods. The two he had spotted earlier were there, the swordsman and the mace-wielder. But there was also a shorter man holding a hunter's bow.

"Take him. Hold him still!"

The voice of the man with the mace had been cultured, learned. His accent had been similar to that of the southern nobility. But Saint-Evremonde had not recognized the voice.

The archer and the swordsman had stripped the wounded nobleman of his broken bow, arrows and knife. They had pinioned his arms behind his back, their grips powerful and punishing. Despite his desire to appear stalwart, Saint-Evremonde had cried out in pain. But the hands holding him had only gripped harder and waited as the third man had stepped near.

The man with the mace had pulled Saint-Evremonde's head back. His dark eyes had become visible; they had held nothing but contempt and fury. The eyes had stared at him for a moment, studying him and becoming even more contemptuous with each passing second.

"Noble Saint-Evremonde. Boon friend of the hellspawn Philippe. For your crimes against the noble Templars, we condemn you to the pits of Lucifer. You and your foul master deserve all the torments of the damned."

The hooded man had released his head and raised his mace. And, after a massive explosion of pain, an inky blackness had enveloped the Marquis.

He had lain in that stygian darkness for what had felt like an eternity. But then, he had opened his eyes. And everything in the world had now seemed quite different to him. He was both more and less than he had been before.

And he was not alone.

The ancient idol had been missing, but a man—or possibly a woman—had stood near him. That being wore a pale robe of some indeterminate color, and a yellow mask.

Saint-Evremonde had learned much from this ancient being, though far less than he would have desired. Then he had been released into the world, transformed.

No longer a mere human, he had become a fearsome power—but not yet an unstoppable force.

He had known, then, that that he would use his new-found powers and his skills as a huntsman to lay in wait and act with the controlled might of a predator. He would become a hidden force, a blood-thirsty specter haunting the halls of power. There would be many pleasures, and even more pain, thanks to his actions.

And blood would flow. Rivers of it, through the centuries. That was his promise to the unspeakable, unknown being in the yellow mask. He would bathe in the blood of thousands, nay, millions. And none would be able to stop him!

It was the perfect destiny for Philippe de Marguetel de Saint-Denis, Marquis de Saint-Evremonde, the future vampire king of France!

CHAPTER XXV

Paris, November 1804

While Jean-Pierre Séverin and Baron Franz von Karnstein were traveling beneath the streets of Paris, the Marquis de Saint-Evremonde didn't remain idle. Ordering his servant to stay silent and in one place, he left their hiding place for an appointment.

Though he wasn't gifted with the manipulative genius of his former master, Louis XI, he was wise enough to play some of the great king's games. Louis had been wiser than most, almost as much as his beloved Philippe. His ability to use others to achieve his goals had been admirable. After all, why dirty one's hands when one can allow others to do one's work?

Saint-Evremonde was wise enough to sense a threat to his plans, not to mention his undead existence. Jean-Pierre Séverin was still in Paris, and far too close to that upstart Corsican, Napoleon Bonaparte. That both men had already spoiled his plans a while ago was important. That, in and of itself, was galling. But as an ageless being, Saint-Evremonde was able to let such small defeats pass. He could bid his time to earn both his goal, and revenge.

Take the grandson of that other fearsome monarch, François I. That one, named Henry III, had been a fourth child and had never been meant to become ruler of France. When, through the foolishness of his brothers, this ill-prepared soft-hearted child had risen to the throne, he had defied the suggestions of Saint-

Evremonde's latest incarnation. Of course, he had not been aware this was the same man who had once served his grandfather and earlier kings of his line. To this lack of knowledge, which mighty François would have found both amusing and criminal, had been added another insult: raising Henri's favorites to a position which should have rightfully gone to Saint-Evremonde.

That was galling enough to the elder vampire, but King Henri had also ended the practice of grand hunts and made a weakling lesser nobleman into his Grand Huntsman. That dreadful insult had been made worse by the king's disinterest in war or blood sports. Henri had been a weakling, one who had preferred soppy, poetry-loving mistresses, none of whom would ever produce an heir.

Happily, Henri had made the situation easier by stupidly antagonizing the Catholics. Religion was always an easy means to destroy an enemy. If they were too devout, cause them to act foolishly believing God was on their side. If not dedicated enough to religion, cause them to act against those who did believe deeply. In the first situation, the fool usually died a sad, silly death. In the second, a host of enemies emerged, all willing to destroy one fighting against their beliefs. Saint-Evremonde loved religion. It had solved so many of his problems!

In the case of Henri III, all that he had had to do was to find a fanatic and whisper a few tales of unholy beliefs and plans. A Dominican friar named Clément had fulfilled that role perfectly. Convincing him that the weak monarch was a heretic, it had been simple enough to get that so-called "holy man" ready to assassinate him. The Marquis had brought the friar's insane hatred of the King to a boiling point by providing proof that

Henri had once courted the English Queen, Elizabeth, the destroyer of the Spanish Armada and leader of the heretics of England.

Clément had viewed killing his monarch as the act of a martyr, and had become the perfect weapon for Saint-Evremonde. And he had succeeded! A dagger, laced with a slow-acting poison killed the man who had dared to defy the power of the undead.

Today, Saint-Evremonde's plans were close to fruition. He could not risk failing again. It had taken years to recover from the last time he had battled Séverin and Napoleon. The would-be Emperor would be destroyed—that was already about to occur. But the hated Séverin needed to die too. It was unfortunate such actions had to being taken in such a rushed fashion, but the destruction of the Corsican was of paramount importance. The Marquis would not, could not, allow his coronation to take place. There was a social order and a Corsican peasant did not belong on the same seat which had once held great men like Louis the Spider King, François the terrifying, and his beloved Philippe the Fair.

Now that there was a spare moment, Saint-Evremonde could act. His contacts in Paris were still numerous and he had discovered an important name a little while ago. This meeting would solve his main, thorny problem: how to get rid of Séverin. Because there was no waiting in this situation, time was of the essence.

Slipping into a warehouse, the Marquis followed the instructions he had received and stopped before a row of packed boxes. The building was large, with the scents of old grain, men's sweat and tobacco in the air. Saint-Evremonde spotted his contact immediately. The human was good, very good, but he was the Marquis de

Saint-Evremonde. No human could match his skills when it came to stalking a prey.

"You may come out," said the Marquis. "I spotted you as soon as I arrived."

Saint-Evremonde stared where the human crouched, a low packing crate in a shadowy aisle.

"You are very good," he added. "I'm merely better."

The figure hopped off from behind the box and stopped, just outside sword range.

"You are not carrying a pistol," she said, "just a long blade and a dagger. Your money is in a pouch attached to your belt."

Saint-Evremonde nodded.

"You are as expert as I was told. I wish to hire your service. There is a man I wish you to kill. His name is Jean-Pierre Séverin. He is a swordmaster…"

The shadowy figure broke in the flow of speech:

"…and the Director of the Paris Morgue. He is also a friend of the First Consul. He is an expert with the blade. He is one of the most dangerous men in Paris."

"I will double your usual fee, and add a bonus if you accomplish your task in the next two days. December 1 is your deadline."

Saint-Evremonde tossed a heavy pouch at the feet of the assassin.

Lisebette (for it was she) picked up the bag and glanced at the gold coins within. Secretly, she knew she would have accepted the job for a mere token fee, because Séverin was the most hated creature in her life. He was the man who had defied her, and defeated her with ease. No being in all of Paris deserved death more than that vile, puritanical, republican son of a poxed whore.

This killing would put to rest a gnawing hunger that lay within her black heart.

"Agreed," said Lisebette.

She bowed to her client and watched him leave. After nine long years, Séverin would die by her hand. The very thought caused Lisebette to shudder with satisfaction.

CHAPTER XXVI

Paris, November 1804

As was his habit, Jean-Pierre Séverin was up with the dawn. Franz von Karnstein could be heard in the room up above. The young exorcist had accepted the old, dusty, disused room formerly reserved for pupils of the sword school. He appeared a short time later, as phlegmatic as ever. A book by Hieronymus Grost was in his hand, borrowed the night.

"That was one of Grost's later works," Séverin observed. "Not as organized as the earlier editions. More a series of memories. And as such, there's no central theme. And he ignored the scholarship in favor of interesting if somewhat irrelevant reminiscences."

The Morgue Director knew this from personal experience. He had acted as the elderly academic's amanuensis. It was the least he could do for a man who had taught him so much of the world.

"That was the reason I chose the book," said Karnstein. "Sometimes more information can be discovered by baring one's soul than quiet contemplation. In this situation, I was sadly unsuccessful."

The Baron carefully straightened the row of books into a neat, clean line. His actions were unconscious, but fit his character. The man appeared to need order in all things in his world.

"It was a good thought," said Séverin. "But the vampire we will battle does not possess the weaknesses common to his breed. He does not fear the cross. Nor do stakes or garlic have any visible affect."

Séverin lifted a practice rapier, frowned and placed it back on the rack.

"Then how did you defeat that creature in your last encounter?" asked Karnstein.

He waited, hands behind his back. His eyes never left the swordmaster as he stepped from weapon to weapon and examined each of them in turn.

"Through a method which would not work a second time," replied Séverin. "As you can see, this was merely a small setback for him. This creature will continue to destroy lives until he is finally put to a final rest."

Séverin studied the rapier in his hands, nodded, and tossed it to Karnstein. The young man caught it and frowned.

"This is a rapier. Is it not an outdated device? All militaries now use sabers in battle."

Séverin clucked his tongue and straightened slightly.

"No sword is ever, as you so quaintly put it, outdated. Weapons are designed with a specific purpose in mind. The skillful use of the sword follows. Therefore, it is important to learn the proper use of all weapons. Look here. Do you recognize this sword?"

The weapon was shorter than the rapier, but far heavier. Its steel edges were sharp and a heavy iron basket protected the grip. An ugly, dangerous sword, possessing none of the elegant beauty of the rapier. A tool for killing and nothing else.

Karnstein shook his head.

"No. It's even heavier than my saber."

"This is a British Navy cutlass. The short length is better for actions in close quarters. The heavy blade can cut ropes or sails in an action. And it requires less skill to use than a smallsword in a navy battle."

"And you possess this blade because..?"

Karnstein looked at the weapon with open revulsion. There was something evil about this type of sword. Perhaps it was its complete lack of artistry. The cutlass was a device only designed for the death of another person. A pure killing tool, nothing more or less.

"Many reasons. First, to master a skill, one must learn its less savory aspects. I reacted as you did when first holding a cutlass. But distaste will not protect me if I am attacked by a man swinging this blade. Second, my second swordmaster insisted that I train with the cutlass to build my strength. He always gave me the heaviest, most difficult to hold, weapon in his racks. Then I would be forced to use the sword in a way for which it was not intended. Try using this cutlass to lunge as if it was a rapier. Or block with the speed of a smallsword. Once mastered, the actual weapons are easier to wield. And finally, physical conditioning. Duels or battles are won by those able to fight beyond the endurance of the equally skilled opposition."

"I comprehend your reasoning. How long does it take to master all weapons?" said Karnstein, looking at the many other swords in Séverin's collections.

He didn't recognize many of them. They ranged in size from several inches above his head to barely the size of his palm. And each possessed a dark luster of their own.

"When I achieve that vaunted goal, I will make it a point of informing you. No, I am not making sport of you, Baron. I still have much to learn myself, no matter my expertise in some small areas."

Séverin put down the cutlass and turned to Karnstein. He noted the young noble's scanning eye, taking in the many odd and ancient armaments he collected over the years.

Karnstein finally stopped looking and shook his head.

"I would not be able to do as much. My studies and work must take precedence."

"Of course. I hope you did not believe such was my suggestion. No, that is clearly not your path in life. The life of a swordmaster is a calling. In a way, it is similar to your own. My reasoning is far simpler. You require training to protect yourself from harm. You possess some basic skill in saber fencing, but not enough to help you deal with truly dangerous situations. And you do not know how to use your hands and feet to protect yourself from assault. This much was clear when we fenced and when you were overwhelmed by the Satanists. Had one of them possessed a small dagger, you might have died. I state this without meaning to offer insult, but also as a fact."

This was the first time in many years that Séverin had offered to teach his skills to another. The loss of his wife and son had transformed his life in many ways. But the young Baron von Karnstein had awakened something within him—a desire to pass on his skills to another. This was the reason why Kronos and Grost had taken him on as their student. The knowledge of those two amazing men had therefore not been lost. Perhaps the young Austrian exorcist would keep the battle alive. His mysterious abilities did make him an impressive weapon against the dangerous powers that lurked in the dark.

"I agree," replied Karnstein. "His Holiness will not begrudge my decision. My attachment to his staff was always somewhat nominal, but I will still be in the service of the Church."

"Which is why you are not being followed at all times. I am guessing, based on our discussions, that your own Emperor does not view you as a traitor."

Séverin was mildly elated that Karnstein had accepted his offer, but the political situation between them was still awkward.

"As I mentioned, Emperor Francis knows of my disinclination for matters political," shrugged Karnstein. "My estates are in careful hands and run in the same fashion as they did under my grandfather. As heir to the Karnstein name, I am considered somewhat suspect, but a nobleman whose main interest lay with the Church and not gaining more temporal power makes me a rarity. His Imperial Majesty's single concern is that I should marry and father an heir. They would prefer the family line to continue through me."

"Based on your history, I am surprised you do not use the Vordenburg name and title instead."

Séverin remembered the pain of loss in Franz's eyes as he had told him of his relative's murder at the hand of Mircalla Karnstein. That, even more than the child's execution of the vampire woman and his mother, had showed a hint of the human side of the man. Franz von Karnstein was one of the coldest, least reactive individuals Séverin had ever met. He was the very image of the classic witch-hunter: dark, saturnine, dangerous, a man whose only interest in life was to fight the forces of darkness. He was the puritanical warrior, disinterested in the common behavior of humanity. His reward came from the devout belief he held dear.

But this was merely the surface of the Austrian exorcist. The loss of his family at a young age had forced the young nobleman to build a mask of cold indifference to the world. These barriers had protected him from the pain he still suffered, buried deep within his soul. Séverin knew this well, for he viewed similar walls every time he looked in the mirror. Best to find a means of preventing that long and painful road to Franz von Karnstein

"I considered it," replied the exorcist, "but why deny the truth? I am a Karnstein as well as a Vordenburg. If I do marry and have children, my house will be that of Vordenburg-Karnstein. The Emperor has agreed as much informally. I think he and his advisors believe it will soften the black history of the Karnstein name."

His mask of calm had returned. He might as well have been speaking of the weather to a stranger.

"That is understandable," agreed Séverin. "Shall we begin your lesson now? I would like to start you on a course of basic skills to determine your strengths and weaknesses. Then a lesson in unarmed combat."

Séverin pointed towards the pale cloth jacket and pants used by students while training in his academy. The clothing had been unused for some time, but would serve for Karnstein.

"Agreed."

Karnstein took the item and left the room to change. Séverin picked out a smallsword, saber, cutlass, Venetian dagger, and a well-used practice rapier. There was so much to teach and so little time in which to do it.

CHAPTER XXVII

Paris, October 1795

"Halt! Identify yourself!"

The uniformed sentry at the gate of the Palais des Tuileries was trying valiantly to sound threatening, but the crack in his voice was a clear signal of his near terror. Still, he had his rifle up and pointed at Séverin's chest. The swordmaster dutifully lifted his arms in surrender.

"I am Jean-Pierre Séverin," he announced. "I must speak to General Bonaparte at once. It is a matter of considerable urgency."

The guard, who possessed only a light fuzz of beard on his cheeks, blinked several times. Clearly, this was an unexpected occurrence for him and he was confused. His orders were simple: none were allowed past this gate without a pass. A man asking for the same general who had recently taken charge of the city defenses was unanticipated—and quite bewildering.

"General Bonaparte said nothing of a visitor," said the guard, attempting to sound strong.

But this was merely an imitation of a senior officer whom he had observed in his short time as a soldier.

Séverin chuckled lightly.

"I was not aware that generals consulted privates as to their actions. Is this a new regulation implemented by the Directory?"

"Um… I… er…" stammered the guard, gripping his rifle tighter.

He stared at the tall, older man and sensed some danger, but he wasn't sure it was the stranger or the odd situation that brought about this feeling.

"May I suggest a course of action?" proposed Séverin. "Send a runner to the general. I will write down my name we will allow him to determine the best course of events. Better for all involved, no?"

Séverin still held his hands up in surrender. Nervous, frightened, men with firearms were a far greater danger to an innocent man than any professional soldier. Best to move as little as possible and keep the young soldier from acting out of fear.

The guard thought for a moment and asked:

"You won't approach? You won't insist on entry?"

Séverin shook his head and kept his hands high.

"I will not move from this spot—unless you would prefer me to step back a little further? If General Bonaparte refuses to see me, I will immediately turn back and walk away."

"Yes, step back. Two steps...yes, there. Thank you, Citizen Séverin."

The guard sighed with relief and lowered his rifle several inches.

"Orderly!" he shouted.

A boy, probably no older than thirteen, appeared. He wore a castoff army uniform which was far too big for his thin-shouldered frame. His tired, pockmarked face made him appear far younger and more vulnerable. But his eyes were bright, lively and active. This was a child and the last place he belonged was at the site of a future battle, but the boy would see it as a great adventure—until the blood began to flow and the limbs fell like twigs in a forest. Then, his youthful innocence would be destroyed forever. No matter his age, if he survived this day, he would no longer be a child.

"How may I assist you, citizen?" asked the orderly in a high-pitched voice, cracking with each word.

"Allow this citizen to write a message. Then present it directly to General Bonaparte."

The guard nodded at Séverin and watched as the latter accepted a pen and ink and a slip of paper. He wrote a few words, handed it to the orderly, and returned the pen. The guard was relieved to see that the dangerous-looking stranger never once tried to approach or make any suspicious motions.

The orderly returned a few moments later with two older soldiers. The guard recognized them instantly as veterans of many battles. They ignored his salute and waved Séverin inside. Respect was evident in their actions; they treated the stranger as if he was a visiting dignitary.

"The Citizen General told me to tell you that you did right. He wanted to see this man," the orderly said, before vanishing back inside the building.

The soldiers lead Séverin deep within the Palais, ignoring all salutes and calls from other soldiers. Within minutes, he was ushered into an office adjoining a larger meeting room.

Bonaparte stepped through an adjoining door. After calling out a quick response to someone within, he shut the door firmly. He smiled briefly at Séverin and extended a hand in greeting. He appeared more alive, more substantial. Though the swordmaster was taller and wider, at that moment, he was almost dwarfed by the magnetic power of the smaller Corsican general. The genius of Napoleon Bonaparte caused him to appear more substantial than any other being.

"Maestro Séverin," said Napoleon. "I was hoping to hear from you."

The General waved a hand, inviting Séverin to sit.

"I took action shortly after we parted" continued Napoleon. "Your information was correct. The Convention ordered me to prepare a plan for the defense of the capital. I agreed on the condition that I would be allowed freedom of movement. Barras and the rest of the newly-appointed Directory agreed to my terms."

"Excellent news," exclaimed Séverin.

This was nothing less than the truth. Paul Barras, though a good man, was not a soldier. He was a former nobleman and a politician. The intricacies of the arts of war were a lost upon such an individual. No, for the Republic to survive this assault from the Royalists, they needed a general. They needed Napoleon Bonaparte.

"Not so excellent. We are out-numbered six or more to our one. We must triumph by superior strategy and tactics. Otherwise the Royalists will overwhelm our position. And only you and I know of the witchcraft they plan to use to destroy my forces. What have you for me, Maestro?"

Napoleon focused his full attention upon Séverin. The force of his will seemed to envelop the powerful swordmaster, though he was not overawed.

"The vampire has his *loups-garous* in hiding. They cannot remain so for long. Such creatures must feed constantly. They will attack your position at first light."

Séverin mentally prayed that Napoleon would come up with a solution to the problem he was about to present.

"I expected this," said the General. "To attack in the early morning makes sense; our men will be tired, and the light will reveal the full horror of the unholy beasts for the first time, thus striking terror in our camp."

"So you are prepared!" said Séverin clapping his hands. "Good! Do you have a map or plans of this building and its surroundings?"

Napoleon led Séverin to the desk and unfolded two large pages.

"Both. I demanded them upon accepting my commission."

Séverin glanced at both papers and pointed to a location.

"The vampire will send them here. This would be in sight of the Palais, as well as the main body of your men."

Napoleon walked around the plans once, examining each area without a sound.

"Agreed," he said.

"Your struggle will be if any *loup-garou* reaches this position. The vision of a werewolf, snarling and howling, tearing apart their fellows, would shatter your soldiers. Seeing such evil often causes the mind of even the strongest man to fail. They must be destroyed at a distance. And rifle bullets might not be enough. You must find another way."

Séverin stepped back and watched as Napoleon's mind considered the problem. This was an obstacle which had vexed many great leaders in the past. And one of the reasons the barbaric hordes had destroyed so many Roman armies in ancient days. But Napoleon was already smiling.

"This is no difficulty for me, merely a small hurdle for the horse to jump."

Stepping over to the door which had admitted Séverin, he threw it open and shouted:

"Sous-lieutenant! To me, at once."

A man appeared at a run, stepping into the room and closing the door at a look from the General. He was as tall as Séverin, rapier-thin with curling black locks which fell just above his shoulders. He was dressed in the uniform of an officer of the 12th Régiment de Chasseurs à Cheval and possessed the same challenging look which always appeared in the eyes of the born cavalry officer.

"Sous-lieutenant Murat, I have a mission for you. The fate of the Republic lies in your hands," said Napoleon, pacing, his attention focused on the two men as well as his battle plans.

"I am at your orders, Citizen General," said Murat, ignoring Séverin.

He grasped the sword on his belt with a white-knuckled grip. He was smiling and appeared to vibrate in place like a horse about to leap into a race.

"Excellent," aid the General. "You are to ride with utmost speed to the plain of Sablons. General Menou has informed me that cannons are there at this moment. Return with these weapons with haste. They must be here long before sunrise. Can you accomplish this much, Murat?"

At the last question, Bonaparte stopped pacing and looked straight up into the eyes of the younger cavalry officer. A cannon's explosion couldn't have disrupted his intense concentration at this moment.

"I will not fail, Citizen General," replied Murat, saluting.

"See that you do not."

Bonaparte spoke these final words to Murat's back and waited until the door was once again closed. He then turned back to Séverin and said:

"Leave Lucifer's pets to my hands. What are your plans? I can make you a Captain and place you on the line. A temporary commission, of course."

Séverin shook his head.

"I must confront the vampire. Otherwise he will order his beasts to retreat and will attempt to use them in another attack. You must destroy these *loups-garous*, Sire. Root and branch. No survivors. They are a menace to all life."

"You called me *Sire* again, Jean-Pierre Séverin. I shall do as you order, but in this matter, it is I who am under your command."

Napoleon shook Séverin's hand and ushered him to the door.

"May the Lord bless your sword in this struggle, my friend," said the General.

"I pray this is so, Sire."

Séverin stepped behind the two veteran soldiers and headed back to the streets. The sun would rise in a mere four hours. He hoped that there would be time enough for Murat to succeed in his mission before the coming struggle.

CHAPTER XXVIII

Paris, November 1804

"We shall stop here," said Séverin. "Well done. You are better than I imagined. Your unique life has taught you some skills. Your saber fighting is based in the Prussian system. You have little skill with the rapier or smallsword, but I expected as much. More impressively, you possess instinctive skills with the Venetian dagger, and in unarmed combat. Your skills are based on survival. Now we will refine you into someone a great deal more dangerous."

The swordmaster handed Karnstein a cup of cold tea. The younger man was dripping with perspiration and breathing hard. And there was some blood flowing from a split lower lip. That had been earned when, in his growing exhaustion, Karnstein had dropped his left hand before throwing a punch. A simple jab to the face had earned him a small injury for this failure.

In contrast, Séverin looked untouched. A light sheen of sweat was visible on his face, but he otherwise appeared unruffled. He sipped his tea while contemplating the last hour's work.

"I think I shall teach you the basics of rapier and smallsword. It would not do to have you sliced to pieces by the first English officer you might encounter. But your training will emphasize your strengths and preferences. You do not have the spirit to be a professional duelist. To you, battle is about defeating your enemy and staying alive."

Séverin poured the Austrian exorcist another mug of tea.

"Is there any other way?" asked the young exorcist. "Weapons are for killing."

Karnstein had regained his composure and was toweling off while drinking the tea. He controlled his desire to gulp down the bitter fluid, knowing the mind was stronger than the body. This had been his way since his childhood. To never allow oneself to fall victim to cravings of any type. Man's body possessed no morals, no comprehension of the results of poor choices. The mind and soul were essential in not falling victim to dangerous desires.

This was a lesson he had learned many times over during his short life. His mother's lust for power had led to her falling victim to the evil of the vampire, Mircalla. This moral had been repeated often before Franz von Karnstein's eyes since that dark day. A priest who had lost his way in favor of riches. A nobleman who had let his jealousy of another's good fortune transform him into a vengeful, hate-filled creature. A pretty girl who had become so entranced by her beauty that she had used it as a weapon to harm friends and foes alike. The list was long and sorrowful. Franz von Karnstein had vowed every day to never follow that sinful path.

Séverin smiled and looked to heaven. Karnstein had to be the most solemn man alive. He needed to learn that the world was not just a battlefield between darkness and light. Perhaps that would be the greatest gift these lessons might impart.

"There is the beauty of the weapon, and the perfection of the technique. These are art forms. They raise a man to a higher standard. Look here..."

He led the young Austrian nobleman to the far end of the weapons shelf. Upon a special rack lay a sword, about three feet in length. The blade was held in a black lacquer sheath and silken cords were bound around the handle.

"This is a special blade from distant shores. It was a gift to my swordmaster for killing a vampire."

Séverin drew the sword and it shimmered in the sunlight.

"A sword smith named Masamune created this weapon over four hundred years ago. It is still as sharp as the day he presented it to its first owner."

Karnstein didn't reach for the sword, but tilted his head to examine the details of the blade in greater detail.

"It looks new. I've seen swords rust after a few years of ownership."

Séverin carefully returned the weapon to the sheath and replaced it in the holder.

"That is the difference between a tool and a weapon made as an art form. But I digress. Your training will stress cutting weapons, small daggers, and unarmed combat. By honing the body into a weapon, both mind and soul will flourish."

"*Do you not know that your bodies are temples of the Holy Spirit, who is in you, whom you have received from God?*" replied Karnstein, quoting *Corinthians*.

"Just so," said Séverin.

He had a vision of the possible future of Franz von Karnstein, just like he'd had foreknowledge that one day all would call Napoleon Bonaparte "Sire."

In this possible future, Franz von Karnstein was still the phlegmatic, somber, soul. Yet there was a dangerous authority to him now. He was a man others respected, even feared, but the light of insane fanaticism was not present in his eyes. This future Franz was not a crazed witchfinder, destroying the good along with the evil in the world. This man was a terror to the forces of darkness, a slayer of evil and a protector of good. A servant of the light.

This, more than anything else, convinced Jean-Pierre Séverin that he had to train Baron Franz von Karnstein. Such a man was needed in the world. Someone who combined the best of Séverin, Grost, Kronos, and whatever unusual teachers the Austrian exorcist had had in the past. The world needed more warriors on the path of heaven.

But he also knew that another pupil would be coming one day. The art of the swordmaster resided within Séverin, and would do so until his time, too, passed. But his heir, who he had once hoped had been his lost son, would be the one who would learn these arts and would not let the ancient knowledge die. The fighting arts were a link to the history of man. To allow them to vanish under the wheels of progress would diminish mankind irrevocably. He would find his pupil, his heir, and the knowledge of humanity's first true art would not vanish into the dust of ages

"You must cleanse yourself first," Séverin said. "If you walk across the square, you will find the home of a Barbary merchant named Selim. Ask to use his bathhouse. He will allow it and will not accept any payment for the use. Take your time, then return here. We will continue our attempts to determine the location of our enemy."

Séverin knew Karnstein would not object to bathing. Though many believed to do so was dangerous to one's health, the Austrian was not one of that number. He smelled of soap, not perfumes.

"Why will he reject payment? Is this a religious objection?" asked Karnstein with interest. There appeared to be no judgment in his tone of voice.

"Selim's religion holds bathing as essential to piety. For a Westerner to follow that tradition is like a form of charity in his mind. Payment would be insulting. To Selim, your acceptance of his bath is proof that you believe in God."

Séverin knew many would object to accepting any form of charity from a Muslim, but he knew Karnstein well enough to know the younger man would find such an act as human kindness. Not a reason to debate religion.

"Then I will merely offer my thanks and pray for his soul to go to heaven."

And with that, Karnstein could be heard walking down the back stairs. The door closed a moment later and all was silent.

"You can come out now, Lisebette," said Séverin.

He kept his hand clearly in view and looked to the main stairs.

Lisebette stepped out of, a wide smile upon her attractive face. She was lovely to behold; her long dark hair fell in ringlets to her shoulders. Her skin was still creamy and flawless and her teeth were like tiny, perfect pearls. Her mouth was still a lovely red cupid's bow, of the type that caused poets to rhapsodize for pages.

But her eyes held the light of madness beneath their stygian loveliness. Lisebette was still a lover of pain and death. She was a predator in a pretty package. Death was all she offered.

"How did you know I was here?" she asked. "I was totally silent this time. Your handsome young student did not know I was waiting and listening."

Lisebette stopped after taking a few more steps and raised the flintlock pistol she gripped in her right hand. Her aim was perfect, unwavering, and without the slightest tremor in her arm.

"You still wear the same scent," answered the Morgue Director. "Very strong and filled with musk. And the gunpowder you used in your weapon is quite fresh. I detected it immediately. Simplicity itself."

Séverin knew he was bearding this beast, but he did not have any choice. Any show of weakness on his part would give her the chance to kill him instantly.

Lisebette's eyes flashed with fury, but her gun hand did not waver.

"Still the same arrogant, sneering eunuch, aren't you, Maestro?"

Séverin shrugged, intentionally making the gesture more elaborate.

"You shall never know, Lisebette. I never embrace reptiles."

She stiffened momentarily, but regained her poise in a heartbeat.

"No, I shall not fall victim to your mocking. I was hired to kill you. And I shall do so, but not by the gun. It is too easy. Too quick."

Séverin bowed and waved to his racks of weapons.

"A duel then?"

"Yes! When you humiliated me, I trained hard. I learned from swordmasters, expert assassins and, oh, so many more. I became skilled in all forms of death. Then I hoped, I prayed to anything listening, that one day I would be paid to put you down like a mad dog. And my wish was granted. I would perform this act for free. Just to have the pleasure of watching that smug look on your face replaced by one of terror. I will slice you to ribbons, old man. Your time has passed. I am now the master of weapons, old man."

Lisebette placed the flintlock on a nearby window sill. She picked up a smallsword and a dagger, tested the edges and smiled.

Séverin drew his favorite smallsword and a Roman dagger. The brass ball on the dagger's handle appeared to twinkle in the sunlight.

"I imagine you spent years practicing that speech. Moliere would probably declare it too long and obvious. I merely call it tiresome. The product of cheap melodrama and poorly written tales of revenge."

"You talk too much, old man. *En garde!*"

Lisebette lunged forward, her smallsword aiming for Séverin's heart.

CHAPTER XXIX

Paris, October 1795

The sun was rising ever so slowly on that crisp morning. It was October 5, 1795, under the real calendar, 13 Vendémiaire, Year 4, under this foolish republican nonsense. This would be the beginning of the end of that rot upon France. Once the Convention and their new ranting leaders, the Directory, were destroyed, a new age would begin. The king would return and the true values of France would again become paramount. Commoners would return to their rightful place, serving their betters. A glorious future.

Saint-Evremonde thought this as he watched the sky, waiting for the light of dawn. He possessed no illusions about the future king, the one who would be called Louis XVIII. He possessed none of the might of his ancestors; he was all too typical of the Bourbons, too weak to fully return France to the *Ancien Régime*, but pigheaded enough to wish to sit his fat fundament on the throne. Still, his willingness to be king was enough for the Marquis.

It was the rash of republican sentiments that had altered Saint-Evremonde's long-standing policies of shadowy involvement. For centuries, he had been content to serve and sit behind the descendents of his beloved Philippe and François—but no longer! The behavior of the former serfs was no longer acceptable.

Consider the present day. The peasants, lowly creatures meant to only serve their betters and till the soil, now controlled France. The county that had once been ruled by great kings was now in the hands of mud-dwellers. This was an offense to the natural order. God had created man and divided him between the small numbers of noble-born and the rest of the common herd. This was in the Bible, somewhere.

But that was not the end to the indignities perpetrated upon this mortal plane. That these commoners had demanded equality under the law had been ludicrous enough, an opium eater's fantasy, but that these creatures had then had the audacity to rise up and overthrow the Bourbons truly meant Hell upon Earth! God's own king, captured and imprisoned by ranting, screeching crowds of farmers and tradesmen. This was the first step to the End of Days.

The day the so-called rulers of France had executed Louis XVI and his Austrian-born queen, Saint-Evremonde had fully expected the heavens to turn black and Satan himself to rise up. That event had not happened—at least not yet. Perhaps both God and the Devil knew there was still one man in France who would return the country to its proper mandate?

His work had begun two years earlier, a great day indeed. Using a puppet of not-too-poor breeding named Charlotte Corday, he had convinced the woman that the horrors of the Jacobins' régime would only grow worse. It had not been especially difficult; the weak little thing had witnessed the infamous September Massacres of the previous year. Having seen the execution of over one thousand humans, some of which were priests, had pretty much destroyed her mind. She had been the perfect tool.

He then had pointed her at one of the worst believers in "equality"—a creature called Jean-Paul Marat, one of the most abysmal of the modern men. Marat had actually believed in the insane theory that people could rule themselves, that they could create laws, and a peaceful society without the noble classes. The final indignity had come when this monster had printed these words in his tract, *L'Ami du peuple*:

"Five or six hundred aristocratic heads lopped off would have assured you repose and happiness; a false humanity has restrained your arm and suspended your blows; it will cost the lives of millions of your brothers."

Pure insanity. One that had to be stamped out—but not by Saint-Evremonde personally. To do so would be to make him into a martyr. Best to have Marat die without dignity, in a way that would add shame his name. Had he been a creature who liked girl or boy whores, he could have died in a pathetic street brawl. But Marat's devotion to duty kept him from such pursuits. But he did bathe constantly, and even met people while immersed in water...

Providing Charlotte Corday with a simple ruse and a sharp knife had been child's play, and she had killed the creature in his bath. A fine end. For all his ranting and demands, history would only remember him as one who'd been stabbed in his bath. An undignified end for a ridiculous little man.

But it had not been enough. When the Jacobins had finally fallen, another horde of Republicans had stepped in their place. They had been less objectionable, ending the murder of aristocrats, but they still had allowed elections and not paid tribute to the monarchy. This would never do. It had been time for the Marquis to become directly involved with the Royalists' counter-revolutionary forces.

Which had led him to this place. It had been a little difficult to become the Marquis de Saint-Evremonde again. His latest descendant was dead, killed by a vengeful commoner who hadn't known his proper place. And the Jacobins had killed the only other known heir—the one time, perhaps, those accursed creatures had been of some use. This had allowed the one true Marquis de Saint-Evremonde to step into the title once more—but with a difference.

No longer would he be content to hide in the shadows. It was time to come into the light and openly be the power behind the throne. Already fat Louis considered him a genius, a great man and the future of the aristocracy. Once the Republicans were slaughtered to a man, Saint-Evremonde would accept a greater title—Prince perhaps? And he would become the puppet master behind the Bourbon *marionette*. What title should he take? *Principal Ministre d'Etat*, like the wily Richelieu two centuries ago? Secretary of State, like the ingenious Colbert? Doubtful; that sounded too English. No matter. The title mattered less than the power associated with it.

The first light of the sun peeked out to the east. It was five a.m., or nearly that time. Saint-Evremonde stood up and raised a hand, causing his werewolves to fall silent. Their inhuman, bestial eyes were filled with one simple burning need. This was the only focus they had in their terrible, savage, blackened souls. Hunger. These creatures were all appetite, filled with an unrestrained lust for the flesh of the living. They were never satiated by their ravenous rampages. This was the reason few survived for many years. Even pathetic humans detected when a creature was feasting upon their fellows daily.

There was a rumor, a tale he had earned over the years, of a *loup-garou* who had learned to control the hunger. With his vampiric mistress, he had learned to hide his inhumanity from the gaze of mankind. Legend held that the vampire had trained her beast secretly and created a terrible weapon. One she could unleash upon her enemies. It was a good story. Perhaps one day Saint-Evremonde would attempt such an experiment. Time was no obstacle, and a *loup-garou* ceased to age upon its transformation.

"My hounds, turn! Look! Run to that building, the Tuileries Palace used by the Convention. Kill them all! Feast until I command you to return. Go! Go now!"

Saint-Evremonde pointed at the building as the growing light revealed its outlines.

That was all that he needed to say to the monsters. They growled and howled. They roared and slavered. Ropes of drool fell from their massive, twisted black lips as they turned towards the seat of Republican France. And then, they lifted their enormous snouts, opened their massive maws, and howled. As a pack, they charged towards the Palais. Their massive black talons and ivory fangs flashed as they stepped into the sunlight.

Saint-Evremonde smiled, a rare show of his pointed fangs. He was looking forward to the screams of terror as his *loup-garou* horde tore apart the soldiers and the peasants. There was something so delightful, so delicious, in being the cause of the fall of the so-called new order. This was a great day, all brought about by his hand.

Suddenly, Jean-Pierre Séverin stepped into view. He had stayed downwind of the *loups-garous* and their vampire master, waiting for the right moment. Saint-Evremonde was typical of the vampires he had fought in the past. Séverin knew the undead creature would not risk his life first—not while he possessed slaves willing to attack upon his orders. The trick was to wait until the werewolves had gone before showing oneself.

"You are the Marquis de Saint-Evremonde, I believe?" said Séverin coldly, not bothering to hide the contempt in his voice. "Your descendant died on the guillotine. I remember that day. Damned by his own father-in-law. How delightful."

In truth, Séverin had despised the former Committee of Public Safety. Robespierre, Saint-Just, and the rest had replaced the ideals of equality with a bloodbath of horror, terror, and death. In many ways, they were as evil as the worst monsters of the aristocracy. They, too, were vampires, in their own way. They fed upon the suffering of the masses, the fears of France. And, in the end, it had been virtually impossible to tell them apart from the creatures of the night.

But Séverin had a plan. And part of that plan was to play the role of a Republican devotee. What better way to insult that ancient monster?

"You dare? I am the Marquis de Saint-Evremonde. I was old when the first spawn of your line cleaned waste from the shoes of their betters. How dare you speak to me thus?"

Saint-Evremonde's normally handsome face transformed as he spat out his speech. His mouth grew wider, his jaw more substantial and each of his ivory incisors looked capable of tearing a man to pieces.

"I dare, ancient monster. For I am Jean-Pierre Séverin, swordmaster, and I am your better. Your kind are relics. You are nothing more than pale reflections of the past. This is a new day and you and your ilk are now the new servant class."

Séverin's smirk was one he had learned from the street duelists of Verona. No people were more expert in the art of insult than the men of Verona. In that city-state, entire families had feuded for generations over minor sneers.

Saint-Evremonde drew his sword in a move that was a blur of motion.

"I shall slice that smile off your peasant face. Then I shall consume the hearts of each member of the Directory. And I shall leave you all to feed my hounds. Draw your sword!"

Séverin bowed slightly and drew his rapier and a short unadorned steel sword.

"If your insults are as sharp as your blade, I am quite safe, Marquis. *En garde!*"

CHAPTER XXX

Paris, November 1804

"*En garde!*"

Séverin's reply to Lisebette had been uttered in an almost bored tone.

He parried her initial lunge and stepped away from her slashing dagger. The young assassin was faster and more precise now, far better trained. Her boasts did not appear to be outrageous.

"You've slowed, old man," she jeered. "Years before, you could have blocked my attack much faster."

Lisebette launched a series of probing attacks, her lunges and slices seeking vulnerable points on his body. Her every attack was meant to weaken him, destroy his endurance. It as the fighting system of a professional duelist and killer.

Séverin continued to block Lisebette and attacked in response. She moved as fast as a bee, her metaphorical stinger seeking his arms, legs, eyes, and hands. His attacks were quick attacks, seeking to overwhelm her defenses.

Lisebette proved up to the challenge, dancing about the floor, a wide smile across her face. She suddenly switched her sword to her other hand, dropping the dagger back into her belt. The young assassin's attacks increased in speed and intensity, forcing Séverin to block, counter and move across the floor with celerity.

"Once I'm done slicing you to ribbons, I'll seduce and murder your priestly student."

Lisebette's voice was mocking, teasing. There was no sign of exertion in her face or voice.

Séverin rolled his eyes.

"You are welcome to try. More likely, he'll shoot you. Or try and convert you to a better path."

Lisebette giggled and threw back her dark curls.

"I've seduced and killed fifteen priests. Two were bishops. I never fail."

"But you have, Lisebette. I defeated you with ease. Your poor attempt at seduction bored me, and your skills were no better than a common street ruffian."

Séverin continued to move defensively, occasionally attacking, but he never pressed hard.

"They're better now, old man. I trained for years, praying to all who would listen for the day I would kill you. Nine long years I've waited, but now I have you!"

Lisebette sliced a bit off Séverin's sleeve, her attack missing the flesh beneath by a mere hair's breadth.

"Nine years? How very sad. To hold so firmly onto hate because I rebuffed your seduction."

Séverin sounded bored and he continued to parry and attack with simple moves. Lisebette evaded or blocked his every move.

"You think that was the reason? You think too highly of yourself. You are old and repulsive. I would sooner lay with a pig in a sty than you. That was not why I wished your death!"

Lisebette's attacks grew more furious, forcing Séverin across the training floor. He was entirely defensive now and a slight sheen of sweat had appeared across his brow.

"There is another motive? Pray, tell me before you strike home. So to speak."

Séverin sounded slightly breathless as he danced back across the floor, his sword just barely stopping the small blade in the hands of the female assassin.

"The Antipope is the reason. At your suggestion, she cast me out. Alone, though with all the money I earned slaying old fools like you. I determined to learn all the tricks you used to defeat me. To become your better. And then wait for the day someone would pay for me, or even ask me, to kill you. For I knew that day would come. One day, your outspoken ways would mean your end. I was so aroused by the thought of killing you that I took and killed two of my lovers before lying in wait for you."

Lisebette smiled as two more slices shredded Séverin's shirt, but she still narrowly missed his skin.

"I will admit to feeling great pleasure from learning of your expulsion from the Court of Miracles. I even assisted them in finding a new secret location as recompense."

Séverin stepped aside and almost stumbled as Lisebette lunged. She missed his heart by mere inches, damaging the wall behind him; several paintings fell, the frames cracking as they clattered across the floor.

"And for revenge, and revenge alone, I slaved away under swordmasters across the globe. I studied saber fighting under Prussian and Hessian experts. Smallsword under English and Parisian duelists. Street-fighting killers in Rome and Venice, rapier experts in Madrid. If there was a skill, I served under its teacher until I mastered the art."

Lisebette knocked the dagger out of Séverin's hand. She kicked it under a rack and smiled even wider.

"How?" he asked. "None would teach a woman. Even if you bedded them daily."

Séverin backpedaled fast, barely eluding the slicing smallsword. Lisebette rolled her eyes and giggled.

"I pretended to be a boy. Cut my hair short and hid my bosom. Only one detected otherwise. An Austrian named Albrecht. I poisoned him and had his servant hanged. Now, enough talk. Time to conclude this, old man."

Séverin straightened and nodded.

"I do agree."

Lisebette screeched and lunged forward, only to be met by a firm parry. She circled her blade, attempting to move the Morgue Director's sword out of position, only to stumble to the side. She barely kept her balance and stepped back. Exhaling through her teeth, she stepped forward into Séverin's line and began to attack.

Her speed was even greater, her precision perfect. Yet Séverin stood still, his sword barely appearing to move. Yet, always it was there, stopping her lunges and swings. His calm face was even more mocking than his look of derision before their duel commenced.

Sliding back, Lisebette looked at him with confusion written across her brow. She pulled out her dagger and began attacking again. Now he did move, but always just slightly away from one of her weapons, all the while his smallsword parried sword or blade with very little effort.

Finally, dripping with sweat, Lisebette stepped back again.

"I had you defeated! What happened? Did you poison me?"

"You never came close to me, madwoman," replied Séverin, shaking his head. "Your skills are impressive, but limited to the practicality of a battle. You never learned the higher art of the blade."

Lisebette spat upon the floor, her attractive face twisted in a sneer.

"Higher art? All you elderly sword teachers are the same. You speak more of peace than battle. The sword is a tool of killing. Not a flower or possession of peace!"

Séverin shook his head again. His expression was sad, his manner somber.

"That depends upon the soul of the wielder. A dark soul turns all beauty into something ugly. And yours is as black as the monster who's employed you to take my life."

Lisebette giggled and threw back her soaking locks.

"I always knew I would die in battle. But I shall do my best to take you with me, old man."

And she flung her dagger straight for his eyes while lunging for his groin. It was an impressive attack. The sword, if not blocked, would result in his groin and the artery nearby to be pierced. The agony would be indescribable and would probably result in Séverin's death. If he blocked the sword, the dagger's solid brass ball might stun him briefly. Or the blade might cut his eye. Either way, he'd be very vulnerable to Lisebette's follow-up assault. These were moves typical of the Italian street duelists, some of the most dangerous men in all of Europe.

But Séverin had served under such men in his life. Catching the dagger with his free hand, he parried Lisebette's sword. Then he struck. A pair of quick slices, exactly timed and placed.

Lisebette shrieked, dropped her sword, and fell backwards, clutching her face. Blood seeped through her fingers and she screamed long and loud. Sadly for her, the heavy walls of Séverin's school and home prevented any noise from entering the street.

Séverin pulled a cloth from the wall and cleaned the blood from his blade. He felt the familiar wave of unhappiness fill him as he looked down at the writhing woman. Such a pathetic waste of a life. Lisebette, though lovely to gaze upon, was a creature of terrible evil. She loved the pain and death of others, and used her beauty as a weapon against the unwary.

Her expulsion from the beggars' guild had been in hope that she might learn the error of her ways. Instead it had further poisoned her black heart. She was like a vampire, a creature of blood and evil. She had fed upon the misery of others and left a trail of corpses throughout her travels. Her only constant trait, beyond a love of pain and death, had been the code imposed upon her by the Antipope. She had treated killing as a contract, a paid compact. Just one that granted her sexual release as well as profit.

And that was why Séverin had waited and probed her. By feigning weakness, he could discover her true character. And with the truth revealed, he could act. Which was why Séverin had spared Lisebette's life. Not out of mercy. A quick end would have been too much mercy to this mad dog in a pretty package. And Jean-Pierre Séverin possessed little to no compassion for such a creature.

"My eyes! My eyes!" Lisebette shrieked, continuing to writhe upon the floor.

The blood seeped from the two destroyed cavities within her face.

"For your crimes against the lives of mankind. And for wasting your beauty and skills on brutality and violence. Your life is now yours to choose. You may allow bitterness to consume what little soul you still possess, or you can try and devote yourself to a better, if limited life. Or…"

Séverin broke off, seeing the fury upon the look of the now blind assassin.

"Or what? Or what, you bastard?"

Lisebette's voice was the hiss of a serpent. An enraged, inhuman sound which caused Séverin to shiver.

"Or you may kill yourself. Throw yourself in the Seine. Or allow a cart to run over you. There are so many methods. But I hope you don't believe in the afterlife. Suicides join Judas in his circle of Hell."

Séverin didn't wait for her answer. He stepped over to Lisebette's side and pressed a cloth to her mouth. She fought for a moment, then fell limp upon his floor.

After covering her bleeding eyes with a bandage, Séverin called in two of his friends. Lisebette was carried out to a cart. She would be brought to the convent of the Sisters of Mercy, who operated as a hospital for the poor. Mother Agnes was an excellent healer and the former assassin would survive her injury. But she would never see again.

"Your life is now your own." Séverin whispered as the cart vanished from view. "Life, death, or rebirth. Your choice, Lisebette."

CHAPTER XXXI

Paris, November 1804

Franz von Karnstein craved a bath. Though many held that baths and cleaning one's body were unnatural, he disagreed. Washing meant he wouldn't stink like many people. That alone was a good enough reason. But a Roman physician, one who had studied all over Europe and even Arabia, always held that cleanliness was a method of ensuring good health.

Spotting the Barbary Merchant's shop, he headed in that direction—and stopped.

His hand dropped to his sword as he glanced behind him to ensure that this was not a trap. But he observed that he was alone on his side of the street. Still, he gripped his blade and whispered a brief quote from the Bible to give him strength and courage.

"...*be strong in the Lord, and in the strength of his might.*"

A simple set of words, but Franz von Karnstein did feel stronger.

"Should I be honored by your fear, my lord?"

The Satanist woman crossed the street and stopped several steps away from Franz. She was taller than he remembered, and dressed in the height of fashion. Her short-waisted dress was long, loose and made of shimmering silk. The effect was powerful, causing her to look nearly naked. Her blonde hair fell in curls across her forehead and ears, and the longer curls were pulled into a Psyche knot on the back of her head.

"No more than a serpent is when confronted by a man with a sword."

Karnstein's face was calm and cold. But there was fury in the tight coils of his sinews.

The Satanic priestess stared at him with open fury. She still looked lovely, but her rage was like a living force, rising from her and causing her to resemble one of the legendary war goddesses of days long past.

A heartbeat later, however, she resumed her sunny smile, causing those pedestrians in the street to stare at her with open admiration.

"Well-spoken, Baron Karnstein. I heard you were... unusual. A Karnstein who destroys vampires, serves the false God, and rejected a spot in the Scholomance. Your family, dead and undead, are disgusted by your betrayal of your legacy."

Karnstein guffawed and shook his head.

"You say that as if it were an insult. I hope you speak the truth for the first time in your short unholy life, witch. To learn that the monsters I descend from consider me an aberration brings joy to my heart."

"Young? You are easily taken by a pretty exterior, priest. I am no callow girl, impressed by the lies of a dark priest. I was old when your people were tribal warlords, dancing upon the entrails of their enemies."

The lovely woman's words were mocking, but they held an odd ring of truth. Karnstein nodded and frowned:

"Possibly so, possibly not. I have no notion of your dark designs. You are no vampire, that much I see from the start. You never attended the Scholomance, the Deep School, the Domdaniel, or the Devil's Dungeon Caves in Spain."

The attractive woman was visibly nonplussed by his knowledge. She stepped back slightly and her eyes narrowed.

"What are you, little Karnstein? No being of your age should know of such places. Not unless they attended as a student in all."

"Incorrect. I am something different. And I will bring about the destruction of many, if not all, of such hell-born academies of evil. If you are as ancient as you claim, be afraid. The time of your kind is passing."

Karnstein was once again the cold inquisitor, the exorcist who confronted children of the night without a trace of fear.

The woman smiled again, her tiny pale teeth causing the rosy bloom to her cheeks to look even darker.

"One man against the schools of the Lightbearer? You must be mad."

Karnstein shrugged, looking unconcerned.

"I quote this to you in response, *Submit yourselves therefore to God. Resist the devil, and he will flee from you. Book of James* 4:7. My path is clear."

"You like to quote the Bible, priest. Then I shall throw one back in your smug face. *Psalm* 106:37-38 *They sacrificed their sons and their daughters to the demons; they poured out innocent blood, the blood of their sons and daughters, whom they sacrificed to the idols of Canaan, and the land was polluted with blood.* That is this world. A land polluted by blood and death. War appears in every corner of the Earth. The Dark One will return."

"If he does, I'll send him back to the lake of fire and brimstone. Mankind was created in the Lord's image. But we do not possess his perfection. War and greed will continue to exist. But that does not give us the right

247

to renounce His name. Oh, and I am no priest. I am an exorcist. You saw that when I sent your demon back to Sheol."

Karnstein appeared taller and more significant as he discussed his life's quest. The woman giggled and covered her mouth with a slim, gloved hand.

"You believe you can defy the will of Lucifer? You must be mad."

"Possibly. It matters not. I did prove I can defy your demonic slaves. That alone is why you are speaking to me with such care, and in the view of the public. I cannot attack you. This time."

Karnstein still held the hilt of his sword, but he knew to draw the weapon would be pure folly. The passers-by would leap upon him and turn him into the authorities. And the pretty Satanist would play the victim. A few tears and some sad looks, and Franz von Karnstein would be held in a jail cell until he was expelled when the Pope returned to the Papal States.

Studying him for a moment, she nodded once.

"I will have you one day, exorcist. You will father my latest child. I last mated with your kind a century ago. My son was terrible, a monster who destroyed the lives of many humans. But it was prophesized that my next offspring would be a beast who would serve the King of Earth when he casts forth the shackles of light."

Now it was Karnstein's turn to laugh. Throwing back his head, he roared and wept, nearly falling over in his mirth.

"You think… you believe you… me… oh, Lord, protect me, I may expire…"

The female Satanist watched the sniggering Austrian, trying to maintain her dignity. But she did flush red when the giggles continued for several minutes.

"You doubt my pledge?"

Karnstein suddenly stopped cackling, his face freezing. His pale eyes were suddenly filled with rage.

"You believe I would soil myself with the Devil's handmaiden? Your physical charms remind me of my ancestor, Mircalla. I ended her undead existence when I was a mere child. She was as lovely to the eye as yourself. And you both possess souls as black as the pits of perdition. Have me? I would sooner mate with a sewer rat."

Her eyes narrowed again, but she did not allow herself to lose her composure again.

"You believe that to be so? You will find that some things in this life are beyond your paltry control. No matter, I have business to be about. We attempted to locate the vampire and his servant, but he moves every few hours, and often in a pattern even we can't follow, or predict. But I can tell you this much, his werewolf is very dangerous."

"All cursed creatures are deadly."

Karnstein sensed an odd moment of sincerity in this very dangerous being. Odd, since lies were the favored tool of the demon worshipper. But she appeared truthful for the moment.

"True. But a *loup-garou* who's survived years? They are as dangerous as a vampire. They hide their evil beneath a mask of innocence."

The Satanist stepped slightly closer, her voice dropping as she spoke of such dark dealings.

"Explain your words, if you please," said Karnstein.

He didn't step back, but his hand did tighten on his sword just a bit.

"As you wish," she replied, smiling again, looking very pretty. "A were-creature is all appetite and little control. They are destroyed in time because they lack the ability to stop feeding upon the living. In particular, they crave the organs within a human body."

"This much I know. I've destroyed such monsters."

Karnstein frowned and fought the urge to retreat again.

"I have no doubt. You have the appearance of one who enjoys burning an innocent woman or three. No matter. If a *loup-garou* or this type survives, it learns to govern its need for flesh. It feeds less often and can cease when ordered to do so by its master. This one, in particular, is terrible. Ten of my people died at its hands."

The Satanist didn't sound unduly concerned about the death of her fellow cultists.

"I will pray for their souls."

Karnstein was at a loss for anything else to say in response. The death of any living being was meant to be a loss for mankind, but he had difficulty feeling sympathy for a devil-worshipper who died beneath the claws of a werewolf. A failing of character, at least in his mind. But the statement did grant him a moment to consider a possibly important point.

"Why is this one so dangerous? It is a giant or some such?"

The woman shook her head and lowered her voice.

"The opposite. A child—or at least the semblance of a small child."

Karnstein looked as if he'd been slapped.

"A child? No, that can't be!"

The woman shook her head.

"It is not. The form is that of a child, but that is merely an illusion. A false form the creature uses. According to the Black Bible, a werewolf gains the power to transform into younger or older versions of their human shape. The true shape of this werewolf is a woman with brown hair and a pretty face. She spoke like one born to luxury, but she prefers to remain in the form of a child because it causes people to overlook or underestimate her."

Karnstein nodded slowly, accepting the truth of her words. It would not make the search for the vampire any easier, but any information could help. Just as important was the slip of the tongue this supposedly ancient woman made a moment earlier. The revelation that the Black Bible, the Satanic Codex, was an existing tome. This knowledge was essential for the future battle between light and dark. But he would not tell this evil being that.

The woman stepped back and waved her hand in a shooing motion.

"That is all we can tell you. For now, we will leave you to your battle. But the day will come when I will have you. And our child will shake the very heavens."

Karnstein shook his head. He didn't bother to refute her nonsensical fantasies. It was a waste of time debating with those pledged to the Prince of Lies. Instead, he would follow Séverin's suggestions. He would bathe and change his clothes. Then return to the training academy and try and discover a strategy in defeating the vampire and his pet werewolf.

CHAPTER XXXII

Paris, October 1795

"You must be mad, but I enjoy killing fools," said the Marquis de Saint-Evremonde. "I shall feed upon you and join my wolves as they consume your republican compatriots. But first I shall revel in your shrieks of agony."

The ancient vampire stepped forward and began attacking with his gold-encrusted saber. He missed the swords of his time. The long, sharp, steel blades were true man-killers. Many a head had fallen from one swing of his mighty arm. But to carry such a blade would be outlandish. No man carried such a blade these days, even those who loved the ancient ways. A heavy cavalry saber was close enough. Unlike the light version of the sword, this blade was straight and possessed some weight. And it was the mark of a nobleman of this era to beautify the hilt with gold filigree. The weapon would serve, but would never be as pleasurable as a sword in Saint-Evremonde's mind.

Séverin parried each attack, moving almost as fast as the undead creature. He was careful to only attack in small ways, forcing the Marquis to parry the occasional slice towards his face or arms. The swordmaster was careful to prevent the ancient vampire from approaching too close. This creature was far stronger than a mortal man. To be caught in such a monster's grasp would result in Séverin's being torn to pieces.

"That is your best?" jeered the Marquis. "This is what you thought would destroy me? I was killing nobles and peasants alike since mighty and beloved Philippe the Fair sat upon the throne. You are like an insect to me. A flea to be crushed beneath my heel."

Saint-Evremonde smiled as he taunted Séverin. His teeth were massive, yet his voice, surprisingly clear. Odd, but vampires did not operate under natural laws.

"Philippe the Fair?" replied Séverin. "Oh, yes. The king who bankrupted France. Whose sly, idiotic ways lead to the Hundred-Year war. One of France's greatest failures. Proof that no man is better than another."

Séverin continued to carefully parry each attack by the vampire. This was not easy. The creature was superhumanly fast, and he wielded a heavy cavalry sword. Were Séverin to block the blade incorrectly, disaster would follow. His rapier would shatter and he would soon be killed by this creature.

"Die! Die! Die!" Saint-Evremonde screamed and began swinging wildly towards Séverin's face, neck and heart.

His speed was incredible, the sword moving with the speed and power of a bolt of lightning, but his technique suffered. His attacks were wild, reckless and unskilled. All power and speed, but no actual technique. Perfect.

They danced back and forth, Séverin always leading Saint-Evremonde further away from the starting point of their duel. He had a very definite plan in mind and needed to keep the vampire engaged and enraged.

"Your precious Philippe is buried at the Basilica of St Denis?" said the swordmaster. "After we've destroyed all the Royalists, we'll dig him and the other royal scoundrels up; then we can use Madam Guillotine upon their bones and toss their remains into the Seine."

Of course, Séverin would never commit such blasphemy upon the dead, no matter what his political beliefs were, but it appeared that Saint-Evremonde was easily goaded by such ridiculous statements.

Grost had once instructed him as they'd left with Kronos to battle a former warlord turned vampire coven leader:

"Ancient vampires are dangerous monsters, young man, but their minds are trapped in a prison of their own making. They are unable to think of a world beyond the one which they experienced while living. Thieves steal more, but receive no joy. Seducers fall in love, but they bring about untimely deaths to their beloved of the moment. Breaking the cycle sends them into a rage, a tantrum if you will."

And, as was to be expected; Saint-Evremonde lost all semblances of control and humanity. His skin turned pale green, his eye pupil-less yellow and a stench of mold and graveyard dirt filled the air. This was the beast within, the true monster beneath the Marquis' handsome façade. Saint-Evremonde was a monster, an undead leech sucking the lifeblood of humanity to maintain his extended existence.

His assaults were even wilder, more crazed. The threat to Philippe's corpse had awakened the demon within. There was a wrongness to the very existence of a vampire. They were beings from the worst nightmare of mankind's subconscious. Their destruction was a mercy in a very real sense. The vampire was a being whose denial of the natural order led to their extended existence, all at the expense of the lives of the living.

Then, the sounds of thunder filled the air. Napoleon's mighty cannons were firing, and the first screams and shrieks of agony and death resounded. Though terrible monsters, the *loups-garous* were little threat to the citizen soldiers. The great General Bonaparte fired upon them with grapeshot, tearing them to pieces with relative ease. The hundreds of yards the beasts had to cross was a zone of death and destruction. But for them, not for the humans inside the Tuileries.

"My hunting hounds! What is happening?" Saint-Evremonde screamed.

He tried to turn away, but Séverin stopped him with a harsh slice across his twisted visage. The ancient vampire shrieked and stepped back. His face was sliced open and black blood seeped slowly from the already closing wound.

"I expect the soldiers protecting the Convention are firing cannons upon your werewolves," said Séverin. "They are following your last orders. To charge in and destroy the humans inside the building. But their mindless charge will fail. They won't even get within sight of the guns shredding their monstrous bodies."

Séverin did not hide the triumph in his tone of voice. The arrogance of this vampire was proving his undoing. A victory for mankind, as well as the hopes of a better future for France.

"You! You did this! I will destroy you and save my wolves for later!" Saint-Evremonde snarled, swinging his sword at Séverin's neck.

The swordmaster batted the slicing blade aside and stabbed the vampire's arm with his rapier. Saint-Evremonde yelped and his sword fell from his grasp. The weapon fell to the ground and bounced off a rock.

Séverin placed one boot upon the sword and shook his head.

"Kill me? No, Monsieur le Marquis. You haven't the skill. For all your extended life, you possess the sword skills of a callow youth. An elderly master of arms from the Directory could slice you to pieces. Which I shall do now."

But Saint-Evremonde reacted differently than Séverin expected. He turned and fled. The ancient vampire ran nearly as fast as a horse and was out-of-sight in seconds. He ran towards the sounds of guns, determined to save his slaves.

"Stop, stop, my hounds!"

His voice was lost in the howls and shrieks of the werewolves as the tiny lead slugs ripped through their bestial forms. Few were left, yet onward they ran. Or stumbled. Or crawled. The last command in their limited minds kept them moving towards their target.

Séverin stopped, recognizing the danger. Though a trained swordmaster, and expert in weapons and close quarter combat, he was still just a man. The blast of a cannon could destroy him with the same apparent ease at it was the *loups-garous*.

The cannons kept firing; long tongues of flame extending towards the *loups-garous* and the furiously running vampire. Clouds of choking, stinking smoke filled the air, obscuring all sight or the werewolves or Saint-Evremonde.

The last sight Séverin caught of the ancient vampire was his being thrown through the air, then falling back to the earth unmoving.

And that was the first battle on 13 Vendémiaire, better known to the world as October 5, 1795. Napoleon Bonaparte led the defense of the Convention, defeating the human Royalist forces hours later. His cannons destroyed them, just as easily as they had Saint-Evremonde's creatures, breaking the back of their attempt to return to power.

Napoleon became a national hero and was immediately promoted to Division General. Joachim Murat also received a promotion, to Colonel, and became his general's favorite cavalry officer. Murat later married his patron's sister, Caroline Bonaparte.

Saint-Evremonde's body was not found among the dead.

CHAPTER XXXIII

Paris, November 1804

Franz von Karnstein found Jean-Pierre Séverin back at the training hall. He was on his hands and knees, a cloth in hand, scrubbing the floor. A battered wooden bucket was at his side and the scent of vinegar filled the air, a pungent but not unpleasant odor.

"May I assist?" asked Karnstein, looking for a second cloth, but not finding any in sight.

"I'm nearly done," replied Séverin. "You have the look of a man with much to say."

The Morgue Director tossed the cloth into the bucket and stood up. He opened the window, looked below and tipped the contents into a back alley. The liquid fell upon a patch of filth, cleansing the passageway.

"I do," replied the young exorcist. "I was met by the woman—the one from the Satanic ceremony. She stated the vampire moves regularly and cannot be tracked. But she also told me of his werewolf servant. The creature is female and able to control her need to feed. And can transform her shape into a young or older version of herself."

Karnstein didn't discuss her statements regarding using him to father her children. That nonsense was mere lies and temptations of a fallen creature. Part of him was fearful at the confidence within that woman. He believed her tale, that she was an ancient being who once birthed a monster. Which was why her self-assurance that she would have him and use him to create an even greater monster was frightening.

Séverin deposited the bucket back inside a cabinet and shook his head.

"An elder werewolf? They are as lethal as a vampire. And clever. We will need to find another means of stopping Saint-Evremonde's plans."

"You've faced such beasts in the past?" asked Karnstein.

He'd never heard of a werewolf that could control their transformations. All his readings stated that such monsters were unable to hide the beasts which consumed their soul.

"Only once. A man at the court of the Grand Turk. He was the son of a powerful official. His father hid him away in the desert for years. When he returned, the animal remained hidden, but he still craved flesh and blood. Secretly, he killed and consumed beggars in the streets. My teacher and I forced him to the surface. The Sultan and his Vizier gifted us much, and the poor man was executed secretly. Always remember, Baron, a werewolf is a victim as well as a monster. Many are infected against their will. Some by magic, others by the bite of another shifter. Their stories are always very sad."

Séverin shook his head. Just like his battle with Lisebette, he acted against the *loups-garous* and their kind for the purpose of saving many lives in the future. But part of him wished there was an alternative path.

Karnstein tried to keep his thoughts upon the current battle. The philosophy of the werewolf was a discussion for another day. One less tense and terrible.

"Does this demon possess any enemies in Paris? The Pope, for instance? It is rare that His Holiness is away from the Papal States."

"Yes, myself and... Oh, Holy Mother! I have been such a fool! The last time this creature acted was on 13 Vendémiaire!" said Séverin, slapping his forehead, amazed that he could have been so blind.

"You must explain further. I fail to understand your meaning."

Karnstein sensed that Séverin knew the plans of the vampire, but he did not follow the older man's words and meaning.

"That is the French Revolutionary Calendar," Séverin explained. "On October 5, 1795 the Marquis de Saint-Evremonde and approximately one hundred *loups-garous* charged the Palais des Tuileries, home of the Convention. They were met by Brigadier-General Napoleon Bonaparte, who commanded the defenses of the city. He and his men destroyed the monsters. The General later defeated the Royalist army with his small force and many cannons."

The Morgue Director led Karnstein back into the library.

"In a few short days, Napoleon will be crowned Emperor by His Holiness, the Pope" considered the exorcist. "Two of the most important men in the world..."

Karnstein dropped into one of the stark wooden chairs in the library.

"Yes, but both men are under constant guard" said Séverin. "To attempt to attack them both would be madness."

The Morgue Director dropped in an opposite seat and placed a hand on his chin.

"As insane as sending a horde of shape-shifting monsters sent to destroy soldiers and politicians?" said Karnstein. "I believe we can dispense with thoughts of mindful action."

Karnstein watched his new teacher, wondering what the man was thinking. Séverin was applying the same method of thinking he had learned over the years. Using the evidence of Saint-Evremonde's actions, he attempted to discover the reasoning behind the ancient vampire's actions. This was the only means they had to act, and possibly save the life of the soon-to-be Emperor of France.

The first detail to consider was that Saint-Evremonde moved about Paris, never settling. That showed greater foresight than years before. Then, he had arrogantly based himself among the Royalist rebels and transformed them into his slaves. This time, his behavior demonstrated cautious circumspection. A significant alteration.

Second was the werewolf. Instead of an army of monsters, he controlled only one. And this *loup-garou* could completely control its change and the burning hunger that controlled all such beasts. Therefore, he must have spent years training this creature, teaching it the method of total body transformation. Karnstein's statements proved that much. A werewolf required years to fight their appetite for living flesh. Once tamed, the ability to transform into other versions of their human form slowly emerged.

Since Saint-Evremonde had a more complex plan in mind, he was not attempting a simple assault. He and his creature planned on killing Napoleon at his most vulnerable moment. Though the Emperor was not above fanciful affairs of the heart, this would not be one of those occasions. He was about to be crowned and start a new dynasty. One with no connection to the former rulers of this land. Seduction would not be attempted. Even an ancient being like Saint-Evremonde would see such an act as ridiculous with no chance of succeeding.

Nor would the assassination occur in one of the many grand balls celebrating Napoleon's impending coronation. The number of dignitaries and their guards would make such an attack a waste of time. A singular werewolf, even with the help of a vampire, would be destroyed by the sheer volume of swords and guns in such a location. In truth, many men present wearing swords had little conception of how to even hold such weapons, but if enough hacked away, the werewolf would fall. No, the moment of the attack would be more precisely timed. A moment when Napoleon's protection would be absent.

"The coronation itself," whispered Séverin.

He was surprised to see that the room was dark and Karnstein was not present. Gazing at the clock above the mantle, he realized that ten hours passed since he had last spoken. That had no occurred since his wife's untimely passing. In truth, Séverin thought that this form of total concentration had been lost to him due to grief. There was some comfort in the knowledge that one of his skills was still residing within his psyche.

No matter. He would sleep and meet with Karnstein the next day. They needed to save Napoleon at his coronation!

CHAPTER XXXIV

Paris, November 1804

The Marquis de Saint-Evremonde listened as his pet consumed her feast in the next room. A family of four. Their house was far enough from the main streets to be private, yet close enough to the center of Paris. A good location for the night. And none would even find the bones of the family. The beast was hungry and this would be her last feeding until she consumed the heart of the usurper, Napoleon Bonaparte.

Her name was Anna and she was his devoted slave. She was the daughter of a farmer, residing outside Paris. Nine years earlier, having barely survived his failure to destroy the Convention, he had stumbled into her barn and slept. This had happened two days after the doomed attack on the Palais des Tuileries, Saint-Evremonde, having hidden in the sewers, had been a wounded, weakened creature. He had survived on rats, their scant life force providing him with just enough sustenance to continue his undead existence.

This had been far from the first-time Saint-Evremonde had received an injury in battle. He had walked a path of violence throughout the ages, and there always had been men and women who had sought his death. Such as the fifteen arrows that had struck him fighting the English at Agincourt. Or the knife in the back he had always blamed on that bitch, Catherine de Medicis. There had been so many other blows. But in every situation, the Marquis had managed to survive.

However, the cannon blast brought about by Jean-Pierre Séverin and Napoleon Bonaparte had nearly been his final death. The tiny shards of lead had ripped through his arms, legs, and torso. Had he been conscious throughout, realizing the damage being wrought and knowing full well that more would follow. Saint-Evremonde's body had been aflame; an agony, greater than any he had felt over the centuries had filled his mind. He had wanted to scream, to shriek as the pain had overwhelmed his whole body, but he knew better. To embrace the pain would have meant his end.

For above all else, the Marquis de Saint-Evremonde was a survivor. He held his existence as more important than any other life on Earth. And he, a nobleman, would not allow himself to be killed by some peasants masquerading as soldiers. He had crawled away, at a rate of speed that would have been the envy of any rat or serpent, into the sewers. There, he had remained for two weeks, slinking out of the stinking tunnels, a nearly mindless creature craving blood. He had fed upon three random people, their faces a blur, before hiding on a cart and leaving the city.

The rest of the trip had been a hazy nightmare, the time he had spent traveling lost in memory. How he had reached that was still a mystery. But the Marquis had woken up with Anna leaning over his body. For the first time, he had felt able to think, to plan. His body had healed, except for a scar across his face. That had been a gift from that sneering swordmaster, Jean-Pierre Séverin., a low-class swine whom he would enjoy torturing to death.

There, in that barn, on a bright winter morning, a brown-haired young woman had studied him with curious, frightened eyes. She had been dressed in a shapeless sack of a gown, appearing dirty and disheveled. Her eyes were dark and wide and she had been trembling like a deer before a wolf. She had looked back over her shoulder, her expression filled with fear.

"Monsieur! You must flee! My father is coming and he will be angry! He will kill you!" she had whispered, flinching as the door to the barn had flown open.

"Who are you talking to, girl? I told you to get my strap... Who in the name of our savior, are you? A tramp looking to steal from a poor farmer?"

The man stepping into the barn had been about the girl's height, but with broader shoulders. He had possessed a thick brown beard, with food visible in the tangles of his fur-like hair. His clothes had been slovenly, old and ill-fitting. In his hand, he had carried a jug of cheap liquor, the scent of which had filled the air with pungent fumes.

"Ah! You must be one of those Royalists on the run!" he had uttered. "Well, my friend, we'll hand you to the guards for a nice reward. Stand still and I'll tie you up. Girl, get the rope. Now!"

He had shoved the young woman with a rough slap. The girl had stumbled towards the wall, reaching towards a heavy cord with a trembling hand.

"Peasant," had growled Saint-Evremonde, stepping forward and lifting the man off the ground by his throat.

The farmer had struggled weakly in the vampire's grasp, unable to break the iron grip.

"Oh, my..."

The girl had dropped the rope and had stared at Saint-Evremonde. She hadn't moved to help her parent.

Saint-Evremonde knew her type. Her progenitors had had a child or three, to turn into virtual slaves. Female children were especially abused. And they were the easiest to manipulate. His plan, which he had made in the sewers, could now unfold. The girl didn't love her parent and she might be happier under his control.

"What is your name, child?" he had asked the girl.

Saint-Evremonde had purposefully ignored the struggling farmer and focused all his attention upon the young woman. With some cleaning, she might prove acceptable. Possibly even pretty.

The girl had looked fearfully at her father, and then had answered in a whisper:

"Anna. Anna Faure."

Saint-Evremonde had bowed slightly and smiled:

"And your father? What's his name?" he had asked.

"Stephan."

The girl's voice was a little louder now. And she wasn't watching her father anymore.

"He treats you like a slave. Beats you. Forces himself upon you when he drinks."

Saint-Evremonde had not asked; he knew this to be so from one look at the pair. The man was a bully. His wife had either deserted him, or died. He had been left alone with their daughter, who had become his servant, cook, farming hand, and, almost definitely, bed mate. But Stephan Faure would despise his lusts afterward, and vent his fury upon young Anna. Then he would drink even more and the cycle would continue until one of them died.

Despite his disgust at such filth, Saint-Evremonde knew that this sequence of events was not limited to their class. Noblemen were just as capable of behaving in a similar manner. And this was not limited to those whose minds still resided in the past. These actions were based in the sins of mankind. Greed, wrath, lust, and pride caused such men to behave as little more than animals.

Anna had nodded, blushing furiously.

"He says... I look like my mother... then he... he..."

Raising a hand to stop her flow of word, Saint-Evremonde had nodded and looked suitably sad. In truth, he hadn't cared in the slightest. Her tale of woe had been unimportant noise. It was what she'd represented to his future that had made her into something useful.

"Do you wish to escape him? To make him pay for all your hurts? And never have another person treat you poorly again?" he had asked, speaking in a low voice, full of seduction.

Anna had held a hand to her face. She had looked frightened, but a new light had entered her eyes.

"I'm just a girl. Father says..."

"He lies. He wants you to stay his weak slave. You can be strong and wear beautiful clothing. And you will never cook or clean again."

Saint-Evremonde had slowly extended his free hand, his smile still bright.

Anna had lifted one of her hands, but had stopped inches away from the vampire's fist.

"You can do this for me?" she had questioned. "Why?"

"Because it is within my power. And also, because you deserve a better life."

The first was truth, the second a lie, but an effective one. Saint-Evremonde had used it often over the centuries. Male or female, young or old. Every man, woman, or child who was not king or queen, believed they deserved a better life. It was an easy lever to get one's way.

Anna had hesitated at first; then, she had taken Saint-Evremonde's hand and looked at her barely moving father with narrowed eyes...

Hours later, Stephan Faure would become her first meal. He was followed by two neighbors, a passing tinker, and a drunken whore stumbling down the lane towards her next customer.

Then, the real work had begun. Training Anna to hide the beast within. Teaching her to control the cravings for flesh. And to speak again, wear clothing, and behave like a human again. No simple mission.

In truth, the first step had been to defeat her in battle. The first night, he had pinned her to the ground and held his fangs against her exposed neck. She had struggled, but eventually had grown limp, signifying submission. Anna had never viewed him as food again. And like her lupine relatives, she had treated him as her pack leader. Saint-Evremonde's word was her command.

Three years of patience had been required to achieve some control. They had moved constantly, staying away from large cities. Travelers and merchants had been the easiest to consume; they were rarely missed and their deaths were always blamed on local bandits. But then the day had come where Anna hadn't moaned for food.

"May I have some water?" she had asked.

Her voice had been just as tentative as that fateful day in the barn. But it was the first sentence she had spoken in years.

Saint-Evremonde had smiled at his servant. Their true work could now begin. Training Anna to behave as a human and comprehend her true powers. Those days had been difficult for them both. But they had achieved much and were ready one year earlier than he had antici-pated.

Now, Anna could dress however the opportunity required. She could play the part of a *grande dame*, a peasant, a slattern, a child, or a crone. She was a protean being, her only thought pleasing his every need. Though a slave once again, she resided in a gilded cage and pos-sessed powers beyond the dreams of man. To Anna, her life was far better under the control of the Marquis de Saint-Evremonde.

Revenge had burned within Saint-Evremonde's breast all those years, a living force within his black heart. He knew that the death of Jean-Pierre Séverin and Napoleon Bonaparte would not be enough to quench that thirst. Their deaths would only be mildly satisfying at best. After all, they had thwarted his will, killed his wolves, and saved the Republic from the proper rulers of France.

That last part was the most galling. Years after the battle, the Republic was stronger than before. And worse of all, Napoleon now ruled the country under the ludi-crous title, "First Citizen"! Napoleon Bonaparte, a Cor-sican peasant, ruled the same country which had once been under Philippe the Fair. Nothing could be more offensive. Just thinking about it such caused Saint-Evremonde to burn with barely contained rage.

Therefore, their deaths had to be not only ignoble, but horrific. The answer had come in a heaven-sent piece of news. Napoleon, like all social climbers, was not sat-isfied using a title once reserved for legendary Roman politicians. No, this disgusting Corsican pig farmer had decided to have himself crowned Emperor. Saint-Evremonde wasn't sure that Napoleon had been an actual swine herder, but in his mind, all such fellows possessed that title.

That had given the Marquis a simple idea. If his servant were to kill the newly-crowned Emperor, as well as the Pope and other random dignitaries, the world would be tossed into chaos. Napoleon's name would become a byword for a person cursed. This was beautiful, as if his beloved Philippe had assisted him in his machinations.

Placing Anna inside Notre-Dame wasn't too difficult. The traditions of coronation, even for parvenus like Napoleon, had remained essentially the same. It had merely taken a bit of work, of planning, and one death. The body had been consumed by Anna and all was in readiness.

The one failure of his plan, so far, had been Séverin. Saint-Evremonde wished to humiliate the man, destroy him in the same manner as Napoleon, but the nosy little creature was too much of a danger. His blade had permanently disfigured Saint-Evremonde's noble profile. Finding out that the peasant swordsman was investigating the recent, suspicious deaths in Paris was too much of a danger. The usurper's death was more important. Hence, the step of hiring the female assassin. No doubt she would succeed and all would be well.

"Master?" said Anna, walking into the room.

She was clean, but smelled of blood and fresh meat.

"Is it time?" she asked.

"Yes, my pet," he replied. "Go along and change your shape and your clothes. You must hide among the humans. Do you remember when to strike?"

Saint-Evremonde stroked her short brown hair.

"Yes, master," she answered, obediently. "Just when the crown is placed upon the usurper's head. Kill him. Then, the Pope. Then, any others nearby."

"Very good! That is correct," said Saint-Evremonde, smiling, looking off into the distance.

The end of the Republic, or whatever the usurper called his perverted version of France, would take place in two days hence. It would be a glorious event—a return to the natural order of the world.

And the Marquis de Saint-Evremonde would at last be the master of all.

CHAPTER XXXV

Paris, December 1st, 1804

Séverin rose shortly after dawn. He was unsurprised that Karnstein was already up and returning from Lauds services. The young exorcist bowed briefly and, without a word, joined the elder swordmaster in breaking his fast. The Austrian nobleman was a serious soul, incapable of thinking past his quest. He would need to learn the pleasures the world had to offer. Otherwise, he might start looking for evil where it did not exist.

"My meditations revealed to me the answer we'd been missing," said Séverin. "The vampire and his werewolf minion's main purpose. Why they are in Paris at this time."

Séverin glanced at the chest he kept the sacred blade.

"Please explain," said Karnstein, remaining inscrutable as he chewed on a piece of cheese

Séverin ticked off his fingers as he made each point:

"First, this vampire hates the Republic. Second, nine years earlier, his plans were spoiled by myself and then-General Bonaparte. Third, he worships the memory of the ancient kings. He referred to Philippe the Fair as his 'beloved Philippe.'"

"I assume that was not a common address of that monarch?' said Karnstein without a note of irony.

"Not in the least," replied Séverin, shaking his head. "He was called the Fair by some. He was a handsome man, but also known as the Iron King because he was such a powerful ruler. Most curse his memory today. He destroyed the Knights Templar for his own personal gain. Saint-Evremonde spoke as a man speaking of his love of God. He visibly worshipped him."

Karnstein's face creased with disgust.

"Thou shalt have no other gods before me."

"Just so. Many men mistake temporal power for absolute power. This vampire is one of them. And, like many of his undead kind, he is incapable of thinking beyond his own past. To him, Philippe was all that was good and right in the world. History disputes his claims, but that is the failing of vampires. Often, they are lost in the past, incapable of changing with the times."

"This much, I am aware," said Karnstein, looking away.

The memories flooded back upon him, Mircalla. His mother. And the others that had followed since that day. It was painful to remember.

"My apologies from bringing up a difficult subject. Shall I go on?" asked Séverin.

Seeing the phlegmatic nod from the exorcist, he continued:

"Third, Napoleon is about to take the throne of France. A Corsican with no connection to the blood of Charles Martel or the ancient kings. This would offend our undead noble."

Karnstein followed the swordsmaster's reasoning and slapped his hands together:

"The coronation!" he exclaimed.

"Correct. If he can get his werewolf inside Notre-Dame cathedral, I doubt the Emperor will survive. Possibly the Pope and others as well might not either."

"It would be a slaughter, but he cannot get her near. The Pope possesses no nuns in attendance. Nor would the Cardinals or the incoming Emperor. The Empress' ladies are all well-known—unless this werewolf can change their face as well?"

Karnstein said a brief prayer, hoping that his last thought was incorrect.

"Not even an ancient *loup-garou* possesses such power," said Séverin. "They are young or old versions of themselves, and their beast. Transformation into others is said to exist in other beings, but not were-beasts."

"Praise the Almighty for that small favor," said the exorcist. "Still, this is a bizarre conundrum. Female nobles are all known and listed. Servants will not be permitted within the cathedral or the grand balls. I fail to see how this Saint-Evremonde can place his werewolf within Notre Dame. The gendarmes, and the Pope's Swiss Guard, regularly search the church. They are still on guard. Not even a mouse could sneak inside."

Karnstein knew this personally, having witnessed the many seen, and unseen, guards within the cathedral.

"Children," said Séverin, ticking off his final point. "Most are unseen, ignored and forgotten by soldiers. They are not viewed as a threat. But the Satanist female articulated to us that Saint-Evremonde's servant can transmute into a younger age."

"I see one difficulty. No girl child will be near the ceremony. The closest might be the children of noble guests, but I doubt one of them is serving a vampire."

Karnstein spotted a gleam in Séverin's eye. The older man was a step ahead of him—again.

"You forget the choir" said the Morgue Director. "Children singing to the Lord. How many will be present—three hundred? More?"

Séverin saw the shock in Karnstein's face. The young Austrian still had much to learn.

"Four hundred, I think, though none are females. All choir boys are male children."

Karnstein liked to listen to the singing of choirs. He himself could not carry a tune or play any musical instrument, but he did exalt those who did so excellently in the name of God.

Séverin rolled his eyes and waved a hand.

"Cut the hair of a young girl and dress her in boy's clothing. Few would bother looking beneath the robes to discover the truth."

Karnstein thought for a moment. Then, he nodded slowly:

"Agreed. But we have only two days. And to demand to see each child naked... I have doubts the church officials would believe our claims."

"Are you permitted within the cathedral before the ceremony? And during?" asked Séverin.

His plan hinged on this point. It would be difficult to complete it without Karnstein's presence.

"Yes. I am one His Holiness's staff. Are you invited?"

Karnstein knew that there was a connection between the Morgue Director and the Emperor, but the details were elusive in his mind.

"I am," replied Séverin.

"Excellent. We can then force this werewolf out in the pen and follow it back to her master."

"Yes. I'm certain Saint-Evremonde will be nearby. He would not wish to miss the shrieks of fear and pain for the world. That, as much as blood, is his sustenance. Come, my friend, we have preparations to make before the ceremony."

Séverin stood up and reached for his cloak.

"Where are we going?" asked Karnstein.

He'd risen up and wrapped himself in his cloak as well.

"First, to a pharmacist shop I patronize. The owner keeps certain items always in stock. Then, to a coffin maker I befriended some years ago."

Séverin lead them out into the growing sunlight, his stride long and fast.

"Pharmacist? Coffin maker? Monsieur Séverin, what are you planning?" asked Karnstein, trotting to catch up to the tall swordmaster.

"Follow and observe, Baron. You will not be sorry," answered Séverin called as they headed down the street.

CHAPTER XXXVI

Paris, 2 December 1804

"This is perfection," Franz von Karnstein whispered to himself as he gazed upon the interior of Notre-Dame.

The coronation procession would start within the an hour and he stood inside the cathedral. As one of the lesser orders, he was not expected to be with the Pope and his party. They would be led by a bishop carrying a crucifix while riding a mule. Pope Pius IV would enter first and take his place upon a throne near the high altar. Then, the Emperor and Empress and their attendants would follow and take their places.

The guests would soon be allowed to enter, but Karnstein wished to take one final moment to look at the ancient church in all its glory. Well placed lights illuminated the vaulted arches and the stained glass threw a heavenly kaleidoscope of colors across the marble floor. It was a scene of perfect serenity, soon to be broken by the masses of people entering to witness the ceremony.

Upon the altar sat the so-called "Crown of Charlemagne." The title was granted to the item out of respect, but not by history. The original ancient crown of the Kings of France had long been destroyed. The revolutionaries of the past days had seized the regalia and smashed the original. The new one looked ancient, but had been newly fashioned on the orders of the Emperor. The scepter and sword, however, were original, having belonged to Charles V and Philippe III respectively.

There was a majesty to these items, but Franz von Karnstein was unmoved. Perhaps it was because of his devotion to battling the forces of darkness, but in his mind, a sword was merely a weapon, and a scepter an archaic instrument representing power. A gilded version of the former was a waste or wealth. And the life of royalty was an empty one. For all their power and wealth, kings lived like servants of the state from birth until death. Karnstein had once read that Louis XVI had loved carpentry and building locks. A weak, timid man, Louis may have been happier performing such work rather than attempting to rule a country. But he had been trapped in his role, a king who was ill-suited to his position.

All that was ultimately unimportant. Karnstein had a duty to perform. If Séverin was correct, he would reveal the identity of the werewolf and save both Napoleon and the Pope. He knew that many in Europe might be happier if both men were torn to pieces, but Franz von Karnstein possessed a complete lack of political interest. The Emperor's death this day would merely strengthen the forces of darkness. Chaos was one of the Devil's greatest weapons. Saint-Evremonde's plot would create havoc on an unprecedented level. Blood would flow in the streets of Paris—and beyond. Death would rule over all of France and the horror would spread throughout the continent.

The revealing of a werewolf, one who would have murdered both the Emperor of France and the Pope, would send a wave of hysteria throughout the world. The very suggestion of witchcraft had once caused entire countries to persecute women in masses, and men to a lesser degree. Cats had been slaughtered merely because a witch-hunter, who hated the poor creatures, had called them familiars of witches.

It would be a nightmare to imagine the insane responses from the weak-minded, fanatical, and torture-loving members of humanity should the truth of werewolves and vampires be revealed. Just the suggestion of that possible future enraged as well as frightened Karnstein. He would die before he let that happen. If that death occurred while protecting Napoleon, so be it. The needs of mankind came before the life of one man.

Turning his back upon the regalia, Karnstein strode to the rear of the cathedral. Climbing down a short flight of steps, he was greeted by the rising sounds of boys' voices. It was the choir, assembled and waiting to take their place in the ceremony. A sea of children's faces met his as he entered a grand, wide vault. The boys, all young, none even close to their teens, filled the chamber. The stood in twenty rows of twenty, each bedecked in new gowns of white. They all were excited, their hushed voices chattering like birds as they awaited the signal to silence. The choirmaster had trained them with the same rigor as the Imperial Hussars before a battle.

The choirmaster spotted Karnstein as he entered, and bowed in respect to one of the Pope's personal staff. The choirmaster was a tall, rakishly thin man with a small pointed beard and a fussy manner. His name was Fabien Fabre and, for all his over-elaborate behavior, he could make a room full of unruly children sound like the angels singing the praises of the Lord in heaven.

"Ah! Just on time, Baron," he said. "How refreshing. Shall we begin? I should think we must to ensure my young ones are in place and singing by the time the Emperor arrives!"

Fabre spoke in a falsetto voice. He had once been an opera singer, but for some unknown reason, had turned his back upon that world. Instead, he had taken priestly vows and chosen a different life. He was an officious man, but his skills made him a natural choice to become the new choirmaster. The previous one had been directly related to a noble family, but had been guillotined during the Terror.

"If you please," said Karnstein.

The Baron was dressed in a finer version of his usual black outfit. Though unadorned, his sword was new and polished. In a severe way, he looked every bit the nobleman.

"Boys! I will have silence!" said Fabre, clapping his hands four times and stepping on a small box.

His servant, an elderly but stolid man named Raoul, kept the wooden box nearby at all times for his master.

The boys, previously sounding like a flock of chattering birds, were brought to a hushed silence. This was accomplished with barely a murmur from their ranks. The occasional false cough and high-pitched titter emerged from the throng, but they were otherwise silent. Almost uniformly, they were smiling and full of cheerful anticipation. Soon, they would sing before the Emperor, the great general and First Consul, Napoleon Bonaparte. This would be a tale and an honor they would hold onto for the rest of their lives.

"We will file up the stairs by ranks," instructed Fabre. "You will walk with the dignity our choir demands! No shoving or fool's play. The Emperor and Pope will remember our perfection, not our mistakes. And, we have been granted a singular honor. A member of the Pope's personal staff brings to us a relic of great age and history. You will each step up and touch your head to it before stepping upon the stairs."

Fabre revealed a battered wooden cross. Holding it above his head for all to see, he waved the first rank of boys forward. Each touched their head to the crucifix and dutifully stepped out of sight.

The "great age and history" of the so-called "relic" was that of one day. Séverin, after stopping briefly at the pharmacy, had led Karnstein to a coffin-maker by the name of René, an elderly man with a skeletal body and a surprisingly young voice. René had greeted the swordmaster with great dignity, bowing deeply, his long white hair and beard nearly touching the floor.

"Jean-Pierre, Jean-Pierre, Jean-Pierre! Son of my oldest friend! It has been too long since you came and visited old René. Have you married again? You should! You are still a young man!"

René had moved slowly, but not as one infirmed. Just as a man who possessed no desire to rush for anything in life.

Séverin shook his head:

"Not I. May I present my new student, Franz von Karnstein, Baron Vordenburg and Karnstein of Styria. He and I require your skills."

Karnstein had exchanged bows with the old man. He did notice that his was not nearly as low as the one granted to Séverin.

"I am honored, Monsieur," he had said.

"Hmpf," had grunted René in return.

The coffin-maker had waved them towards a door in the rear of the shop.

"Come into my workshop and tell all. If it is within my feeble powers, I shall grant whatever you wish."

And grant he had. The old man had created this cross, his gnarled fists moving with the careful dignity of a concert violinist as he had shaped the difficult material. The result, handed to them within a few, short hours, had been a work of art. The crucifix resembled an ancient relic, one seized by the Crusaders while fighting in the Holy Lands. It was perfect. Séverin's plan had a chance of working.

Ten minutes later, while the eighth rank filed past, a brown-haired boy stopped before the cross. He sniffed once and appeared to visibly recoil. His dark eyes whirled about and then, he spotted Karnstein. The Austrian was an austere, imposing figure, resembling an ancient knight poised before battle. His pale eyes were like chips of ice and he was as still as one of the statues above their heads.

"I need to use the… umm..." said the boy, his voice a mere squeak as he stepped from line.

Fabre waved him away with a light swat to the back of his skull.

Karnstein smiled as the boy—who was in reality a werewolf woman—pushed through the crowd.

Séverin was a genius, as wise as a biblical prophet, he thought. By correctly surmising the location of the attack, he had been able to prepare a defense. Through his knowledge of the monster who would perform the evil act, the Morgue Director had designed a perfect response. Is they could cause the creature to flee, the only lives at risk would be Séverin's and Karnstein's, which was acceptable.

This defense was truly inspired. This one method of repelling a werewolf had been known to peasants for centuries. Turning it into an ancient-looking cross was something no one had ever considered before—except Maestro Jean-Pierre Séverin.

For the cross had been made of wolfsbane, a plant that was anathema to werewolves!

CHAPTER XXXVII

Paris, 2 December 1804

Anna fled from the scent of wolfsbane, her whole body shaking and quaking. She needed her master, she needed to scream, or transform, or run away into the dark tunnels. Though she was strong and powerful, dangerous, nearly unstoppable, the little plant made her sick. Its touch wracked her entire body with burning pain and made her feel weak and very small. She hated wolfsbane and was always grateful when her master burned the houses that kept it upon the doors and windows.

Running down three flights of steps and a narrow passage, she entered a small, narrow vault. The room was made of a gray stone with a light film of white dirt upon its floor. The walls were unadorned and the only way inside was through that single small arch. What this room had once been used for was a mystery. It was a small gap in the tunnel, easily overlooked and forgotten.

Saint-Evremonde paced across the floor, a small plume of dust filling the air by his feet. He spun around hearing her entry, his face full of questions and growing rage. He was anxious to learn of the death of Napoleon and the Pope. Anna's presence meant that his plan was now at risk.

"Wolfsbane, master!" she rushed to explain. "A German baron wanted us all to touch our heads to a cross made of wolfsbane. I smelled it! The German brought wolfsbane!"

Anna's words spilled out of her in a flood. She remained a small child, but her teeth and talons were lengthening as she cried out.

"I happen to be Austrian," said Karnstein, stepping into view.

He and Séverin stood together, the latter holding a cutlass and a smallsword in hand.

"Séverin!" snarled Saint-Evremonde.

His skin turned a pale grey and his teeth grew enormous in the split second it took to breathe that single word.

The Morgue Director gave the Marquis a small bow.

"In the flesh. Baron Karnstein, may I present to you Philippe de Marguetel de Saint-Denis, Marquis de Saint-Evremonde. He is a vampire of some age."

Karnstein suppressed a smile, seeing the rage growing hotter in the nobleman's yellow eyes. By introducing Karnstein first, Séverin had just implied that the lower-ranked Karnstein was, in fact, a highest ranking noble than the elder vampire. A subtle insult, but a telling one.

"You again!"growled the Marquis. "But you shall not stop me now. My servant and I shall kill you both, and then she shall destroy the usurper when he arrives. The Pope and many others shall fall beneath her wicked teeth and claws!"

Saint-Evremonde pulled out a pair of sabers and spun them with impressive dexterity.

"You failed in your last two attempts," replied Séverin, contemptuously. "You failed to kill me on 13 Vendémiaire. Then, no doubt out of great fear for your undead existence, you sent in an assassin. She failed, too. In truth, ancient monster, you've failed throughout the centuries. Nothing you attempted to protect or create has survived—not even your precious monarchy. Napoleon will, in a very short time, be consecrated as the man the people chose as the new ruler of France. Like your precious Philippe, you are little more than dust. Lost in the ages."

Séverin kept his swords pointed at Saint-Evremonde, hoping that his words would wound the evil undead creature. He was not, by nature, a cruel man, but insane vampires did cause him to occasionally demonstrate the darker aspect of his soul. A failing, but one he would continue to strive to control.

"Kill the German, my pet," Saint-Evremonde said in a voice that was a barely human croak—a whisper from a being of the deepest, darkest circle of Hell.

Anna snarled and her body grew enormous in less than a second. The clothing she wore and the white choir gown shredded in her explosive transformation, and a thick coat of grey and black fur covered her body. Her face changed last, an almost instantaneous explosion. Human to monstrous oversized lupine in a heartbeat.

The very vision was a nightmare to witness. Even the strongest minded man could have turned mad beholding the inhuman transformation of a young girl into an eight-foot-tall, fur-covered, massive-mawed mix of beast and human. The wicked claws in the creature's huge paw-like hands looked capable of rending a man limb-from-limb with little effort.

"I'm Austrian," repeated Karnstein, drawing a pair of pistols.

He fired both at the same instant. The deafening retort deafened all and the werewolf was tossed backwards. Anna struck the far wall, dark blood spurting from her chest. But she rose again...

"DALKHU TARU SERU..." Karnstein began to say, a silver white mist emerging from his body.

Anna stood and howled, then snarled and charged forward. Her massive talons would strike the exorcist's chest in seconds, and he would die...

Séverin didn't waste any more words on Saint-Evremonde. He merely leaped into the fray. His cutlass flashed out and met the vampire's saber. Sparks flashed across the chamber, illuminating the gloom and shadows. The Morgue Director parried the vampire's other blade, his very skill the only reason he was able to stop the lightning attack.

Saint-Evremonde responded in fury, attacking high and low, his razor-sharp blades whistling through the air as they attempted to slice Séverin open. The sabers flashed like bolts of lightning seeking to strike with lethal force. The vampire moved with a swiftness that was closer to an elemental assault than something even approaching human. Yet, for all his inhuman strength, uncanny speed, and furious attacks, he was still inadequate. His blows were easily met and only his undead powers had kept him from being slashed into pieces.

Séverin ducked a slice towards his neck and stabbed upward with his smallsword. Saint-Evremonde screamed and dropped his sword, jumping back and staring at his bleeding arm. The flesh around the cut was blackened and felt cold to the touch.

"Do you remember this blade, my lord?" chuckled the Morgue Director. "It gave you that scar across your ignoble, undead, horror of a face. And that was merely the tip. This blade was made of a cross. And it will mean the end of your bloodstained, undead, existence."

Séverin sliced the sword in the air and stepped forward. This sword, made by Grost decades earlier, had been the death of many an undead monster.

Meanwhile, the *loup-garou* snarled as its claws pierced Karnstein's chest. The enormous jaws snapped forward, reaching down towards the Austrian's head. In a heartbeat, the exorcist would be no more.

"...SERU ESERU ETUTU INA ETUTI ASBU DARISAM!"

Karnstein's voice was a snarl and the ancient eldritch sigil appeared between his body and that of the werewolf. The silver and white light flowed over the creature, pushing it backwards, and grew in intensity with each passing second.

The *loup-garou* froze and howled again. But this time, it was a mournful sound, the cry of a creature about to exit this world. It filled the air, rising and then falling, transforming into a very human moan of sadness and loss. The werewolf, once an abused woman named Anna Faure, shook and uttered a very human wail before toppling backwards. The inhuman shape was still present, but its mighty chest no longer rose and fell. The werewolf and the sad woman within were finally at peace.

Franz von Karnstein stared at the blood across his chest and suddenly felt cold. He dropped to one knee, numb and having difficulty breathing. The pain was rising, a living force overwhelming his body and mind.

"You shall not defeat me, peasant scum! I trained for years and I am your master!"

Saint-Evremonde's voice sounded even less human as he assaulted Séverin with his flashing blade. The speed and strength behind the attacks were formidable.

The Morgue Director was on the defensive, skirting across the floor and using both of his weapons to parry, block, and feint. One strike landing from the ancient vampire would be a death blow. But for all his insane attacks, the undead creature was still a lesser swordsman. He relied on his physical prowess, but had very little skill.

Séverin feinted and quickly stepped to his left. Saint-Evremonde's sword lashed out where the Morgue Director had previously stood. The blade struck the wall and shattered upon the unyielding stone. Shards of metal dropped to the floor, a gentle tinkling sound quite incongruous from the clashing steel a moment earlier.

Saint-Evremonde's massive maw dropped open in shock. And then he shrieked, black blood bubbling from his mouth.

Séverin, standing in the undead Marquis's blind spot, had lunged forward and stabbed him in the heart with the lethal smallsword.

The swordmaster pressed the blade deeper and watched as the wound, and the dead flesh near the blade, turned black and began crumbling into gray dust.

"*Kings, aristocrats, tyrants, whoever they be, are slaves rebelling against the sovereign of the Earth, which is the human race, and against the legislator of the universe, which is nature.* Maximilien de Robespierre," quoted Séverin as he twisted the blade a little deeper.

In truth, the Morgue Director had despised the late Jacobin as a tyrant in his own right. But quoting the killer of kings, making them the last words the Marquis would ever hear, was a final insult in the face of this undead monster, a fitting punishment for the endless river of blood and pain he'd caused throughout the centuries.

"You…"

Saint-Evremonde pointed a withering finger at Séverin, then collapsed.

A moment later, all that remained were gray bones and a twisted, inhuman, snarling skull. Even in death, the Marquis was a horror upon the eyes of the world.

Sheathing his swords, Séverin stepped to Karnstein's side. He examined the wounds with a critical eye and helped the young Austrian to his feet.

"The wounds are deep, but I believe you will survive," he said.

Séverin assisted the exorcist as they left the chamber.

"How nice. I was wondering," replied Karnstein. "We cannot be seen at the coronation. His Holiness's guards would demand that he leave out of fear for his safety."

Karnstein knew enough about politics to believe that that would cause a scandal, one perhaps capable of starting a war, given the magnitude of the ceremony about to take place.

"We will not," said Séverin. "I will take you to Doctor Patou. He is the most brilliant physician in Paris. Then we shall write our reports for the Emperor and Pope. They must learn of this day. And ensure that the remains of those sad creatures are never discovered by the eyes of man."

They climbed a different set of stairs towards the light of the day.

CHAPTER XXXVIII

Paris, 4 December 1804

Karnstein kissed the Pope's signet ring and sat on a proffered stool several feet from the throne. His Holiness read the report once again in silence and, after several minutes, looked at his chief secretary.

"Place Exorcist Karnstein's report in the sealed records. In a red cover, if you please."

Pope Pius VII emphasized the color with a degree of gravity that gave weight to that simple phrase. Whatever that meant was a mystery known only to those two powerful men.

The secretary bowed and then looked at the Swiss Guard. He waved them away, forcing the men to more distant posts. The professional soldiers bowed and, within a few moments, were out-of-sight. They were used to such secret conferences and possessed little interest in their contents. Their only interest was the safety of the Pope and his retinue.

The secretary stepped forward. He was an imposing figure in his own right. Karnstein knew his name was Annibale Francesco Clemente Melchiore Girolamo Nicola Sermattei della Genga, Titular Archbishop of Tyre. The man had a strong future in the Church, though the politics in his position could be a pitfall.

"His Holiness is grateful for your actions. Saving the lives of his holy personage and of Emperor Napoleon. He wishes to honor you, as well as encourage your pursuit of Satan's minions."

Archbishop Genga handed Karnstein two sealed envelopes.

"Exorcist Baron Franz Karl Joseph Vordenburg-Karnstein. You are hereby granted the duties, rights, and powers of a member of the Holy Inquisition. You will answer only to His Holiness. Do as you must in the name of our Lord, Jesus Christ."

Archbishop Genga crossed himself, and the Pope and Karnstein echoed, "Amen."

"As thanks for services to the Holy See," he continued, "His Holiness wishes to make you Knight of the Sovereign Military Order of Malta. Kneel, Exorcist Karnstein..."

Archbishop Genga waved Karnstein down to the steps before the holy throne.

The young Austrian painful lowered himself to his knees. The honor of the knighthood meant little to him, in truth. He would normally reject such rewards, but had been warned that to do so would be considered an insult to the Pope.

"Even one as politically disinterested as you must see that as a poor idea," Séverin had stated before they had parted ways.

Sadly, Karnstein had agreed. Which was why he bowed his head and tried to hide the pain across his chest as he was knighted. Later, he would cast-off the award and return to work. For he had a duty to the world. Only the Pope and Archbishop Genga knew the truth of his powers.

But that would change in time. One day, he would tell Jean-Pierre Séverin of the days that had followed his execution of Mircalla Karnstein and his own vampire mother. But not today...

CHAPTER XXXIX

Paris, 4 December 1804

"Quite a story, Maestro," said Napoleon, dropping the report on his desk. "I had Murat and his most trusted men burn the remains and seal off the room. As for this report, I may be forced to burn it too. Such information, even kept in secret, could become dangerous."

"Agreed," replied Séverin.

He sat on the proffered chair as the new Emperor met him in his private office. Napoleon smiled slightly.

"Murat suggested I make you a Count in my new nobility, as a reward for our lives, and a means of placing you in my debt. But I told him that you would reject such a gesture."

"You are correct, Sire. I am still a Republican at heart."

"I said as much" chuckled the Emperor. "Just as I am a soldier first. And in the army, the reward for a job well-done is further duties. You will remain Director the Morgue of Paris, of course, but I am also appointing you Inspector General. You will have the rights to request assistance from the police, the army, the navy... whatever is necessary to the success of your missions. Your true work will be known only by myself and Murat. I am hereby appointing you as the Empire's first vampire hunter. Do you accept, Jean-Pierre Séverin?"

Séverin stood and bowed deeply.

"I accept this duty and honor, Sire."

"Good, good. Because I have received some very troubling reports from the Gendarmes d'élite de la Garde Impériale. It appears someone is intent on killing the great nobles of France. And then, there is the Countess Marcian Gregoryi..."

Napoleon handed Séverin the charter of his new position and opened a file upon his desk.

Séverin placed his hands at his side and listened. The newly-created vampire hunter of Emperor Napoleon was already being put to work. Life would be even more interesting from this day forward...

SF & FANTASY

Adolphe Alhaiza. *Cybele*

Alphonse Allais. *The Adventures of Captain Cap*

Henri Allorge. *The Great Cataclysm*

Guy d'Armen. *Doc Ardan: The City of Gold and Lepers; The Troglodytes of Mount Everest/The Giants of Black Lake; The Abominable Snowman*

G.-J. Arnaud. *The Ice Company*

André Arnyvelde. *The Ark; The Mutilated Bacchus*

Charles Asselineau. *The Double Life*

Henri Austruy. *The Eupantophone; The Olotelepan; The Petitpaon Era*

Barillet-Lagargousse. *The Final War*

Barbot de Villeneuve.*The Naiads/Beauty & The Beast*

Cyprien Bérard. *The Vampire Lord Ruthwen*

S. Henry Berthoud. *Martyrs of Science; The Angel Asrael*

Aloysius Bertrand. *Gaspard de la Nuit*

Richard Bessière. *The Gardens of the Apocalypse; The Masters of Silence*

Chevalier de Béthune. *The World of Mercury*

Albert Bleunard. *Ever Smaller*

Félix Bodin. *The Novel of the Future*

Pierre Boitard. *Journey to the Sun*

Louis Boussenard. *Monsieur Synthesis*

Alphonse Brown. *City of Glass; The Conquest of the Air*

Émile Calvet. *In a Thousand Years*

André Caroff. *The Terror of Madame Atomos; Miss Atomos; The Return of Madame Atomos; The Mistake of Madame Atomos; The Monsters of Madame Atomos; The Revenge of Madame Atomos; The Resurrection of Madame Atomos; The Mark of Madame Atomos; The Spheres of Madame Atomos; The Wrath of Madame Atomos* (w/M. & Sylvie Stéphan)

Jean Carrère. *The End of Atlantis*

Félicien Champsaur. *Homo-Deus; The Human Arrow; Nora, The Ape-Woman; Ouha, King of the Apes; Pharaoh's Wife*

Didier de Chousy. *Ignis*

Jules Clarétie. *Obsession*

Jacques Collin de Plancy. *Voyage to the Center of the Earth*

Michel Corday. *The Eternal Flame; The Lynx* (w/André Couvreur)

André Couvreur. *Caresco, Superman; The Exploits of Professor Tornada* (3 vols.); *The Necessary Evil*
Gaston Danville. *The Perfume of Lust*
Camille Debans. *The Misfortunes of John Bull*
Captain Danrit. *Undersea Odyssey*
C. I. Defontenay. *Star (Psi Cassiopeia)*
Charles Derennes. *The People of the Pole*
Georges Dodds (anthologist). *The Missing Link*
Charles Dodeman. *The Silent Bomb*
Harry Dickson. *The Heir of Dracula; Harry Dickson vs. The Spider*
Jules Dornay. *Lord Ruthven Begins*
Alfred Driou. *The Adventures of a Parisian Aeronaut*
Odette Dulac. *The War of the Sexes*
Alexandre Dumas. *The Return of Lord Ruthven; The Man who Married a Mermaid* (w/P. Lacroix)
Renée Dunan. *Baal; The Ultimate Pleasure*
J.-C. Dunyach. *The Night Orchid; The Thieves of Silence*
Henri Duvernois. *The Man Who Found Himself*
Achille Eyraud. *Voyage to Venus*
Henri Falk. *The Age of Lead*
Paul Féval. *Anne of the Isles; Knightshade; Revenants; Vampire City; The Vampire Countess; The Wandering Jew's Daughter*
Paul Féval, *fils. Felifax, the Tiger-Man*
Charles de Fieux. *Lamékis*
Fernand Fleuret. *Jim Click*
Charles-Marie Flor O'Squarr. *Phantoms*
Louis Forest. *Someone is Stealing Children in Paris*
Arnould Galopin. *Doctor Omega; Doctor Omega and the Shadowmen* (anthology)
Judith Gautier. *Isoline and the Serpent-Flower*
H. Gayar. *The Marvelous Adventures of Serge Myrandhal on Mars*
Louis Geoffroy. *The Apocryphal Napoleon*
G.L. Gick. *Harry Dickson and the Werewolf of Rutherford Grange*
Raoul Gineste. *The Second Life of Doctor Albin*
Delphine de Girardin. *Balzac's Cane*
Léon Gozlan. *The Vampire of the Val-de-Grâce*
Jules Gros. *The Fossil Man*
Jimmy Guieu. *The Polarian-Denebian War* (2 vols.)
Edmond Haraucourt. *Daah, the First Human; Illusions of Immortality*
Nathalie Henneberg. *The Green Gods*
Eugène Hennebert. *The Enchanted City*

Jules Hoche. *The Maker of Men and His Formula*
V. Hugo, P. Foucher & P. Meurice. *The Hunchback of Notre-Dame*
Romain d'Huissier. *Hexagon: Dark Matter*
Jules Janin. *The Magnetized Corpse*
Gustave Kahn. *The Tale of Gold and Silence*
Gérard Klein. *The Mote in Time's Eye*
Fernand Kolney. *Love in 5000 Years*
Paul Lacroix. *Danse Macabre; The Man who Married a Mermaid* (w/Alexandre Dumas)
Louis-Guillaume de La Follie. *The Unpretentious Philosopher*
Jean de La Hire. *The Fiery Wheel; Enter the Nyctalope; The Nyctalope on Mars; The Nyctalope vs. Lucifer; The Nyctalope Steps In; Night of the Nyctalope; Return of the Nyctalope*
Etienne-Léon de Lamothe-Langon. *The Virgin Vampire*
André Laurie. *Spiridon*
Gabriel de Lautrec. *The Vengeance of the Oval Portrait*
Alain le Drimeur. *The Future City*
Georges Le Faure & Henri de Graffigny. *The Extraordinary Adventures of a Russian Scientist Across the Solar System* (2 vols.)
Gustave Le Rouge. *The Dominion of the World* (w/Gustave Guitton) (4 vols.); *The Mysterious Doctor Cornelius* (3 vols.); *The Vampires of Mars*
Jules Lermina. *The Battle of Strasbourg; Mysteryville; Panic in Paris; The Secret of Zippelius; To-Ho and the Gold Destroyers*
Maurice Level. *The Gates of Hell*
André Lichtenberger. *The Centaurs; The Children of the Crab*
Maurice Limat. *Mephista*
Listonai. *The Philosophical Voyager*
Jean-Marc & Randy Lofficier. *Edgar Allan Poe on Mars; The Katrina Protocol; Pacifica 1, 2; Robonocchio; Return of the Nyctalope;* (anthologists) *Tales of the Shadowmen 1-13; The Vampire Almanac* (2 vols.)
Ch. Lomon & P.-B. Gheuzi. *The Last Days of Atlantis*
Camille Mauclair. *The Virgin Orient*
Xavier Mauméjean. *The League of Heroes*
Joseph Méry. *The Tower of Destiny*
Hippolyte Mettais. *Paris Before the Deluge; The Year 5865*
Louise Michel. *The Human Microbes; The New World*
Tony Moilin. *Paris in the Year 2000*
Michael Moorcock's *Legends of the Multiverse*
José Moselli. *Illa's End*

John-Antoine Nau. *Enemy Force*
Marie Nizet. *Captain Vampire*
Charles Nodier. *Trilby and The Crumb Fairy*
C. Nodier, A. Beraud & Toussaint-Merle. *Frankenstein*
Henri de Parville. *An Inhabitant of the Planet Mars*
Gaston de Pawlowski. *Journey to the Land of the 4th Dimension*
Georges Pellerin. *The World in 2000 Years*
Ernest Pérochon. *The Frenetic People*
Pierre Pelot. *The Child Who Walked on the Sky*
Jean Petithuguenin. *An International Mission to the Moon*
J. Polidori, C. Nodier, E. Scribe. *Lord Ruthven the Vampire*
P.-A. Ponson du Terrail. *The Immortal Woman; The Vampire and the Devil's Son; The Police Agent*
Georges Price. *The Missing Men of the* Sirius
René Pujol. *The Chimerical Quest*
Edgar Quinet. *Ahasuerus; The Enchanter Merlin*
Jean Rameau. *Arrival; in the Stars*
Henri de Régnier. *A Surfeit of Mirrors*
Maurice Renard. *The Blue Peril; Doctor Lerne; The Doctored Man; A Man Among the Microbes; The Master of Light*
Restif de la Bretonne. *The Discovery of the Austral Continent by a Flying Man; Posthumous Correspondence* (3 vols.); *The Fay Ouroucoucou* (2 vols.)
Jean Richepin. *The Crazy Corner; The Wing*
Albert Robida. *The Adventures of Saturnin Farandoul; Chalet in the Sky; The Clock of the Centuries; The Electric Life; The Engineer Von Satanas*
J.-H. Rosny Aîné. *Helgvor of the Blue River; The Givreuse Enigma; The Mysterious Force; The Navigators of Space; Vamireh; The World of the Variants; The Young Vampire*
Marcel Rouff. *Journey to the Inverted World*
Marie-Anne de Roumier-Robert. *The Voyage of Lord Seaton to the Seven Planets*
Léonie Rouzade. *The World Turned Upside Down*
Han Ryner. *The Human Ant; The Superhumans*
Henri de Saint-Georges. *The Green Eyes*
Louis-Claude de Saint-Martin. *The Crocodile*
Frank Schildiner. *The Quest of Frankenstein; The Triumph of Frankenstein*
Nicolas Ségur. *The Human Paradise*
Pierre de Selenes: *An Unknown World*

Norbert Sevestre. *Sâr Dubnotal: Vs. Jack the Ripper; The Astral Trail*

Angelo de Sorr. *The Vampires of London*

Brian Stableford. *The Empire of the Necromancers (1. The Shadow of Frankenstein; 2. Frankenstein and the Vampire Countess; 3. Frankenstein in London); The Wayward Muse; Eurydice's Lament; The Mirror of Dionysius; The New Faust at the Tragicomique; Sherlock Holmes and The Vampires of Eternity; The Stones of Camelot* (anthologist) *News from the Moon; The Germans on Venus; The Supreme Progress; The World Above the World; Nemoville; Investigations of the Future; The Conqueror of Death; The Revolt of the Machines; The Man With the Blue Face; The Aerial Valley; The New Moon; The Nickel Man; On the Brink of the World's End; The Mirror of Present Events; The Humanisphere*

Jacques Spitz. *The Eye of Purgatory*

Kurt Steiner. *Ortog*

Eugène Thébault. *Radio-Terror*

C.-F. Tiphaigne de La Roche. *Amilec*

Simon Tyssot de Patot. *The Strange Voyages of Jacques Massé and Pierre de Mésange*

Louis Ulbach. *Prince Bonifacio*

Théo Varlet. *The Castaways of Eros; The Golden Rock.; The Martian Epic* (w/Octave Joncquel); *Timeslip Troopers* (w/André Blandin); *The Xenobiotic Invasion*

Pierre Véron. *The Merchants of Health*

Paul Vibert. *The Mysterious Fluid*

Villiers de l'Isle-Adam. *The Scaffold; The Vampire Soul*

Gaston de Wailly. *The Murderer of the World*

Philippepe Ward. *Artahe; Manhattan Ghost* (w/Mickael Laguerre); *The Song of Montségur* (w/Sylvie Miller)

Victor Margueritte. *The Bacheloress; The Companion; The Couple*

www.ingramcontent.com/pod-product-compliance
Lightning Source LLC
Chambersburg PA
CBHW060431030726
47495CB00003B/824